PR

SIGH

"Wow! Nonstop action and incredible chemistry between the main characters . . . Samantha Graves's writing is superb. Bravo!"

—RomRevToday.com

"Full of twists and turns . . . Samantha Graves has a gift for creating sexual tension and coming up with some great ways to bring her characters together."

—OnceUponaRomance.com

"Get ready for the most intriguing wild ride you can ever imagine . . . I highly recommend this one!"

—TheBestReviews.com

"A delightfully well-told story with plenty of action and passion."

—MyShelf.com

"Exceptional . . . Graves keeps the suspense one step ahead of the reader."

—FallenAngelReviews.com

ALSO BY SAMANTHA GRAVES

Sight Unseen

SAMANTHA GRAVES

OUT OF TIME

FOREVER

NEW YORK   BOSTON

Copyright © 2008 by C. J. Barry
All rights reserved. Except as permitted under the U.S. Copyright Act of 1976, no part of this publication may be reproduced, distributed, or transmitted in any form or by any means, or stored in a database or retrieval system, without the prior written permission of the publisher.

Forever is an imprint of Grand Central Publishing. The Forever name and logo is a trademark of Hachette Book Group USA, Inc.

Cover design and art by Rob Wood

Forever
Hachette Book Group USA
237 Park Avenue
New York, NY 10017
Visit our Web site at www.HachetteBookGroupUSA.com

Printed in the United States of America

First Printing: August 2008

10 9 8 7 6 5 4 3 2 1

This book is dedicated to my fabulous and fearless agent,
Roberta Brown.

Acknowledgments

My sincere and heartfelt thanks to:

My terrific editor, Frances Jalet-Miller, and everyone at Grand Central Publishing for helping to bring this book to you.

Lani Diane Rich for her critiquing skills, for dragging me kicking and screaming into the Will Writc for Wine podcast, and for a friendship I wouldn't trade for the world. My awesome beta-readers, Patti Newel and Jill Purinton. Friends and authors Patrick Picciarelli, Susan St. Thomas, and Rae Monet for sharing their expertise.

My mom and dad for showing me that life is nothing without a lot of love and a little risk. Chris and Cheri, my two sisters and fellow published authors, for their courage and beauty. Tom, my brother, for his musical talent, dry wit, and unique way of looking at life.

My cat Oliver for never letting me sleep past 6:00 a.m.,

viii   Acknowledgments

and of course, my beautiful family—Ed, Rachel, and Ryan—for all their support and love.

I am the luckiest person to ever write a book.

CHAPTER
1

Simon had been asleep all of twelve minutes when the doorbell started to buzz.

Go away, he thought through a fog of exhaustion and slipped back into the peace of safe, sound sleep.

Bzzzzz.

He surfaced long enough to register the rain pelting his bedroom windows and the fact that he hadn't eaten today but was too tired to do anything about it. Should have taken that sexy flight attendant up on her offer for more nuts. Now, *there* was a good point to go back to sleep. He rolled over, his weary thirty-seven-year-old body grateful.

Bzzzzzzzzzzzzzzzzzzzzzzzzzz.

"Sonofabitch." He tossed the covers aside and looked at the clock. 7:15 p.m. What kind of moron would be visiting at this time of day in the middle of a thunderstorm?

Whoever it was lay on the buzzer with a vengeance. Simon sat on the edge of his bed and rubbed the stubble on his face. He didn't need this. For three months he hadn't been home. All he wanted was one solid night of sleep without worrying about someone shooting at him. Was that too much to ask?

Simon walked to the security monitor. If it was that old bat next door nosing around in his business again, he'd seriously consider killing her. Okay, maybe a warning shot. But someone was going to pay for waking him.

The front-door camera showed a lone figure hunched and leaning against the outside wall, his hand pressed against the doorbell. The face was hidden in shadow.

Hell.

The good news was the enemy rarely came through the front door. The bad news was it sure didn't look like the Avon lady.

Maybe if he waited long enough, the moron would get the hint and go away.

Then the buzzing was accompanied by the man pounding on the door with his fists.

Or not. Whoever it was didn't look like he was leaving any time soon. First thing tomorrow, Simon was ripping that damn doorbell out.

He grabbed a pair of jeans off the floor and pulled them on. Then he stuffed his gun in the middle of his back and headed downstairs to get rid of whoever it was so he could go back to sleep.

Thunder echoed down the hall as he made his way through his Tudor-style house, unwelcome adrenaline pushing fatigue aside. A lightning crack rattled the windows, and a stormy haze tinted everything. He pressed against the cold steel front door and peered out the one-way sidelight window. He still couldn't recognize the visitor.

He hit the intercom. "Who is it?"

The buzzing and banging stopped, and a muffled male voice answered, "Jackson. Let me in."

"You have got to be kidding me," Simon muttered as big, bad memories surfaced in a flash. He did not want to face Jackson again. At least not alive. He yanked open the door and aimed his gun at Jackson's head. "What the hell do *you* want?"

The tomb raider stared back, eyes red and weary. Rainwater had plastered short black hair to his head. His face was pale, and a long overcoat hung shapelessly over his lean body. He'd aged twenty years since Simon saw him two years ago, and he smelled like wet dog.

The hair on the back of Simon's neck prickled. Something told him this was not a social visit.

Jackson raised one hand and waved him off. The other hand he kept inside his coat. "I'm not armed."

"You'd be surprised how often I hear that and wind up in ICU," Simon said. "What do you want?"

Jackson turned his head toward the quiet neighborhood. "I'll tell you inside," he said, his voice rough. Then he stumbled past Simon without waiting for an invite.

Simon kicked the door shut, keeping his gun leveled at Jackson, who gave a painful groan before settling on the stairs in the dark entry. His breathing was labored as he rested his head against the wall and peered up at Simon. "You're the only one I can trust."

Simon gritted his teeth. "Let's recap. Two years ago, you jumped my single biggest find in South America, and then you jumped my wife. We're a long way from trust, you and I."

"Hey, you poached on my turf. Can't have other

raiders thinking I'm soft. As for Celina—" Jackson gave a guttural groan and clutched his stomach.

What the hell? Simon reached over and hit the vestibule lights. The trail of rainwater that stretched from the door to the stairs was turning bright red.

"Christ, Jackson," Simon said, stowing the gun in his jeans. He knelt and ripped open the trench coat. Blood soaked Jackson's shirt and pants from a gaping hole in his side. "What happened?"

Jackson gave a weak laugh. "I forgot to duck."

"No shit." *And recently, too,* Simon noted. The fact that Jackson was still walking meant it had been only a few hours, at most. And as much as he hated Jackson, he didn't want him dying in his foyer. The cops would be everywhere. "You need to get to an ER."

Simon stood up, but Jackson grabbed his forearm with surprising strength for a man bleeding all over his floor. "No. Listen to me. You have to save her."

"Who?"

"Celina. They're going to kill her."

Simon let out a groan. Aw, shit. Why was it every time there was trouble, she was in the middle of it?

"She didn't come home day before yesterday." Jackson spoke fast and sloppy. He pulled a manila envelope out of his coat. "Then I got this in the mail and a text message on my cell phone. Said if I didn't find some lost treasure, they'd kill her."

Simon looked at him incredulously. "Uh-huh. And you believed them?"

Jackson reached into his pocket and handed Simon his cell phone. "Open it."

Simon flipped the cover up. The background was a

picture of Celina bound and gagged in a chair. His ex-wife's tear-stained, panic-stricken face cut through the years of betrayal. Emotions he'd thought long buried rose with alarming speed.

"Shit," he said softly.

Jackson added, "I know you loved her—"

"Don't go there," Simon warned him. "I'll shoot you myself."

"Fair enough," Jackson said, nodding weakly. "There's more. Check out the pouch in the envelope."

Simon removed a small cloth bag and untied the leather strings. A crystal lens dropped out into his palm. It was perfectly concave and clear. Simon held it up to the light and peered through it, but all he could see was a distorted view of his hallway. "Rock crystal. So?"

"More than it appears. It's old. Like prehistory old. And according to these guys, it leads to a legendary find—the Archives of Man—somewhere in Mexico. That's what they want. Find it. Get Celina back." Jackson gave a sickly, hacking cough. "You got ten days."

Ten days? This was just insane. Jackson was insane. Simon slid the lens into the pouch. "I have to get you to a hospital. We'll figure this out after that."

"No . . . no time."

Simon froze at the raw desperation in Jackson's voice. The rain had stopped outside, and it had become very quiet in the house. The hairs on his neck were standing straight up.

Jackson was dead serious, and his breathing was slowing down. "There's a woman. Photo's in there. I was going to see her, but—" He winced in pain. "Name and details are on the back. You'll need her."

Simon retrieved the photo from the envelope and scanned the professional pose. Charcoal suit, blond hair, blue eyes, nice mouth, and a Mona Lisa smile. "I need *her?* For what?"

"They said she's the key. She knows how to use the lens or something like that. I don't know. All I know is that you need both to find the archives."

Simon tried to think with his sleep-deprived brain. This didn't add up. If they had the lens and the woman, why wouldn't they just go after it themselves? And another thought entered his mind. A really bad one.

"If these guys are so hot to get the treasure, then who shot you?" Simon asked.

"I'm not the only one who knows about this," Jackson said, his voice fading out. "Can't imagine how. I didn't tell anyone."

"Do they know about the woman?"

"Wouldn't doubt it. You need to move fast." Jackson coughed and gave a short, harsh laugh. "You want to know something funny?"

Simon couldn't think of anything funny at the moment. Jackson was about to meet his maker, Celina wasn't far behind, and Simon was getting a bad feeling that he might be next in line.

Jackson beamed for a brief moment. "I finally did the right thing, and it killed me."

Outside, Simon heard a car door slam. He stood up and looked through the sidelight. A tan sedan was parked on the other side of the street behind a green Volvo that Simon didn't recognize. One very large man in a long coat walked over to the Volvo and peered inside.

"The Volvo yours?" Simon asked.

Jackson grunted in acknowledgment.

The man lifted his head and scanned the neighborhood. He looked familiar, and not in a good way. Every self-preserving fiber of Simon's being kicked into high gear. "Friend of yours?"

Jackson replied weakly, "'Fraid not. Kesel."

Well, that explained the hole in Jackson's gut. Kesel was as ruthless and nasty as tomb raiders came. And he was on Jackson's trail, which just made this entire affair a hell of a lot hotter. If Kesel weren't so good at killing, Simon wouldn't be so worried. *What have you gotten me into this time, Celina?*

"I take it he wants that lens," Simon surmised.

"Yup. It won't be long before he trails me to your door. You're a marked man now," Jackson said.

Simon gave him a hard look. "You set me up, you bastard."

Blood dribbled out of the corner of Jackson's mouth as he talked, his words slurring together. "Sure did. So for once in your miserable life, do the right thing. Finish this."

"You just said doing the right thing killed you."

Jackson gave a pained laugh. "But you're better than me."

That was debatable, and Simon had the scars to prove it.

He looked outside. Kesel was walking toward the house directly across the street. Simon exhaled a breath he didn't realize he'd been holding, but Jackson was right about one thing. It was only a matter of time before Kesel came knocking. Doing the right thing had brought Simon nothing but pain, misfortune, and medical bills. Survival, however, was an excellent motivator.

He went back to the stairs to collect his Angel of Death. "Time to move, Jackson. You're coming with me."

Icy-cold hands waved Simon aside. "Yeah, okay, okay. Just give me a minute to rest. Get your gear and come back for me."

Simon cast a quick glance at the front door and nodded. "Don't move."

He took the stairs two at a time, grabbed his cell phone and the duffel bag he hadn't even had a chance to unpack yet. Then he heard the front door shut.

Had Kesel found them already?

Simon dropped the bag and hit the top of the stairs with his gun drawn.

Jackson was gone.

"Shit." He ran down the stairs and looked out the sidelight in time to see Jackson swerve down the street in the Volvo. Kesel had spotted him and was already running back to his tan sedan to give chase.

Simon turned and looked at the envelope Jackson had left by the stairs. He checked inside. Sure enough, everything was there—Jackson's cell phone, the photo, and the pouch with the crystal. Simon considered tossing them all in the trash and forgetting any of this had ever happened.

For a long time, he stood there trying to come up with a good reason not to get involved. There were plenty— Kesel, death, dismemberment. None of them helped to wipe the image of Celina out of his mind. Jackson might be a bastard, but whether or not Kesel caught up with him, he was a dead man. He'd just spent his last bit of strength giving Simon a head start.

Because Kesel would be back.

CHAPTER
2

Jillian loved the Linden Museum at night, after all the guests had left and the small staff had shuffled out. By 8:00 p.m. on a Friday night, the place was empty and all hers. It was one of the benefits of being the head curator in a small private museum in Harlem. She could be alone with some of the finest objects that history had to offer.

Her heels clicked over the marble tiles as she made her way through the cases, pedestals, and enclosures. Long shadows prostrated themselves across the floors of every room as if paying silent homage to the treasures within.

She slowed in front of the eighteenth-century Chinese jewelry exhibit that opened last month. She had personally laid it out in careful detail, every tiny piece meticulously arranged to make the most of the modest collection she'd found packed away in crates in the basement. The research and signage alone had taken weeks. Finally, the jewels had their chance to shine.

In the six months since she had started working here, she'd uncovered many such neglected treasures in storage. After more long weekends and late nights than she wanted to think about, she'd unearthed and inventoried every piece of the vast collection accumulated over seven generations of the Linden family.

She passed the sixteenth-century European rapier collection she had just restored. The metal edges looked as deadly now as they had been three hundred years ago. It always amazed her how beautiful even an instrument of grizzly violence could be when laced with history.

She glanced at each glass enclosure with satisfaction as she passed beneath gracefully arched doorways. If she were still at the Met, she'd never have had the opportunity to work with so many different kinds of artifacts. Everyone thought she was crazy to leave the security and prestige of such an excellent museum, but she had her reasons.

And here's one of them, she thought as she entered her favorite room, the sculpture chamber that housed the museum's single most valuable artifact.

Sitting center stage, the white marble of *Nymph and Angel,* by the French sculptor Emil Crozalles, gleamed under recessed lighting. Unabashedly naked and intimately tangled in spontaneous celebration, the couple had an unbridled joy that shone through their amorous embrace. Each piece the master sculptor created was playful and full of motion, but this one was special to her for a whole other reason.

She glanced around to make sure she was alone. Then silence descended over her as she concentrated on the marble lines. Slowly, a vision appeared as if through rippled glass—hands chipping, rubbing, and caressing the marble with a lover's touch. Then the face of the young sculptor, his hair white from dust, his expression feverish with excitement. The hazy scene filled her vision, blocking out the present as it stole into the past.

After a few seconds, Crozalles turned away from the statue, and Jillian held her breath. This was the moment she waited for every time. Then, like sunshine, the sculptor beamed at the woman entering the picture as she joined him. They fell upon the marble and kissed—like the nymph and the angel.

And the artist becomes the art.

Jillian gave a sigh of envy. That Crozalles. He could still steal a woman's breath away two hundred years later. But she bet he never could have imagined that his work would be admired by so many. Or that there would be one person who knew his true passion and the inspiration behind his most famous work.

Jillian had researched his life, and there was no mention of the woman he had loved, whom he'd encapsulated in marble for eternity. And without hard proof, Jillian's hands were tied. His secret would remain just that.

Heavy footsteps wrenched her from her sadness, and she turned to find the museum's night security guard approaching.

"Hello, Charlie," she said. "I didn't think you were still here."

As he entered the circle of light around the statue, he smiled, and his ruddy Irish complexion reddened, making his white hair even whiter and his blue eyes bluer. "Evening, Miss Talbot. Working late again?"

"The pre-Columbian vase shipment came today. I wanted to make sure everything arrived intact."

He shook his head. "Friday evening. You should be out enjoying yourself and breaking hearts."

Any time the conversation turned to her personal life—or lack thereof—was a signal that the game had begun. It was a battle of wits she and Charlie had played many times. The man was a happily married hopeless romantic.

She said, "Hearts come along every day. Ancient vases don't."

"Yes, but vases are the past. Used and discarded. Hearts are the future."

She countered. "Love is fleeting. Vases last forever."

"But vases are also easily broken."

She had him. "At least you can fix a vase. You can't mend a broken heart."

He raised an eyebrow. "Then that makes hearts far more valuable."

She laughed. He'd won that one.

Charlie grinned in victory. "Would you like an escort out?"

"No, but thank you anyway. Give Marilee and the kids my best."

"I'll do that." He tipped his hat. "Have a nice evening."

"You, too, Charlie." She hiked her bag over her shoulder and took the stairs to the first floor and the front entrance. She stepped outside, and the door closed and locked automatically behind her.

A warm August rain pelted West Harlem's concrete as she exited the building and stood under the granite portico. Steam rose from the hot sidewalks, the vapor swirling softly. This small business district was quiet after hours, most shops gated for the night. Trees had recently been planted along both sides of the block, breaking the monotony of concrete and brick and making the neighborhood more welcoming amid all the neon lights and cityscape.

A yellow cab cruised by, squeezing around the construction cones blocking one lane across the street where a historic building was undergoing renovation, its facade covered by scaffolding used to reface the scarred brick. Right now, ugly plywood covered the front doors, but after years of neglect, the building would soon be beautiful once again and converted into apartments, small boutiques, and cafés. She smiled at the thought of bringing life back to something that was once forgotten.

The rain continued, and Jillian waited in the portico, hoping it would ease up, but as if on cue, it turned into a torrential downpour. *Rats.* Well, she wasn't getting any closer to the subway by standing here.

Jillian cinched the belt of her lightweight trench coat and popped open her umbrella. She walked between the portico columns toward home. No work this weekend. She needed to catch up on her bills and laundry. Maybe she'd cook up some gazpacho for dinner. Review the recipes for tomorrow's cooking class and—

Up ahead, she saw a shadow move and realized too late that she'd let her guard down. A tall, thin man with a long face and darkened features stepped between her and the street. He wore a black trench coat, open in the front, and for a split second she was hoping he was nothing more than a flasher. A freak show would be the least of her worries.

"Jillian Talbot," the man said in a gravelly voice.

She blinked. *What?*

He took a step forward and gave her a lopsided smile that sent chills racing up her spine. A rush of adrenaline moved her back, but the man matched her step and grabbed her by the arm.

"You are Jillian Talbot, are you not?" he said, his grip firm as he studied her face.

"I'm not," she managed to say over the sudden pounding of blood in her ears that muffled her hearing. How did he know her name?

He grinned. "Oh, I think you are." He pulled a gun from inside his coat and pointed it at her. "My employer would very much like to speak to you."

"I'm not interested," she said, her voice shaking.

He leaned in closer, the smell of cigarettes and bad cologne clinging to him. "It wasn't a question. This way. Quietly."

Then he spun her around, and she felt the gun's barrel jammed in her side. A shiver crawled over her as she descended the museum steps slowly on wobbly legs with him close behind. Her mind struggled to remain calm so she could figure out what was happening. Desperately, she hatched the street for help. Few people were braving the rain tonight.

"Stop here," he whispered harshly.

"Who are you?" she asked.

"Unimportant." His hand tightened around her arm as he watched the street. Her heart beat painfully in her chest as they waited. *For what?*

A young man wearing earbuds exited one of the apartment buildings down the block and walked right past them, oblivious to her danger. Jillian tried to get his attention, but he was head-down against the rain, lost in his music. Damn iPods.

A few more people and cars passed without giving her a second look. Her mind grappled with options as calmly as possible under the circumstances. She could fake fainting, but then what? Even if she could break free, the gun pressed to her ribs told her she wouldn't get very far.

Halfway down the long street, a car shuddered and stalled in the single open lane, blocking a big black car behind it. The second car honked its horn and flashed its headlights three times as it waited. In her peripheral vision, Jillian noticed the man purse his lips.

Oh, God, she thought. *That's what we're waiting for.* She knew if she got in that car, she was in serious trouble.

Jillian closed her eyes. Not again. It was hell living in a family full of ex-thieves. Which one of them had gotten her into trouble this time? Her sister? Her father?

"Walk," the man said to her.

"Where are we going?" she asked as she put one foot ahead of the other toward Eighth Avenue.

"A little trip south," he said.

She noted the indifference in his voice. He was a killer. She didn't even need her psychic abilities to figure that one out.

As they walked, she tried to think positively. Maybe they would just kidnap her and ransom her for a priceless painting like last time. Force her sister or her father to steal it, and she'd be free.

Maybe this time, no one would die.

So much for positive.

Up ahead, a big man in a leather jacket and jeans

crossed the street and staggered up the sidewalk. Any hope she felt sank as she watched him stop to balance himself on a parked car. Even if she could draw his attention, he looked too loaded to help her. He veered toward them, and her abductor pulled her to one side.

"Hey." The drunk cut them off, forcing them to stop. He waved a bottle of liquor at their faces and swayed. "How 'bout a couple bucks for a good cause?" he asked her kidnapper.

"Get lost."

Jillian's eyes were locked on the man in front of her. His wavy dark hair was wet, unkempt, and curled over his forehead. Beneath the scruffy stubble was a square jaw. His eyes were hooded, bloodshot, and red-rimmed like he hadn't slept in a while. His gaze flickered past her—holding hers for a fraction of second before returning to her kidnapper. But in that brief connection, she saw intelligence. *Hope.*

The drunk grinned, and something lucid and dangerous flashed across his face. He raised his arms. "Just askin' for a dime, dude. Chill."

She winced as the kidnapper jabbed her in the ribs with the gun and pulled her around. "I don't have one. Now get out of my way."

The next thing Jillian knew, the drunk stumbled into them. A hand shoved her aside. She nearly lost her footing and grabbed a nearby lamppost for support. Behind her she heard a crack, then a grunt of pain, and she turned around just in time to see the kidnapper slump forward into the drunk.

The situation changed so fast, all she could do was stare as the drunk pushed the wheezing, incapacitated kidnapper to the sidewalk. Then he tucked the kidnapper's gun in his jacket.

Who was he? How had he known—then she spotted a man exit the black car and race toward them.

"Move!" she yelled to her rescuer. She tossed her umbrella, turned, and ran for her life. She passed the museum. It was locked up tight, and by the time she found her keycard, she'd be dead. Her heels pounded across the wet pavement toward Seventh Avenue.

The wind picked up, and she leaned into the driving rain. She never heard the drunk come up behind her. He wrapped his arm around her waist and ran with her. Jillian cast him a quick glance and inhaled at the stark, harsh lines of his face. Gone was the clumsy drunk. His eyes were sharp now, taking everything in. Watching. She checked behind them but couldn't see the men.

"Are they following?" she asked.

"Not yet," he answered, his voice oddly calm. When they reached Seventh Avenue, he said, "This way." They crossed the intersection and melted into the pedestrian traffic heading north, still keeping a fast pace.

"They tried to kidnap me," she finally said. "We need to go to the police."

Simon heard the fear in her voice. Great. Cops. Just what he needed—her to spend all night in a precinct when he was trying to kidnap her.

"I'm a cop."

She blinked at him with the clearest blue eyes he'd ever seen. The photo Jackson had given him didn't do her justice.

"You are?"

She sounded relieved, so he nodded and slowed them to a brisk walk. "Off-duty. Your lucky day."

Her whole body seemed to relax, and he contemplated his next brilliant move. He needed to turn at the next block, to where he'd parked his Lexus, then get her into the car and out of the city without a fuss. One scream and he'd have a big mess on his hands.

He glanced back. No sign of the Men in Black or their car. They might have missed her this time, but they wouldn't give up easily. Obviously, he wasn't the only one with her photo. Not that he should be surprised.

It had been easy enough to find her. Her number was in the white pages, for chrissakes. But when her answering machine picked up at home, he'd taken a chance that she was still at work. He hadn't expected them to be waiting for her, too, which meant that she was hot. And not in a good way.

Not only that, but also it was damn near impossible to hide the blond-haired, blue-eyed beauty, even in New York City. Tall, willowy, and dressed in designer clothes, she was hard to miss. He'd had no problem picking her out on the street.

"Let's turn here," he told her and guided her around the next corner. They were partway down the block when she started to slow down. "Can I ask where we're going?"

He needed to keep her moving. His Lexus was just coming into sight now. "I have a car. I'll drive you to my precinct. You can file a report there."

He held his breath. Would she believe him?

"That would be very nice of you. I'm not sure I can walk any farther." Then she gave him a quick smile. Perfect. She thought he was her savior. He figured that would last until about Yonkers.

"I'm Jillian," she said.

"Simon."

"Thank you for coming to my rescue."

"No problem."

They walked in silence for few more steps, and then she slowed to a stop. He turned and found her staring at him with a strange look on her face.

"How did you know I was in trouble?" she asked.

He shrugged. "Cops. We can tell these things."

Suspicion clouded her face. "Did you know he had a gun on me?"

Simon paused. *Careful.* "It's always a possibility."

Her expression turned serious. "Attempted kidnapping. Guns. Shouldn't you be calling for backup or something?"

Didn't even make it to Yonkers. Time to turn on the charm. He gave her his most endearing smile. "Backup isn't going to help if those guys catch up with us. Safety first." He swept a hand gallantly toward his car.

Apparently unconvinced and wholly unmoved by his charm, she took a step back. "I see. Well. Thank you for your help. I think I can walk, after all."

Christ. Nothing was going to be easy today. He cast a quick glance up and down the sidewalk. Everyone in the vicinity was minding their own damned business, just like they should. Simon opened his jacket to show her his gun. "Keep walking."

When she saw the weapon, her mouth dropped open in outrage. Anger flashed in her eyes, turning them dark and narrow. "Are you kidding me? After what I've been through tonight, are you *kidding* me?"

"Do I look like a comedian?"

She put her hands on her hips. "You're no cop, either."

Then he saw a black Cadillac whiz by the intersection at the end of the block. Was that them? He wasn't taking any chances. If they got his plate number, there'd be real trouble.

He grabbed her arm and yanked her toward his car.

"What are you doing?" she said, dragging her feet.

"They're back," he said and unlocked his Lexus from twenty feet away.

They reached the car. "Well, I didn't see them."

"Well, I did." Simon opened the door. "Get in."

She turned back to him, fury mixed with fear. Fury won. "No."

He pinned her between him and the car. Her pupils dilated when he got close. Her breath hitched. Her heat and subtle perfume swept over his tired, aching body. It was a cheap thrill, but it was probably going to be the highlight of his day.

"Get in, lady," he said with admirable self-control, all things considered. "Or I'll put you back where I found you."

Her gaze flickered toward Seventh Avenue as if she were trying to decide which was the lesser evil. Her eyes narrowed, studying him with laserlike focus. A thousand unspoken thoughts flashed across her face, but she didn't say them, and for that, he was grateful. He just wasn't up to it.

Seconds later, she climbed into the passenger side. "Fine."

"Fine." Simon slammed the door shut and cursed Jackson's eternal soul.

CHAPTER
3

Simon—the kidnapper—drove them to the heart of the Bronx and parked in a scary back alley behind a small Italian restaurant called simply Giovanni's. It looked like the perfect hangout for the mob, which of course figured. Because that was the way the night was going. In fact, Jillian wasn't sure what was more dangerous—the abductor or his driving. Her fingernails were almost permanently embedded in the armrests.

She hadn't dared engage in conversation en route for fear of distracting a man hell-bent on crossing four lanes of traffic in one move, hitting every side street, and taking the corners on two wheels. She was pretty sure he'd been a cabdriver at some point.

She studied him as he shut off the ignition. Despite everything, she wasn't afraid of him. He didn't have the cold, soulless eyes of a killer or the dark shadows that drifted around true evil. In fact, he seemed mostly sane aside from the Mario Andretti complex and the gun. And he *had* saved her from the other kidnapper. She shook her head at the lunacy of it all and unlatched her seat belt. "You always drive like that?"

"Only when I want to make sure I'm not being followed."

She squinted at him. "Who *are* you? And what do you want with me?"

The question gave him pause. He appeared younger now in the glow of a single floodlight. Maybe thirty-eight, thirty-nine. But he looked at her with weary eyes like he'd seen it all and more.

He hitched his head to the back door of the restaurant. "I'll tell you inside."

Sudden fear swept through her. In the car she felt relatively safe. There was a link to the outside world through the windows, and when he was busy driving, nothing horribly bad could happen to her. Not true once she was inside a building. "I'm not hungry."

"I am," he replied firmly.

He got out on his side, and she got out on hers. For a moment she considered trying to escape, but her high-heeled boots weren't made for running through back alleys. Besides, he didn't appear too worried about it, which meant he knew he'd catch her. And if she screamed, the only thing she'd probably scare up would be a rat.

He escorted her to the back door and knocked. A few moments later, it opened to a short, compact fiftyish man wearing a white apron that strained from one too many meatballs. A big grin spread across his face when he saw them.

"Simon," he said in a booming voice and clapped him on each shoulder.

"Hey, Giovanni," he replied with an easy grin. "Is the kitchen still open?"

"For you, always," the man said and turned his attention to her. *Thank God.* This was her chance.

Simon tugged on her arm and pulled her forward. "This is Jillian."

The man gave her a long once-over and smiled, teeth white against his olive skin. "Pleasure to meet you."

She stepped forward. "He kidnapped me."

Giovanni gave a good-natured laugh. "He must really like you."

Simon leaned past her. "She's had a few drinks. Mind if we use the back room?"

"I have *not* been drinking," she sputtered.

Giovanni just laughed harder. "Sure, sure. Come in."

He let them pass. Simon smirked at her knowingly, and Jillian threw her hands up in defeat. So much for rescue. Did she not look like she was in trouble?

A dark hallway led to the front room and a glimpse of quaint tables on one side and wooden stools lined up against a bar on the other. Lively Italian music played in the background. The aroma of tomato sauce and garlic made her stomach growl.

Giovanni showed them into a small room and turned on the lights. In the center of the room, an orange swag light hung over a single table, four chairs, and a vintage hand-painted teapot stuffed with plastic flowers.

It looked safe enough. No mob bosses in sight. No implements of torture. No bullet holes in the walls. But the night was young.

Simon murmured something to Giovanni. "Coming right up," he replied, winked at her, and left.

Jillian set her handbag down on the table and muttered, "I can't believe I got kidnapped *again*."

Simon dropped into the chair across from her and regarded her with skepticism. "Does this happen to you a lot?"

She glowered at him and then decided it wasn't worth the effort. Besides, who would believe she'd been kidnapped three times in the span of six months? And twice in under two minutes? No one. She barely believed it herself.

She narrowed her eyes at him. "Okay, what do *you* want with me?"

Simon slipped off his leather jacket, revealing a blue oxford shirt, tanned forearms, and a gun holster. He threw a passport and a wallet on the table and rubbed his eyes. "I have no fucking idea. I was hoping you could tell me."

She gaped at him. "You don't know why you grabbed me?"

"Nope." He opened the wallet and pulled out a license. "Franco Baldwin. That's your kidnapper. Know him?"

He held up the picture of the first man who'd tried to abduct her, and she shook her head. "Never seen him before tonight. Where did you get his wallet?"

"Lifted it off him." He frowned after he opened the passport, and his gaze rose to hers. He turned it around to face her. "This is *your* passport."

Her mouth went dry as she took it. It *was* hers. How would anyone get her passport?

"Franco had this. Where was it stored?" Simon asked her.

"In my file cabinet—" She froze. They had been to her apartment. *In* her apartment. In her things. She suddenly lost her appetite. "Why would they want my passport? Why would they need it?"

"To leave the country?"

Oh, God. She rubbed her throbbing head. This was getting weirder by the minute.

Simon leaned back in his chair and crossed his arms. "Ever hear from a man named Dennis Jackson?"

She looked over the top of her passport. "No. Who is he?"

Simon shrugged. "Just checking. I thought he might be involved. Do you have any idea why Franco would want you?"

"No," she said. That much was true. "I have no enemies." Which was also true. She'd just leave out the part about her family of former thieves. They had plenty of enemies.

Simon asked, "Okay. What do you do for a living?"

She put the passport in her bag. "Curator. Most of the things I work with are already dead."

He was silent, as if waiting for something else. But there was nothing else. That was her life. Work, home, some continuing adult education classes, and a rare night out with friends.

Simon finally said, "You told me you were kidnapped before."

"Six months ago. He was caught. It's not the same man," she said and narrowed her eyes as a thought occurred to her. "You were following them. Who are they?"

He looked very unhappy. "I was following you, because *they* were following you."

"And you haven't a clue why," she stated.

His eyes narrowed. "Not exactly."

"Not exactly? What's that supposed to mean?" she asked, a feeling of dread washing over her. "How do you know who I am and where to find me? Why is everyone trying to grab me? And who are you?"

He watched her for a few long beats before reaching into his jacket pocket and pulling out a velvet bag. From it, he removed a rudimentary concave lens. Jillian's breath caught at the way it reflected the faint light, and she forgot about her million questions. There was something about it....

Simon handed it over, and she took it in utter fascination. The two-inch-diameter lens was smooth and perfectly clear in the center, but the outer edge was thick and rough, hand-hewn. Not glass. Rock crystal, but of superior quality. She held the lens up to the light, and facets emerged as if embedded in the crystal itself. At just the right angle, the light fractured into a thousand spokes.

"Where did you get this?" she whispered.

"Was left on my doorstep today, with a message."

She dragged her concentration back to him. "On your doorstep? Do you get presents like this often?"

"More than I'd like. What is it?" Something about the way he didn't blink made her nervous. On the other hand, it was all pretty relative at this point.

"It's a rock crystal lens."

Simon stared at her in all seriousness. "I think it's more than your average rock. The message said it was prehistory. That puts it at least ten thousand plus years in the past."

She gave a short laugh. "I doubt that. We have no evidence of any civilization during that time period having this type of technology. Was it found with any other artifacts?"

"Don't know."

"Where was it found?"

"Message said Mexico."

She raised an eyebrow. "Can you be more specific?"

"No."

"Then I'm sorry, but I can't help you," she said with a sigh. As soon as the words came out, she knew she'd made a big mistake, and her gaze shot to his.

Nothing. No emotion on his face. Either he didn't believe her or he just realized he didn't need her, after all. That would be bad, and considering how the evening was going, possibly fatal.

"Of course, this is not my area of expertise. Perhaps I could find someone to help you," she added hastily, trying to act like she wasn't bargaining for her life.

"You're the key," he said, his voice tight.

"What?"

Giovanni emerged through the doorway at that moment carrying a tray balanced on one hand and a bottle of Chianti in the other.

"I hope you're hungry," he announced and set the tray on the edge of the table.

Jillian covered the lens with her hand while he placed two heaping plates of ravioli, a basket of crusty bread, and wineglasses before them. She thanked him, and he chuckled and mumbled something about kidnapping as he left.

She leaned forward. "What key?"

Simon poured wine into the glasses. "Message said that I would need you to find whatever this led to. That you would know how to use it."

A shiver ran up her back. Why on Earth would she be the key to anything? "I don't. That must be a mistake."

Simon looked at her over his glass. "Had your name."

How did all these people know her name?

He added, "My guess is that Franco and company have also heard this story. Ringing any bells yet?"

She clenched her teeth. "Will you stop asking me that? If I knew what was going on, I'd tell you."

Simon stabbed a ravioli. "Would you?"

She watched him eat and realized she was starving, but she was too furious to let him have the last word. "Look, I don't know who you are or where you came from, but I've had enough."

She started to rise, but he latched on to her wrist so fast and with so much strength that she nearly yelped. His eyes were dark now, humorless and angry. His soft voice sent a chill across her skin.

"Lady, let me tell you a little something about my day. I've been out of the country for three months in the fucking jungles of Africa donating my blood to every damn bug known to man. I get home after the plane ride from hell to find a big pile of crap on my doorstep. Next thing I know I'm tied up into some kind of mess with people who play with guns. If I don't get some answers, I'm dog meat. And so are you."

Jillian stared at him. He wasn't kidding.

"Sit down so we can figure this out." He released her wrist and went back to eating.

She couldn't believe this was happening to her, of all people. A thought struck her. "There must be other Jillian Talbots in this cit—"

He cut her off. "You're the one." He reached into his

shirt pocket and tossed a photo of her on the table. It was her old official Met picture. She swallowed. This wasn't about her sister or her father or some ransom. She lifted her hand off the lens and looked at it. This was about her.

She was the key, and the lens was part of it. How? What could she possibly know about any of this? She'd never even seen it before Simon showed it to her.

She held the lens around the edges. Why would anyone put them together? Then she lifted it to look through it, and a ghostly movement flashed on the table. Her breath froze in her throat as she zeroed in on the hand-painted teapot. Brush to ceramic, the ghost of an old woman painted each flower petal. The vision emerged perfect, clearer than any she'd ever seen before, and she wasn't even trying. The old woman leaned back to admire her work, and Jillian was transfixed at the details—weathered hands, wise brown eyes, a wisp of gray under a bright red kerchief. Her past visions had always been blurry and muted, but this . . . this was extraordinary.

"Something wrong?"

Simon's question ripped her from the scene. The lens trembled in her fingers as she worked to compose herself. Nothing like that had ever happened to her before.

Her gift.

Her curse.

Oh, God. Maybe all this *was* true.

Warm fingers wrapped around her wrist, and she looked up at Simon.

"Tell me," he insisted. "You see something?"

It was more of an order than a request, and she shook her hand free. "Don't be ridiculous. I was studying it, try-ing to recall any historical precedence."

His eyes were steady on hers, and she realized he didn't know about her vision. He couldn't see what she just saw through the lens. *No one could.* She didn't flinch. *You aren't getting close to this. I don't even want to be close to this.*

He reached over to take the lens from her and slipped it back into his coat pocket. "You might want to eat some food, because this night isn't over with yet."

She frowned. "Why not?"

"We're going to Boston."

Her mouth dropped open. "I am *not* going to Boston with you."

His expression mocked her. "Oh, yes, you are. Unless you'd rather wait around for Tweedledee and Tweedledum to find you."

"Or I could just call the police, like most *normal* people do when they're in trouble."

Simon met her gaze. "And what are you going to tell them? That a couple of goons are after you because of some old lens that, by the way, you don't have possession of? You think New York's finest will protect you day and night for that?"

She hated to admit he was right. For all she knew, those men could be waiting in her apartment or hanging around work to pick her off the street again. How would she stop them? It came down to who was she more afraid of—them or Simon?

"Maybe if I just talked to this Franco person and explained that I don't know anything—"

Simon started laughing. At her.

Red-hot embarrassment burned in her face. Bastard.

She pushed back from the table, grabbed her bag, and headed for the door. She didn't make it three steps.

Simon came from behind, spun her around, and backed her up to the wall.

"You can't go out there," he said.

She tried to shove him away, but his hands were like steel bands around her arms. "Regardless of what you think, I am perfectly capable of taking care of myself. I have lived in this city my entire life—"

"These guys aren't fooling around. They're pros," he said. "*You* don't stand a chance."

Rage rose in her belly, and she had to rein in her temper. "If I'm such a big target, why are you here? Why did you rescue me?"

"I didn't rescue you. I kept my meal ticket alive," he said, leaning closer.

She stared at him in disbelief. "Are you saying that if you didn't need me, you would have let Franco kidnap me?"

His gaze was unwavering. "That's what I'm saying. Trust me when I tell you I'm the best thing that's happened to you today," he said, like he meant it. "So unless you have something useful to offer to this train wreck, we're going to Boston to the one place I know we'll be safe until I can figure out what the hell is going on and where you fit in."

Unfortunately, she didn't have a better idea. At least not at the moment. She'd been kidnapped—twice—and she was getting the bad feeling that there were no safe places to hide in New York City from the people chasing her. Her entire extended family was out bonding in the Mediterranean, and she couldn't think of another soul she'd want to drag into this.

She narrowed her gaze at him. "So if you don't rescue, what's in this for you?"

"My life," he said bluntly. "Because the guys who are after you are after me, too."

So that was it. He was here to save himself. Not for her, and certainly not for the lens.

"You don't care about that crystal, do you?" she asked.

"If I could get rid of it this second, I would."

Her eyes cut to the teapot, and yearning flooded her. She tried to tell herself that she didn't care. Just ignore it. Leave it. But somewhere in the back of her mind, the whisper rose: *I want answers.*

Besides, she was sure of one thing: Simon would keep her safe. At least until he decided he didn't need her anymore. Which might not be a bad thing, unless, of course, it got her killed. Which would be very bad.

She looked back at Simon, who was watching her. She wanted to tell him to go to hell. She wanted to tell him that she didn't need his help or his protection or his cocky, condescending attitude. And if she had an ounce of her sister's skills, she would. Truth was, she needed his help and protection, and she'd put up with his cocky, condescending attitude until she got her answers, too.

So she lifted her chin and said, "Fine, we go to Boston."

CHAPTER
4

Just after midnight, Simon pulled into Yancy's driveway and parked on the lawn in the back. The rain clouds had parted, and the moon cast a blue glow over the quiet Waltham neighborhood. He killed the engine and rolled his stiff neck. If he closed his eyes, he'd be gone for at least six hours. And since Jillian had slept most of the way, he'd had to keep himself awake with silent questions he didn't have answers to.

He looked over at Jillian. She was pressed into the corner of the seat, her body wound tight even in sleep. He'd bet his eyeteeth she didn't have a spontaneous bone in her body. Everything she did had purpose, was pondered and measured. From the top of her tidy hair clipped back in a barrette to the perfect crease in her black pants to the tips of her designer boots, she was in complete control.

Which led him to the next question: Why was she involved?

He couldn't picture her in the jungles of any country. Hell, he couldn't picture her outside Manhattan. She sure wasn't a tomb raider, and she wasn't part of his world or Jackson's. She didn't belong here, yet here she was.

Everyone had come for her at once—Jackson, Kesel, and Franco. Which meant that they must have just discovered they needed her, or they decided now was the time to move. Or they were following each other. Or some of them knew about the crystal and some knew about her. Or they knew about both and had split up the job between them.

And then there was the crystal lens. Which didn't fit in at all, because she claimed to not know what it was. Unless she was lying. Maybe she knew damn well what it was and exactly what was going on. Maybe she was double-crossing someone. Maybe this whole thing was set up to pull him in and find out what was at the end of the rainbow.

He was giving himself a headache. He rested his forehead on the steering wheel, unable to get the picture of Celina bound and gagged out of his mind. Despite two years of wedded hell and as crazy as she was, she still topped his short list of people he gave a damn about. He couldn't leave her hanging.

This was not the way he'd envisioned his early retirement. All he wanted was to live quietly and not have to look over his shoulder every second of every day. It'd taken a year to finally pay back all his debts and markers, and now he had the sinking feeling he was about to cash them all back in again.

"You can't go home, either." Jillian's voice broke the stillness.

He straightened and turned to her. "No."

She tilted her head slightly, and moonlight grazed her

delicate features. Soft eyes, high cheekbones, full lips. She was beautiful, no doubt about it.

"I'm sorry," she said so earnestly that he almost believed her. Almost. Every soul on this planet was here for one reason—to get their fair share. Women were especially dangerous, and he had a long string of disasters to prove it. Besides, how could she be so generous after he'd kidnapped her? No one was that decent. She was playing him. It was always the gorgeous ones that caused the most trouble.

"Me, too," he said and opened his door. Cool air filled his lungs and cleared his head. Time to crash Yancy's Home for Wayward Screwups. Some things never change, no matter how hard you try.

Jillian came up beside him and stared at Yancy's traditional brick colonial with wide white trim and graceful porches. Inside, there were five bedrooms, two bathrooms, and the best liquor cabinet this side of the Mississippi.

"Wow," she said. "Beautiful place. This man is a friend of yours?"

He eyed her. "What's that supposed to mean?"

She blinked once, deliberately. "Nothing."

Bullshit. It meant something. *Say it, lady.* But she didn't. "I have friends."

She got a funny look on her face. "I'm sure you do."

"Damn right," he said, mad and not knowing exactly why. What did he care what she was thinking, anyway? He crossed the back porch with Jillian behind him and knocked on the door. A few raps later, the light came on in the kitchen, and Yancy cracked open the door. One eye appeared over a door chain. "Who is it?"

"Bonner."

There was a lot of swearing on the other side, and the door slammed shut.

"He's not going to shoot at us, is he?" Jillian whispered.

Simon gave her a warning look, and then the door swung wide.

Yancy was not a sight to behold at midnight. His thick white hair stuck out in every direction, his bushy eyebrows were all askew, and his big nose was red and puffy. Over his lanky frame he wore a ratty pair of pajamas that had seen better days.

"Fetching. No wonder you never remarried," Simon said to him.

"Why the hell are you waking me up in the middle of the night?" Yancy asked in a surly voice.

"The nights are getting cooler," Simon said. It was a code phrase they had shared over the past fifteen-odd years for when everything went to hell.

"Are you kidding me? I talked to you less than ten hours ago and everything was fine," Yancy said. "In fact, you told me you were retired."

"Trying to. Not having much luck," Simon said and brushed by him with Jillian in tow. The kitchen was large and white and smelled like cinnamon.

Yancy closed the door behind them and locked it. Then he extended his hand to Jillian. He grinned at her, surprising Simon, because he couldn't remember ever seeing Yancy smile. "Simon has no manners. The name is Elwood Yancy."

"Jillian Talbot," she said and returned his handshake. "He kidnapped me."

Yancy's smile abruptly ended, and he regarded Simon

with a deep frown. Simon raised his hands in defense. "No choice. We had some trouble."

Yancy glanced out the back window. "Cops?"

"No. Worse."

"How much trouble?" Yancy asked, his tone serious.

Simon hesitated. "Enough."

"Scale of one to ten."

"Eleven."

Yancy shook his head in wonder. "It takes real talent to find as much trouble as you do."

"Not my fault. Not this time."

"It never is." Yancy sighed. "What do you need?"

"A place to stay for a night or two. And your expertise."

Yancy nodded, and said to Jillian, "You're safe here. Even from him." He hitched his head at Simon. "I'll show you to your rooms."

At 3:00 a.m., Jillian lay alone in bed staring at the ceiling of Yancy's home. Long silk curtains framed two tall windows and pooled on the hardwood floors. Moonlight gleamed over authentic Shaker furniture. Lace sheers hung from the rails of the huge four-poster canopy bed. It was comfortable and quiet, and she should have been asleep, secure for now and exhausted from the day she'd had. But instead she lay wide-awake, trembling with pent-up energy as the evening played out over and over in her mind.

What happened to her life? Yesterday, everything was in order. Everything was just the way it was supposed to be. Where did she go wrong?

It didn't even appear to have anything to do with her

family this time. Her father had given up a life of art theft long ago. Her sister, Raven, had found love with a former cop and was no longer working as an art recovery specialist stealing back stolen art from the bad guys. That chapter of their lives was over. Everyone had found something legal to do. Even now, her father and Raven were off the coast of Spain, bonding over a shipwreck salvage after years of estrangement. For the first time in a decade and a half, her family was back together. Things were good. Great, in fact.

Jillian sighed. Wait until they heard about this.

Hey, Raven. Been kidnapped again. Can you come and rescue me like always?

Jillian watched the time change on the clock next to the bed. So why didn't she pick up the phone? Why hadn't she fought Simon more? Screamed? Run? Scratched and clawed?

The lens.

She inhaled deeply just thinking about it. She didn't know why she knew the lens was made just for her, but she did. Ever since she was a child and the visions had appeared, she'd asked herself, Why? What was her second sight for? For almost twenty years, she'd tried to find out—pursuing every avenue and finding nothing.

In fact, she'd gone into the art world thinking that was where she belonged. That perhaps her vision was a gift she could use to solve history's great mysteries. But it had proved more frustrating than useful. She knew when the experts were wrong, but she couldn't correct them without proof, which was nearly impossible to find.

Her other choice was to tell everyone about her second

sight. But she was pretty sure that would be the kiss of death in the art world she'd worked so hard to break into.

Which left her as the sole custodian of ancient and unknown history. If there was a way to unlock that past—not just for her—this might be the only chance.

She blinked back the emotion that clouded her sight. Yes, the answer to *why* was worth getting kidnapped for, and *why* was worth staying kidnapped. If it didn't kill her first.

Even though Yancy seemed harmless enough in their short introduction, Simon was another matter. She certainly couldn't trust him to watch out for her best interests, and she definitely had no intention of telling him about her second vision until she figured out what his deal was.

Of course, if any of her family called her, they'd discover she was missing. Even if it was the weekend, they would expect her to tell them if she was leaving town.

That could make staying kidnapped a problem.

She sat up in bed. What if she changed her home answering machine message? Just for the weekend, just until she knew what was going on. And if Simon didn't come through with some answers by Sunday, she'd call in the cavalry. She still had her cell phone in case things got ugly.

Jillian threw back the covers, padded over to her handbag. She riffled through the contents. Her cell phone was nowhere to be found. She *knew* she had it in her bag at work yesterday. Three guesses where it was right now.

"That rat," she muttered. He didn't trust her. Her. Like she was the one kidnapping people.

Fine, there were other phones in this house. Determined, she opened her bedroom door and peered out. Moonlight cast the long hallway in shadow. She stepped out and headed down the stairs, keeping to the edges, where the stairs creaked less.

Once on the first floor, she stopped to make sure no one was following her. Then her stomach growled, and she realized she never did have dinner. The kitchen was as good a place as any to find a phone.

Radiant-heated floors warmed her feet as she opened the refrigerator, flooding the kitchen with light, and pulled out a gallon of milk. It took three tries before she found the cupboard with glasses.

Then she snagged a few chocolate-chip cookies from a cookie jar and the cordless phone from its cradle and settled on a stool at the center island.

She ate a cookie while hitting the Talk button. Dead. No dial tone.

"Unbelievable."

A rustling noise from the doorway startled her, and she nearly choked on her cookie.

Simon stood in the doorway, taking up most of the height and a good chunk of the width, as well. He turned on the light, and they both groaned and put their hands up to shield their eyes from the bright halogens overhead.

"Calling someone?" he asked her roughly.

Her eyes adjusted to the light, and her mouth went a little dry. Simon was wearing long, loose flannel pants, but above that, nothing but beautiful bronzed skin and lean, rippled muscle. *Wow.*

"You stole my cell phone," she said, trying to sound indignant, but it came out mostly distracted.

"Sure did." He grabbed a glass from the right cupboard

like he'd been here before. He'd said Yancy was a friend. She just didn't realize how good a friend. For him to let them spend the night—

Then Simon's back muscles flexed, and she was distracted again. He snagged the cookie jar off the counter, and she tried not to stare at his chiseled torso when he straddled the stool across from her.

"How did you know I was down here?" she asked, trying and failing to take her eyes off his shoulders.

He poured milk into the glass and said, "You set off the security alarm upstairs in Yancy's bedroom. Yancy slept through it. You probably should be grateful for that."

She noticed a thin, jagged scar on his left shoulder. It didn't look like a surgical scar. Was he in a car accident or something? "But you didn't."

He took a drink and said nothing.

"Afraid I'll call the police?" she asked.

He grinned. "Among other things. Wouldn't be much of a kidnapper if I just let you go without getting something in return."

She didn't like the sound of that at all. "And what do I have that you want?"

He polished off the rest of his milk. "I plan on finding out tomorrow. So if you have anything you'd like to get off your chest, now would be the opportune time."

She crossed her arms tightly over her breasts. "What *exactly* do you do for a living? You know, since Good Samaritan is out."

He gave a short laugh. "Babe, there are no Good Samaritans."

She bristled. "I'm not your 'babe.' And the majority of

people I know are decent human beings. They have souls and consciences and everything."

Simon leaned back and shook his head slowly. "I'm surprised you've lasted this long."

She fumed. That was her cue to leave. She got up and put her empty glass in the sink. "I live my life by my own principles. What do you live by?"

"I take good care of myself."

"So basically that's your whole goal in life," she stated.

He looked thoughtful for a moment. "Yup."

"What about the fact that these guys are kidnapping innocent people at gunpoint?"

He shrugged, showing no sign of remorse or conscience. "Not my problem."

Unbelievable. How could anyone be so callous and so cynical? "You don't give to charities? Help out the unfortunate? Do anything for anyone else?"

Something dangerous flashed in his eyes. "I tried that once. It didn't work so well."

"So you just gave up?" she pressed.

He nodded slowly. "Now you're getting it."

Her life was in the hands of a man with the moral code of a hyena. "Well, I'm sure you'll be very happy taking care of yourself *alone* in your old age," she said and headed for the door before she said something along the lines of "You're a sorry excuse for a human being."

Normally, she didn't let people get to her. Normally, she could handle difficult types, or at least ignore them. But he was impossible. Not only that, he thought she was naive. She could see it in his eyes. Well, fine. He could think that all he wanted, because she was going to use him to get her answers.

Halfway up the stairs, she realized she still didn't know what he did for a living, and now she wasn't sure she wanted to.

CHAPTER
5

Simon came down the stairs at 9:00 a.m., feeling almost human again after a decent night's sleep, and headed for coffee.

The kitchen was empty, which meant Yancy must be in his study already. Simon filled the biggest coffee mug he could find, grabbed a donut, and wandered down the hall.

The old man glanced up and grunted a "Good morning" when Simon dropped into a chair across from his cluttered work desk. The study was lined with thick texts, old and new—stuff you'd never find on the Internet. Antiquities filled any empty spaces on the shelves and walls. A faded old globe sat on the corner of the desk.

Yancy held the crystal lens under a magnifying light and made humming noises as Simon ate. The man hadn't changed in fifteen years. Still grumpy. Still in love with old stuff. Still taking in strays.

"So what do you think?" Simon said, breaching the silence.

"I think you got yourself a nice girl there," the man said.

Simon glowered into his coffee. "First off, she's not my girl. Secondly, she's not as sweet as you think. And she's hiding something."

"Sounds like a challenge to me," Yancy said, eyes still fixed on the lens. "So you want to tell me why you kidnapped her?"

"You're looking at it. Seems someone thinks she's the key to this thing. And if I don't figure out how in the next ten days, they are going to kill Celina."

Yancy's eyes cut to him. "Celina? The hell you say?"

Simon filled him in on what Jackson had told him. "Ever hear of the Archives of Man? Mexico legend."

The old man's face twisted in deep thought. "Not familiar with that one. Mexico, eh?"

"Yeah." Simon felt the bitterness rise in his belly. He hated Mexico. "See what you can find in your books."

Yancy nodded. "I'll try. Any idea who the players are?"

"Got the wallet off the guy who tried to grab Jillian. Don't suppose you have access to any personal info databases these days?"

"Sorry, no," Yancy said. "Gave that up long ago."

Simon was on his own. Too bad he didn't have a laptop in his bag. If he could find out who Franco was, he might be able to figure out who he was working for.

He took a deep breath. "And Kesel killed Jackson."

Yancy closed his eyes and let out a groan. "I hoped to God I would never hear that name again. He's still working for whoever will pay him the most?"

"Apparently so. And right now, he's after *that*."

Yancy frowned at the crystal. "You don't want to tangle with him."

"I won't if I don't have to. What I don't get is why Kesel was out for Jackson. Why kill the one man who can get the archives? And why would Franco grab Jillian, for that matter? Jackson said *he* was supposed to find her. Someone beat him to her."

"Unless Kesel and Franco aren't working for the same people holding Celina," Yancy pointed out. "In which case, you've got more trouble than you know what to do with. Have you told Jillian what she's involved in?"

Simon took a sip of coffee.

Yancy shook his head. "Of course not. So she doesn't know you're a tomb raider?"

"Nope."

"I see. What about Celina? The archives?"

"No, haven't mentioned them, either."

"So you just kidnapped Jillian and dragged her along for the ride?"

Simon said magnanimously, "Saved her from the clutches of the bad guys. *Then* I kidnapped her."

Yancy blew out a long breath. "Boy. You gotta learn finesse. She's never going to cooperate if you don't tell her the truth. You owe her that much."

Right. And she'd bolt like a scared rabbit. "Would you risk your life for someone you'd never met? Didn't care about?"

Yancy eyed him seriously. "Not everyone is like you, Simon."

"Enough of them are. I'm keeping her alive, which is plenty, trust me. If I hadn't been there, she'd be bound and gagged and heading out of the country by now. The woman has no survival instincts. If she did, she wouldn't still be here."

Yancy made a humming noise, and Simon stared at him. "What?"

He shrugged one shoulder. "You know what happens when you underestimate people."

"I don't underestimate people. I have lousy timing and shitty luck."

"Well, I hope your luck improves, because you're going to need it." Then Yancy's expression morphed from stern to a strange, awkward kindliness as he gazed past Simon. "Good morning, my dear. Sleep well?"

Crap, Simon thought. How much had she heard of that lovely conversation? He turned around to find her standing behind him wearing an oversized robe tied neatly at her waist, coffee in hand, glaring a hole through the back of his head. His guess would be she heard enough.

He lifted his mug and grinned. "Morning."

She ignored him and spoke to Yancy. "I slept fine, thank you. I finished the last of the coffee. I hope you don't mind."

"Help yourself to anything you want," Yancy said with a goofy smile.

Simon rolled his eyes. The old man was toast.

She walked by him as she surveyed Yancy's various artifacts. Simon eyed her legs. Not bad. In fact, he'd gotten a pretty good look at a lot more than that last night when she stormed out all indignant-like. Which, he had to admit, was more fun than he'd had in a while.

She wandered over to Yancy's desk. "I didn't know you were an antiquities collector, Elwood."

Elwood? Simon frowned. Since when were they on a

first-name basis? *He* didn't even call Yancy by his first name.

"I have a passion for history," Yancy replied with a straight face.

"Christ," Simon muttered into his coffee.

Jillian shot him a fierce look and leaned over so she could see through the magnifying glass.

Simon watched her as she studied the lens, a little crease forming between her eyebrows. Her hair was down and still wet from a shower. Even without makeup, she was a beauty. Almond-shaped blue eyes, a straight nose, high cheekbones, perfect lips, and flawless ivory skin. Everything about her was long, elegant, and fine-boned. She'd never last a day in his world.

"Do you have any idea what this is?" she asked Yancy, their heads side by side behind the magnifier.

"It appears to be rock crystal. Extraordinary quality. I'm not even seeing any scratch marks on the lens. I'd say laser-cut, but the outer edges are very rough."

Jillian said, "Seems strange that they would laser the surface yet hand-cut the edges."

Yancy grunted agreement. He looked up at Simon. "Any idea how old it is?"

"Prehistory."

Jillian shook her head. "That's impossible. There is no archaeological evidence to support this level of technology during that time."

Yancy said, "Perhaps there is and archaeologists just don't want to accept it. Ancient lenses have been discovered before. Usually, they are dismissed as hoaxes, because they don't fit conveniently into our current knowledge base. Or they screw up someone's timeline."

As Simon expected, Jillian stiffened and said, "Speculation is not science."

Yancy chuckled. "You mean crackpot theories are not science. Everything begins with a theory. Whether or not the science follows is up to the scientist." Then Yancy focused on the edge of the lens. "Is that writing?"

Jillian took the lens from him and turned it upright. Slowly, she rolled it like a wheel.

"Glyphs," she said so reverently that Simon was mesmerized. She didn't even look like she was breathing. "Mesoamerican, I think," she added in a whisper.

Simon stilled. This damn thing might be authentic, after all. Crap.

Her voice rose in excitement. "We have designs in between each one. Intricately woven rows. I've never come across anything like this."

Simon watched the color rise in her cheeks. He'd seen it before, from grave robbers and raiders when they struck it big. His gut twisted.

"Could be writing, but it's almost too simplistic. Just lines," Yancy added, sounding as winded as she did.

"How could anyone make such minute etchings by hand? Maybe they were added later? A forgery, perhaps?"

"Look at the wear here. You can't fake that."

Simon shook his head. *Eggheads.* "So what does it *say?*"

Jillian cut her gaze to him like she wished he would just go away. Fat chance.

"I'm afraid my books on glyphs are quite limited," Yancy said, peering over the magnifying glass. "How long are you planning on being here?"

Simon asked, "You need more time, or are you trying to get rid of us?"

"Jillian can stay," Yancy said without missing a beat.

Simon met her eyes. They were cool and blue. "No, I think she needs to stick with me for a while longer."

"In that case, we'll need groceries." Yancy pushed back from the table and rubbed his eyes.

Jillian said, "I could use some clothes."

"I'll take you today," Simon told her.

She frowned. "What if someone sees us?"

"No one followed us here. We're safe for a while."

She didn't look too sure about that. Then a cell phone rang and Simon pulled it out of his pocket.

Jillian narrowed her eyes. "Is that *my* cell phone?"

He checked the number. "Who's Paulie?"

"Friend of the family. I have to take this call, or you'll get to meet all my relatives."

She sounded serious and extremely annoyed, so he handed her the phone. "Speaker phone."

She made a face and answered, "Hello?"

The voice of a young man came over. "Hey, Jillian. How you doing?"

She turned serious. "I'm fine. Is Raven okay? My father? Dax?"

"Oh, yeah. They're great. They're just out of calling range, and I'm kind of holding down the fort here. Thought I'd let you know so if you have any problems or something comes up, you can reach me on my cell."

She gave Simon a smug smile. "Thank you, I'll remember that. Any idea when they'll be back?"

"Probably a week. Maybe less. Depends on how good the fishing is. So, what are you up to?"

She gave Simon a this-is-all-your-fault look. "Oh, you know, a nice, quiet weekend at home."

Paulie asked, "And everything is okay? Because your sister left me in charge of you."

Simon raised an eyebrow as her expression tightened.

"Everything is fine. I don't need a babysitter."

The intensity of her stillness spoke volumes. Anyone looking at her would simply think she *was* fine, but the fingers wrapped tightly around the phone told a different story.

There was a short pause on the other end of the phone. "Okay, sorry. Just wanted to make sure you were safe."

"Perfectly, thank you," she said, a little too sharply. "When you see my family, give them my best. Good-bye." Then she hung up.

Simon held out his hand for the phone. Jillian cut her eyes to him, and he could tell by the heightened color in her face that she was working for her self-control. There was a lot more to that conversation than he'd realized.

He withdrew his hand.

She spoke curtly, "You want my help? Then you have to trust me."

"I don't trust anyone, babe."

"Stop calling me 'babe.' Trust me or do this without me."

They stared at each other for a few moments. Her blue eyes didn't waver. He couldn't bully her any harder. He needed her help to save Celina. "Fine. Keep the phone."

"I'm going to call home for any messages. If that's okay with you," she said, one eyebrow raised in challenge.

"Whatever makes you happy," he said.

"You don't want to know what would make me happy," she replied and walked out of the room.

Yancy grinned at him in triumph. "Never underestimate."

Kesel stood beside a puddle of blood where Jackson had sat two hours ago. Two hours before he'd run out of this house and led Kesel all over Brooklyn. By the time Kesel caught up with him, he'd bled to death and the lens wasn't with him. Which meant it was here or with someone who lived here. The problem was, he'd already checked the house and no one was home. A bad sign.

The foyer was dark and silent as he walked through the first-floor rooms to the kitchen. Jackson wouldn't give the lens to just anyone. He'd pick someone who knew what to do with it, and Kesel needed the homeowner's identity fast. He pulled on a pair of leather gloves and began going through the drawers.

His cell phone rang, and he answered with a curt, "What?"

Carlos started swearing in Spanish and then switched to English. "We lost her. It's over. We have nothing without her."

Kesel took a deep breath and let Carlos's paranoia roll off him until he was once again centered.

"Explain. Slowly," he finally said in a lull of swearing.

"Franco checked Talbot's apartment. She wasn't home, but he found her passport."

Kesel pulled out drawer after drawer, finding nothing. No phone book, no address book, no personal information. Interesting.

Carlos continued, "So then he went to where she works and waited until she came out."

Kesel opened the refrigerator. It was nearly empty, containing only condiments and beer. Nothing perishable.

"And?" he prompted Carlos.

Kesel made his way through the rooms looking for the crap that most people kept in their homes. But there were no photos on the walls or tables. No mementos. No toys. No sentimental touches.

"He had her in his hands, and then a man attacked him and took her away."

Kesel stopped in the middle of the living room and stared at a stone statue of the Hindu god Ganesha sitting on the mantel.

Carlos broke into Spanish again. "Franco said he was pro, and one of his men recognized him."

Kesel walked over to the statue. "Give me a name."

"Simon Bonner."

Bonner. He should have guessed that. He hadn't heard that name in many years. Not since they'd come to blows over a find that Kesel needed for a very persistent customer. Bonner had gotten lucky and won that one, leaving Kesel empty-handed. A rare failure.

Carlos continued, "And now Bonner has her, and we don't."

Kesel moved to the stairs. "And he has the lens, too."

"How do you know that?"

"Because I'm in his house looking at the spot where Jackson gave it to him."

Jackson would have told him everything he knew about the lens and the legend attached to it. So what would Bonner do next?

"He has her and the lens?" Carlos starting swearing again.

Kesel wandered back to the kitchen. He was missing something. "Relax, Carlos. He still has to put it all together. I doubt Jackson even knew what he really had."

Carlos moaned. "If only I hadn't trusted Celina in the first place.

Kesel clenched his teeth. "That's what you get for letting your dick think for you. Next time you decide to play footsie with the hired help, keep your mouth shut and your inventory locked up. Because one way or another, someone is going to pay for Celina stealing my lens out from under your care. Starting with you."

"I know, I know. I was sloppy," Carlos said quickly. "What do we do? Bonner could be anywhere. Hell, he could be in Mexico by now."

That much was true, and highly possible.

Kesel spotted the phone in the kitchen. He picked it up and pressed Redial. The last outgoing phone number began dialing. The date was yesterday, and the digital display read "Elwood Yancy." Kesel hung up before the phone started ringing.

Elwood Yancy. An expert in antiquities. The perfect man to hide Bonner and help him figure out the mystery of the lens. If Bonner went there, it meant only one thing—he was going after the archives.

Kesel let himself out the back door and removed his gloves. "I'm heading back to Mexico. Tell Franco I have another job for him, and this time, he better not fuck it up."

CHAPTER
6

It was early Saturday afternoon when Simon stepped through the kitchen doorway with Jillian hot on his heels. He dropped the groceries on the counter.

"I realize you owe me for the whole kidnapping thing and for just plain being a jerk, but tell me again why I couldn't use my own charge cards?" she asked.

"We don't want to leave a trail someone can find."

She'd stopped just inside the doorway, her hands full of Macy's bags.

Her face was set in a frown. "What about *your* charge cards? Someone could trace those."

He leaned back against the counter and crossed his arms. Damn, she was gorgeous when she was mad. What else could he pick a fight about? "They know who *you* are, but it'll take them a while to identify me."

Suspicion flashed in her eyes. "And why would that be?"

He wasn't ready to give her that much yet. "Let's just say that I know how to keep a low profile."

For a few long moments, she stood there studying him. "I will repay you for my purchases as soon as possible. I won't be beholden to you," she said and then walked out of the kitchen.

She didn't want to be *beholden* to him? Huh. He started putting the groceries away.

As much as he had enjoyed this afternoon, it was tougher to read her than he had originally thought. When she closed up, there was no telling what was on her mind. That could be a problem down the road. He lived by instincts and the ability to read people. The ones he couldn't read always seemed to be the ones who bit him in the ass.

One thing he had discovered was that when Jillian Talbot focused on something, she focused one hundred percent. She'd purchased her clothes quietly and decisively. Nothing frivolous, nothing extravagant—jeans, two tops, a pair of shoes, a jacket, and some intimates he'd tried really hard to ignore but failed.

Black lace bra. Bikini panties. Satin pajamas.

A vision of Jillian's long legs and silky skin in black lace lying on a bed, flashed in his mind. Blond hair fanned across the smooth sheets. Blue eyes hooded and watchful. She smiled that Mona Lisa smile and crooked a finger at him.

He paused while putting the cereal in the cupboard. He was getting a hard-on just thinking about a woman in sexy lingerie. How pathetic was that? He shoved the box onto the shelf. As soon as this was all over with, he was going to start dating and getting laid on a regular basis like normal men.

"Need any help?"

Shit. She was right behind him.

He took a deep breath, cursed his gender, and turned around. "I'm almost done."

She had changed into a pair of hip-hugging jeans and a floral, fitted blouse that showed off a bit of black lace bra. Gone was the professional curator. She'd transformed into one sexy woman.

It registered slowly in his head that that was bad.

Think about something else. Baseball. Getting hit in the groin with a baseball.

"Thank you for using your charge card for the clothes. I didn't mean to sound ungrateful. But I will repay you," she said.

"Whatever you want." It came out a little rough.

She stepped closer, and he noticed she'd put on a little lip gloss and mascara that gave her blue eyes a smoky, sensual quality. Her hair cascaded down over her shoulders, brushing the long line of her throat. A little peek of cleavage showed through the V of the button-up blouse every time she took a breath. And he wasn't getting any less hard.

He moved to put the island between them.

She tilted her head a fraction of an inch as she watched him. "Are you okay?"

He had never noticed how amazing her lips were. Damn. He needed to get rid of her before he embarrassed himself. "Yancy should have something for us by now. I'll be there in a minute."

With one final puzzled look, she walked out of the kitchen, leaving him to his self-induced torture. He gripped the countertop. What the hell was wrong with him? He was a sucker for a beautiful woman, but this was unusual, even for him. It was more than a little scary how easily the fantasies were popping up with her. She was not his type. Not even close. Too uptight. Too conservative. And too damned righteous.

He blew out a long breath and thought back over the long string of disastrous relationships he'd had since he discovered women and what they were good for. The ones who had landed him in debt or in jail or in the hospital. The ones who had lied through their teeth so sweetly that he couldn't resist the trap. The ones who had broken his heart and shaped a cynicism that now defined his every move.

By the time he was done, he could walk again.

"Works every time," he muttered.

Jillian still couldn't believe Simon bought her clothes without even asking her. Just told the cashier to put it on his card before she even had a chance to get that far. But she couldn't risk making a scene in the store. He didn't do it out of the goodness of his heart, she knew that much, and it was going to make her crazy until she paid him back. Maybe he'd take a check.

And then there was the incident in the kitchen. She wasn't sure what happened, but it had gotten really warm, really fast. She was too young for hot flashes, which meant trouble in a big way. There was a kind of attraction for him like she'd never felt before. Lusting after a man who was going to ditch her the moment he didn't need her anymore—not in her best interest.

At least she'd gotten her phone back. It wasn't much, just a cell phone. But that small victory made up for Paulie's babysitting crack. She'd call him if he was her only and last choice. Until then, she could take care of herself.

Jillian found Elwood Yancy at his desk, buried in a thick volume of glyphs, mumbling to himself.

"How are you doing?" she asked, crossing the room.

He rubbed his eyes and looked up at her. "I found as much as I could."

She leaned over to read his notes but couldn't make any sense of them. "What does it say?"

"At first, I thought the glyphs were Olmec. They are close, but I believe far older. The closest I could get was Epi-Olmec."

Jillian blinked at him in disbelief. Pre-Olmec. Good God. This was easily the oldest object she had ever worked with. Jillian picked up the crystal and studied the glyphs. Many of them had been worn off, nearly illegible without magnification. "Were you able to decipher anything?"

Elwood looked at the notes. "Not really. I think we might have an eye and a hand glyph, but I can't be certain. And I have nothing at all on the linear images in between. This is not my area. You need Mancuso."

Simon walked in, and Jillian felt her body tense automatically. He gave her a strange, humorless look and walked over to them. What was his problem?

"Who's Mancuso?" Jillian asked.

"An old friend in Mexico," Simon chimed in.

Elwood added, "And an expert on the Olmec civilization," then looked directly at Simon. "All roads lead to Mexico. If you want answers, you'll need to go there."

Jillian frowned. "*Go* to Mexico?"

"You're positive?" Simon asked.

"Afraid so."

She shook her head. "Why can't we just fax or e-mail Mancuso?"

Elwood chuckled. "Not Mancuso. He doesn't like technology. He doesn't even have a phone."

Simon glanced at her. "It'd just be a quick trip. I'll pay for everything."

She pursed her lips. "That's not the point. I can't simply take off and go to Mexico. I have a job, and Monday morning they are going to expect to see my smiling face."

Simon grew serious. "You don't get it. You can't go back to work until this is over. You won't be safe. Call them and tell them you're taking a few vacation days. I'm sure you have some. In fact, I'll bet you have a lot."

Jillian glared at him, angry more because he was right than anything else. She hadn't taken a single day off since she started the new job. But that wasn't the issue. She couldn't leave the country on a whim just to show a man a lens. She'd never done anything like that in her life.

She looked at the piece of glass in her hand. All this for one lens. Was it worth it? She didn't know, but if she wanted an answer, she didn't have much of a choice.

She asked Elwood, "You're sure this is absolutely necessary?"

He nodded. "I'm afraid so."

"We have to be back Wednesday," she said to Simon. "That's it." Of course, she had no idea what she'd *do* if they weren't back on Wednesday, but she had three days to figure that out. At least by then she'd know more than she knew now.

A corner of Simon's mouth rose. "Deal."

A deal with the devil, she realized. What had she done?

If it weren't for that moment in Giovanni's . . . Her thoughts trailed off as she rubbed her fingers over the lens.

While Elwood and Simon talked airports, she held the crystal up to a window and looked through it. The light caught and fractured brilliantly. Just like it would for anyone. Maybe she'd just imagined the woman in the restaurant. She moved the lens away from the window and scanned the room with it. Maybe there really was nothing special—

Shadows leapt from the artifacts on the shelves with sudden clarity. She inhaled sharply and focused the lens on a Chinese ceremonial cup. Just like in the restaurant, the artisan emerged clearly, working the turquoise with swift, sure strokes. She could see his dark hair and eyes, the hunch of his back, the threads of his tunic.

Destiny, whispered in her mind. *This is for you.*

The scenery morphed as the cup changed hands several times until finally she recognized one man. Her heart sank. No.

"Jillian?"

She broke from the vision and blinked her eyes to find Simon and Elwood watching her intently. She shook off the past as the present returned and a hundred scattered thoughts ran through her mind at once.

She knew why Franco wanted her. Why they thought she was the key. She was, but how could they know? It wasn't like she broadcast her gift. Her heart pounded because she knew. *She knew.* This was no coincidence.

Simon asked, "Problem with the lens?"

She gripped it in her hand. As much as she hated him at this moment, he deserved to know. She wasn't like him. It would be unforgivable if she endangered anyone's life in any way. It was the right thing to do. She took a deep breath.

"I think I know why they believe I'm the key." She lifted her gaze to Simon's. "I have a gift. A kind of extrasensory vision."

His eyes narrowed slightly, and a muscle tightened in his jaw. "And?"

"I can see ghosts of the past around ancient artifacts. Not clearly, but usually enough to see who the creator was. Or anyone else who may have a strong emotional attachment to the object."

Elwood said in awe, "I'll be damned."

"So you see dead people," Simon said.

She shot him a glare. "Only in connection with objects."

"That's quite a claim," Simon said to her. He crossed his arms. "Can you prove it?"

Could she prove it? Jillian felt the heat rise in her face. She'd just told him her biggest, most intimate secret, and he didn't believe her.

"I can tell you that the turquoise cup on that shelf is authentic and was carved by a craftsman in the early 1800s in China. He was about forty years old, wore an ivory linen tunic with a black sash, and worked barefoot."

Simon shrugged. "Educated guess."

"And you looted it from a grave."

Simon didn't even blink as he watched her. "That's not a strong emotional attachment."

"Brutality is the strongest emotion there is," she said. "You're a tomb raider."

"*Retired* tomb raider," he said without a hint of shame.

It got really quiet, and she realized that Elwood wasn't saying a word. She could only assume he knew Simon's occupation, too. Everyone knew but her. Lovely.

"So what does the lens do for you?" Simon asked.

She opened her hand to look at it. "Normally, my vision is blurred. Fuzzy, like a piece of gauze is between the past and me. And it's limited to the immediate proximity of the object. Sometimes all I get are the hands or a flash of movement. But not with this crystal. It's a perfectly focused vision, and I see a lot more detail and a much wider range."

There was an uncomfortable silence while she waited for them to digest that little tidbit. This lens was made for *her*. Thousands of years ago. No one else could use it like she could.

Well, she had wanted to handle this one herself. Here she was.

Elwood cleared his throat, and Simon studied her intently. "Does the museum know about your vision?"

"Of course not. I'd be laughed out of the art world."

Simon's lips thinned. "Don't be too sure. A gift like that could be very profitable to certain people. Like Franco."

Or like you? she thought. *Would you use me?*

But he was right. Was Franco planning on abducting her to use her gift for some illegal venture out of the country? And for how long? She shuddered. Whatever the reason, this just turned very personal. It also meant the cops were definitely out of the picture. The last thing she needed was publicity about how *special* she was. No museum would touch her after that.

"Who knows about your vision?" Simon asked.

"Just my family."

"Friends?" he pressed.

"No."

"Lovers?"

The word echoed in her ears. Elwood's face turned red.

"None of your damn business," she said.

Simon stepped forward and closed the space between them. "It is now. Who did you tell?"

She closed her eyes. Could this get any worse? Couldn't she at least keep her dignity? "Lance Fairfax. He worked at MOMA. We dated until he moved to Arizona a few years ago to open his own gallery."

"You dated a guy named Lance?"

She opened her eyes and glared at Simon, who was clearly enjoying her torment. "He was a decent man with a good, *honest* job."

That bounced off Simon without any effect. "Is he still in Arizona?"

"I don't know." Then she stared at Simon, realizing where he was going with this. "Lance would never tell anyone. He understood how personal this is to me."

"So you trust *Lance.*" Simon emphasized the name. "To do the right thing and not use this amazing ability you have for his own selfish gain."

She raised her chin. "Yes, I do."

The look on Simon's face told her he thought she was crazy or stupid. Maybe she was. But married people shouldn't have secrets between them, and Lance had been more than a lover. They'd been serious. When he brought up the subject of marriage, she'd told him all her secrets. And *then* he'd left.

"Anyone else?"

"No one."

They all jumped when the doorbell chimed. For a moment, none of them moved.

Simon turned to Yancy, and ventured, "Expecting company?"

"No." Yancy jabbed a bony at finger at him. "And if you brought this to my doorstep, you won't be invited back again."

Simon winced. "I'll get my gun."

"I got it covered." Yancy walked over to a cabinet and pulled out a shotgun for himself. He gave Simon a handgun. "It's loaded. Don't shoot yourself. You take the front door. I'll head out the back door and cover them from behind."

"Go to the kitchen," Simon told Jillian as he checked the gun. He pulled the car keys from his pocket and handed them to her. "If you hear shots, get in the car and leave. Don't look back. Don't stop for anything."

He glanced up to find her eyes narrowed in deep thought.

"What?" he said.

"I thought you didn't care."

Christ. "Don't get any bullet holes in my car."

He moved to the front door. He pressed himself against the wall and looked through the door's stained-glass window. Unfortunately, all he could see was a fuzzy outline of a man.

The bell rang again. After he'd given Yancy enough time to get into position, Simon reached over and unlocked and turned the door handle. As the door swung open, he came around the doorjamb, gun first, at the same time that Yancy stepped out from the bushes with the shotgun.

A twentysomething kid wearing a Rolling Stones T-shirt and black jeans stood, slack-jawed, on the front steps staring at the gun. His head was shaved, and he weighed all of 150 pounds. He swallowed hard and slowly raised his hands.

Then he looked at Simon and said, "Is Jillian here?"

"Who else did you call?" Simon asked, standing over her with his hands on his hips and fury in his eyes. Paulie was on the other side of her, dancing from one foot to the other and squinting at Simon like he was ready to rumble, even though Simon outweighed him by fifty pounds. Elwood sat back in his chair, enjoying the show with his hands behind his head and his feet up on his desk.

"I didn't call him. He called me," she said, holding her ground. "You were there, remember?"

"Then how did he find us?" Simon asked.

Paulie pointed a finger at him. "Hey, stop talking to her like that." Then he looked at Jillian. "What is going on? Who is this bozo?"

Jillian closed her eyes and pinched the bridge of her nose where a really nasty headache was forming. "It's a long story."

"Okay. Let's start with, is he a good guy or a bad guy?" Paulie asked.

"I don't know," Jillian muttered.

"I save your life, and that's the thanks I get," Simon said.

She opened one eye to look at him. "You also kidnapped me."

"He what?" Paulie said and took a step forward, ready to do battle in her honor. Jillian held him back. "Easy, Paulie."

"So if you didn't give him your location, how did he find you?" Simon asked her.

Paulie rolled his eyes. "Integrated GPS receiver in her cell phone. *Duh.*"

She turned to look at him. "I didn't know I had a GPS receiver in my phone."

Paulie shut up and looked suddenly guilty.

Jillian felt the heat rise in her face. "Are you saying Raven gave me a GPS cell phone as a Christmas present so she could track me? Like a dog? And you knew about it?"

"It was just in case of an emergency, because of the, you know, kidnapping last year," Paulie stammered.

Lovely. Her sister was tracking her. Wait 'til their next conversation.

"What kind of life do you live?" Simon asked her.

She glared at him.

Paulie added, "And I figured this *was* an emergency, since your apartment was trashed and you weren't home alone having a nice, quiet weekend."

Blood began to pound in her ears. "You checked my apartment? I told you I was fine. Didn't you believe me? You had to see for yourself?"

He winced. "I know it sounds bad when you put it that way, but the GPS put you here when you said you were home, and—"

"And then you *followed* me," Jillian said, holding on to every word with all the self-control she had. "As if I'm a child?"

He relented. "Okay, okay. I'm sorry I infringed on your privacy, and I promise to deactivate the GPS as soon as possible, but then when I saw you pull into the driveway with this bozo—"

"Watch it," Simon warned.

"I ran the check on his plates and discovered that he has about fifteen aliases and a bunch of offshore accounts."

Simon frowned. "How did you get that information?"

Paulie ignored him. "Not to mention some really interesting expenses on his charge cards in every third-world country on the planet."

"You gained access to my charge cards? What are you, some kind of hacker?" Simon asked.

Paulie continued, "So there was no way I was going to let you get anywhere near him. Raven would kill me."

"Who's Raven?" Simon asked.

"My sister," Jillian answered tightly.

Paulie stood on his toes and stabbed a finger at Simon over Jillian. "Who can kick your ass."

Jillian put her hand up to Paulie. "She's doing salvaging with her husband, Dax—"

Paulie interjected, "Former police officer and *very* tight with NYPD."

"And my father," Jillian finished.

"Who's no one's fool," Paulie said, bobbing his head in challenge.

Simon leaned over her. "Tell him to stop doing that or I'm going to kill him."

Jillian put a hand on each of their chests and pushed them apart and said, "Knock it off!"

Both men took a step back, and the room got real quiet except for the potent mix of humiliation and resentment throbbing in her head. She clenched her fists at her sides and tried to pull herself together from the indignity of it all. Didn't anyone think she could do anything by herself? Didn't anyone believe in her?

She took a deep breath. Enough was enough.

She pointed at Paulie. "This is my business. Not yours. Not Raven's. Not even my father's. Clear?"

Paulie's eyes grew huge. "Crystal."

Then she turned to Simon, who was watching her with surprise on his face. "And you. If you don't start trusting me a little, I'm going to sic my entire family on you. Because if you think Paulie has skills, you haven't seen anything."

Her entire body vibrated with fury as she stood there staring him down. He almost called her "babe" and then decided that he liked living and breathing. So he just grunted agreement.

She glared at them in turn. "Good. Now I'm going to go into the kitchen and find something alcoholic to drink. Then I'm calling in to work so no one *else* comes looking for me. You two have your differences worked out by the time I get back. If I ever hear the word 'babysit', some-one's going to get hurt." She walked out of the room.

Paulie looked after her. "Jeez. I've never seen her like that. She's usually really cool. What did you do to her?"

"It hasn't been a good twenty-four hours," Simon told him.

Paulie eyed him suspiciously. "Feel free to fill me in, because I'm not going anywhere. She wasn't kidding about her family. You don't *know* trouble."

Oh, yes, I do, Simon thought. Still he could use the

kid's skills. "So, Hacker Boy, how are you at locating old boyfriends and wannabe kidnappers?"

Paulie shrugged. "If I have Internet access, I can get you anything you want."

Simon slapped Paulie on the shoulder. "Glad to hear it. And we're leaving for Mexico tomorrow."

His mouth dropped open. "Mexico? Are you serious?"

Simon glanced at Yancy, who nodded back. "Looks like."

Paulie rubbed his shaved head. "Crap. Is there a chance I'll get shot at?"

"Yup."

Paulie sighed. "I knew it. Her family's going to kill me one of these days."

CHAPTER
7

Simon woke to someone grabbing his shoulder. Everything registered in a flash—night, dark, strange house, strange hand. He spun around, wide-awake, and nearly broke Yancy's face with his fist.

"It's me," Yancy said, dodging the swing like a pro.

Simon swore and sat up in the bed. His heart was pounding out of his chest as he took stock of the situation. Moonlight streaming through the second-floor bedroom illuminated Yancy's gaunt frame. He was still dressed in his day clothes at 3:00 a.m., which meant that the old man had pulled an all-nighter. Well, good for him. Simon needed sleep.

"You have a death wish, Yance?"

He grinned knowingly. "It never goes away, does it? Even after you retire."

Simon eyed him. "Is there a *reason* you nearly gave me heart failure, or was this payback for crashing at your place one too many times?"

Yancy hitched his head toward the door. "Your girl is up again."

Simon gritted his teeth. "She's not my girl. She's just trouble."

The old man nodded a few times. "I can see that. But there's a lot worse ways for you to go."

There was a grimness to Yancy's joke, and Simon waited for bad news.

Finally Yancy coughed it up. "It took me all night, but I found your legend."

Simon swung his feet to the floor and turned on the nightstand lamp. Yancy handed him a clutch of papers, mostly handwritten scrawl. His mind sharpened as he scanned the pictures and notes.

"Shit," he said when the full weight of the situation dawned on him.

"My thoughts exactly. This is big, Simon. And as you well know, the bigger it is, the better the chance it'll kill you."

No wonder they were ready to murder and kidnap. And no wonder Kesel was hot on the trail. "How much of this do you think they know?"

Yancy shrugged. "Obviously, the lens and the Seer. According to this legend, the Seer is the *only* one who can figure this out. They can't find it without Jillian."

And that was Simon's only advantage. They knew the legend but not the location.

Yancy said, "My trail ends here, Simon. You and Jillian want answers, you'll need to see Mancuso." He stabbed a finger at the notes. "And you *better* tell Jillian about this."

Simon rubbed the back of his neck. "Yeah, yeah."

"And about Jackson and Celina," Yancy added. "She deserves to know just how dangerous this little gambit is."

"I will." And he would, as soon as he could think of a way to keep her from freaking out.

Yancy exhaled. "Watch your back. Don't trust anyone. And always make sure you have a plan B. I know that's your weakness."

Screw plan B. He needed plans C through Z.

"Especially in Mexico," Yancy added.

For a split second, it was fifteen years ago. The walls were concrete and stained. The dirt floor was soaked with urine and blood. Screams of fellow prisoners haunted his sleep. Guards joked in Spanish about what they were going to do to them. And every day was a new nightmare.

They sat for a few long minutes before Yancy said, "I won't be able to help you this time if you have a run-in with the authorities."

Simon heard the worry in his voice. "I know. I'll be careful."

Neither of them looked at each other, but there was a silent understanding. If Simon got thrown in jail again, there would be no one to bail him out.

"Keep an eye on your girl, too. She's worth saving."

Simon smirked. "Lots of beautiful women out there worth saving."

"Not like this one. She's one in six billion." He clapped him on the back. "I'm heading to bed. Probably won't be up until noon. If you need me, you know where to find me." Then he stood up and made his way to the door.

"Yance?"

The old man stopped halfway across the room and turned. Moonlight shone across his aged face, making him look older and more fragile than the sum of his years. Simon cleared the emotion in his throat. "I'm not sure if I ever properly thanked you. So, thank you."

The moon smoothed out Yancy's aged features as he smiled. "You were worth saving, too. Don't ever forget that." Then he walked out. "Lock up when you leave in the morning."

Simon shook the memories from his mind and concentrated on the present. As much as he hated being the messenger, Jillian deserved to know at least the condensed version. He tossed the papers on the bed and headed downstairs.

He found Jillian at the kitchen island sitting in front of a tall glass of milk, the cookie jar, and a small, neat stack of chocolate-chip cookies. She looked up in mild surprise when he walked in and got himself a glass. It took only a second for his body to register the flimsy camisole top and the nipples imprinted through it before she pulled her robe across her chest.

This was getting pitiful. He needed a woman. Just not *this* woman. He grabbed the milk out of the fridge and sat across from her at the island.

"Can't sleep?" he asked while he poured the milk.

"Too much on my mind." She smiled a little, but weariness haunted her eyes.

"Paulie have any luck tracking down Lance yet?"

She shook her head. "Nothing yet."

"We need to talk to him."

She blew out a breath. "I still can't believe he'd tell anyone."

People had been betrayed for less, Simon wanted to say, but he didn't. Besides, Lance was a moron. Any man who had Jillian and let her go must be a complete idiot. Not that *he* wanted her. He was just saying. If he did, which he didn't... *Shut up, Simon.*

He reached over and stole one of her cookies. "What I can't figure out is why you haven't tried to take my car yet."

"I don't have a license."

Simon realized that wouldn't stop most people, but it was enough for Jillian Talbot. "Okay. So why are you still here? You could run away, take off with Paulie or just call 911."

She was about to dunk a cookie into her milk and stopped. A strange look crossed her face. "Do you trust *anyone?*"

"Nope." He popped the cookie into his mouth.

"Even yourself?"

He frowned. "What's that supposed to mean?"

"Nothing. I'm here because I'm part of this, whether I want to be or not. I won't leave you at the mercy of the likes of Franco."

That might keep her around for a while, but as soon as he mentioned death, she'd reconsider. And if he mentioned that a man like Kesel was tracking them, she'd be smart to run.

Then she dipped the cookie in the milk and sucked on it gently. He was about to address the legend but froze as her lips wrapped around the chocolate-chip cookie and her eyes closed slightly. Then she took a bite of it, revealing even white teeth before chewing it slowly. He was pretty sure she wasn't doing this to him on purpose, but if she kept that up, he'd never be able to leave this island.

She opened her eyes and caught him staring. He didn't

even try to look away. He didn't want to miss out if she did it again.

Her eyebrows rose as she put the cookie down. "Sorry," she said, and for a fleeting moment, he thought she could read every lascivious thought in his mind.

Instead, she reached in the jar and slid him three cookies. "I didn't mean to hog the jar."

He stared at the chocolate-chip cookies. It wasn't cookies he wanted.

"So how long have you been a tomb raider?" she asked.

His mind did a whiplash 180 from some nicely forming fantasies to ugly reality. "About fifteen years, but you'll be glad to know I'm retired now."

"The damage is done. You've already plundered history." She took a bite out of her cookie.

And just like that, the fantasy was over. Her view of him and his occupation was as righteous and stubborn as the rest of her. What would happen if he told her everything right now? What would she do? Refuse to help him? He decided he couldn't risk it. He'd give her just enough to get her into Mexico and figure out the rest from there.

He tipped his glass to her. "Someone had to. Those precious artifacts don't do anyone any good buried in the ground."

Anger darkened her face. "As opposed to being in some private collection with no historical reference. What you do is illegal and immoral."

"Did," he corrected and raised a hand to stop her before she stepped up on her soapbox. "Babe, don't even bother to argue with me. Can't fix the past. Don't want to. We got enough problems in the here and now."

She narrowed her eyes. "I really wish you'd stop calling me 'babe.'"

He grinned and watched her take a mental count to ten. She was so tightly wound. What would it take to unleash what lay underneath? It was the quiet ones you had to watch out for. Years of pent-up energy, frustration, emotion. Bet he'd have his hands full. But since that wasn't going to happen in his lifetime, he might put his energy into worrying about how long his lifetime was going to be.

Simon picked up another cookie. "Yancy found a legend that might answer some questions about the lens."

Jillian's expression brightened in a flash. "He did? Where?"

"He has connections."

Her excitement dimmed. "I'm sure."

Simon took a drink of his milk while weighing his options. Just enough info to keep her close to him, needing his protection. Not enough to send her packing. Finally he said, "Supposedly the lens leads to an ancient treasure in Mexico. Only one lens was created to find the location—"

Jillian's mouth dropped open slightly. "Only one?"

"To be used by the chosen Seer when the world was ready. That's all Yancy could find," he finished. He watched her to see how she handled that.

"Chosen—me? Seriously?" she asked, suddenly hanging on every word he said, the cookies and milk forgotten.

"Seriously."

She pulled the robe tighter over her chest. "And that's why they want me. They believe I can find this treasure for them?"

"And if they believe that, there will be no stopping them until proven otherwise," he added.

She frowned, deep in thought. "What if the legend isn't true?"

He replied, "Then we might have a problem."

Her eyes met his. "I see."

She got it. And so far, she didn't look like she was planning a getaway. "Does that vision of yours work on *anything?*" he asked.

Jillian tensed. "Not people, if that's what you mean."

And even if it did, you wouldn't use it, he thought immediately and wondered how he knew that to be true. "So just objects. What about newer items, like a chair or this glass?"

"It depends if there is a strong emotional imprint. Even then, I may only get shadows of movement. A flash of a hand. A burst of darkness or light."

"What if you used the crystal?"

"So far it's only worked on old objects. Unfortunately, I haven't had a chance to test it, since you keep hiding it on me."

He smiled. And that was the way it was going to stay. "You'll get plenty of practice. Mexico is full of old stuff."

"Mexico," she said with a sigh. "I've never been there."

"I have. At the very least, we need to learn more about this legend and what we're up against. Even better if we get to it first. Then you have something to bargain with."

He watched her to see if she bought it.

Her gaze fixed on him for a long count. "You mean *we* can bargain with."

He finished his milk and stood up to rinse the glass. "*We.* I'd like to live to cash in my 401K."

She watched him intently. "And what if this really does lead to something significant? Something historically irreplaceable?"

He leaned against the counter and studied her. What if she wouldn't part with it? What if she refused to let him trade it for Celina? That would be a problem. He had to quash any notion she might get of "saving" this find. "Which would make it all the more valuable. Feel free to sacrifice yourself, but don't expect me to."

She gave him a look like she was thinking about it, so for good measure he added, "And you can't find it without me. Believe it or not, there is some skill involved in tracking down treasure."

She blinked at him, clearly unimpressed by his skill set. "There must be another way."

He shook his head. "If you've got a better plan, let's hear it. The way I see it, you can turn both yourself and that crystal over now and see what good ol' Franco has in store for you, or we can find the treasure and use it to save both our hides. Not to mention Paulie and Yancy and anyone else you might bring into this."

He could tell he hit pay dirt by the way she blanched. "I didn't bring anyone else in."

"It might be a good idea to keep it that way," he added.

She bit her lip. "What about the police?"

"You'll always have that vision. The cops can't help you. You don't find this, you spend the rest of your life on the run. Short of destroying the crystal—"

Her eyes widened in alarm. "No. Never."

He almost felt guilty for playing that card, but a desperate man couldn't be choosey. He couldn't save Celina without her, and he couldn't risk losing her.

Jillian stood up and put the cookie jar on the counter next to him. She was so close he could smell her. Like spring. He didn't remember women smelling like that before. Her blue eyes held his, and he couldn't look away. *Don't be an idiot, Simon.*

"We'll go to Mexico and talk to your friend Mancuso. But if I think of another way out of this, we discuss it," she said firmly.

Discuss it. Sure. And then they'd do things his way.

"Agreed?" she asked.

He inhaled her one more time, even though he knew it was a mistake. "Agreed."

"Scout's honor?" she added, her gaze steady.

She was catching on quick. But what did he care? He'd never been a Boy Scout. "Scout's honor. Now go to bed. We're on the first flight out tomorrow."

CHAPTER
8

Be careful what you wish for, Jillian thought as she and
Paulie waited for Simon outside the Veracruz airport car
rental at 10:00 p.m. The evening air was heavy with the
smell of oil and lingering heat. Yet, in the darkness, there
was color and motion in the people and vehicles and buildings. A curious mix of old and new, shiny and shabby.

A long flight from Boston to Mexico City to Veracruz,
security checks, customs inspections, and the visitor ap-
plication had Jillian feeling the weight of jet lag. Her bag
was full of paperwork and forms that she was too tired to
concentrate on.

Still, the excitement of change had her mind racing
and her body full of restless energy. This must be what
Raven felt like all the time. No wonder she was so hooked
on it. On the other hand, Raven had the skills and experi-
ence. The excitement faded as Jillian realized just how
ill-equipped she felt.

She strained to understand the rapid-fire Spanish
of passing locals with her limited language skills. She

caught a few words—*caliente,* "hot," and *cerveza,* "beer." But everything was pretty much lost on her, since her entire language study had been a few short weeks of an Introduction to Spanish class. Too bad she hadn't kept up with it. Who knew she'd need it? Who knew she'd be in Mexico with zero days' notice?

She turned to Paulie, who looked perfectly rested in a loud Hawaiian shirt and khaki shorts. "Thank you for coming along."

He shrugged a shoulder. "No problemo. I wouldn't leave you alone with him for nothing. I know he told me that this was the only way to save your necks, but I gotta bad feeling this is bigger than we think."

She had that feeling, too. Especially since the closer they'd gotten to Mexico, the quieter and more surly Simon had become.

"I'm surprised you had your passport with you," she said.

Paulie laughed. "I work for your sister. I *always* have my passport with me. At least this time I didn't get a call in the middle of the night telling me to be in Jakarta in twenty-four hours. This? This is cake."

If you say so, she thought. "Have you been to Mexico before?"

"A few times," Paulie said. "Quick one-day trips, mostly. It's better than some places I've been."

Jillian pursed her lips. "Simon doesn't like Mexico."

Paulie wiped his sweaty forehead on his sleeve. "I noticed. Makes you wonder why, doesn't it?"

Yes, it does. And since he was running the show, any secrets he might be keeping made her very nervous. That was quite a feat, considering. First thing she needed to find was a map. She wanted to know where they were and where they were going.

She yawned despite herself, and Paulie asked, "You okay?"

She nodded. "Just a little tired. Didn't sleep much last night or on the way here."

"I slept like a rock." He rubbed his shaved head. "Traveling is a bitch, though. You gotta learn the fine art of sleeping on a plane."

"Never happen," she said, half to herself. She would never become a road warrior. It was just too hectic. "Any word from Lance?"

Paulie shoved his hands in his pockets and rocked on his heels. "He's not in Arizona. In fact, it's like he disappeared off the face of the Earth. I hate to say it—"

"Don't," she interrupted, more sharply than she intended. She smiled apologetically at Paulie. "Sorry."

He nodded. "I understand."

Did he? Did he know what it was like to bare your soul to someone and be rejected? She hoped not. She wouldn't wish that on anyone.

A white Jeep barreled from around the side of the rental building and screeched to a halt in front of them. Simon stepped out and started loading their bags in the back.

Paulie asked, "So. Simon. Why are we walking into the lion's den, again?"

"Because it's the last place Franco would think to look for us," Simon told him as he kept his eyes on the surrounding action. But he wasn't sightseeing like she was. He was working. And from the irritable look on his face, he wasn't liking what he saw.

"Right. Hate getting shot at." Paulie kept his laptop but tossed his bag into the back with the others. "And Yancy couldn't come *because?*"

"Legal issues." Simon opened the front door for Jillian, and she climbed in.

Paulie got into the backseat and leaned forward to murmur in Jillian's ear, "Legal issues, my ass."

She gave him a smile. "Worried?"

"I'm always worried. Paranoia keeps me alive," Paulie said.

"You haven't seen Simon drive yet," she said. "Buckle up."

Simon took the driver's seat, and the Jeep lurched into traffic with a vengeance, narrowly missing a cab. She heard Paulie swear in the back and grinned.

The windows were wide open, and the wind whipped her hair across her face. She corralled it into a loose braid as she took in the city of Veracruz.

Cheap neon lights vied for attention in the midst of the rich colonial and Spanish architecture. Tall cathedrals pierced the night sky. Illuminated by spotlights, domed white roofs shone. Smells of food and spices dominated the air. It was a lovely city. As they drove through street after street, her excitement grew. The museums must be magnificent. She couldn't wait until morning.

But then she noticed that the landscape began to flatten out, leaving the tall clusters of buildings behind them. Her exhilaration took a dive.

"I thought we were going to stay in the city," she said to Simon.

He glanced at her. "Heading to a small town called Cielo Azul. About thirty kilometers south."

She looked back as the city slipped into the background. Obviously Simon didn't do sightseeing. He was completely focused on getting himself off the hook. She couldn't blame him. None of this was his fault. Plus he was a tomb raider, which meant that he wasn't dealing with the kind of guilt she was. If the legend was true and if the lens was authentic and if it led them to something historically important, it was a curator's dream. And she was going to use it as a payoff to save her own skin. Might as well stick a knife in her heart. On the other hand, that was a lot of ifs.

Still, the lens was special to her. Made for her. She was special; she'd always known that. But never would she have guessed this would be the reason. For so long, questions had occupied her mind and her life. In her bones, she knew the answers were out there, just a glance away.

You have a gift, Jillie, her mother used to tell her. Jillian looked out the window at the black sea.

Maybe. Maybe not. There were times when history was best forgotten. There were things she wished she could forget seeing. Things that turned a gift into a curse.

"What are you thinking?" Simon asked, interrupting an increasingly depressing stream of consciousness.

She turned to him and raised an eyebrow. "Wow. A complete sentence."

He gave her a warning look, brown eyes narrowing. The dashboard cast a green light over the shadow of a beard over his stubborn jaw. She suddenly realized how comfortable he looked driving the Jeep, in a blue T-shirt and cotton pants. Wind ruffled his hair, adding to the rebel look.

They didn't make men like him in Manhattan—rough,

tough, real, fearless, and mean. He didn't hone that amazing body at the gym with all the muscleheads. He didn't worry about his hair or his manicure. He didn't care what anyone thought of him. He just lived his life his way with complete ease. As much as she hated his occupation, she had to respect him for knowing who he was.

That, and the amazing body. It flashed in her mind just long enough to raise her temperature a little. Maybe Mancuso had a cookie jar. She gave a mental sigh. *Don't even go there, Jillian. You've got all the trouble you can handle.*

"Is Mancuso expecting us?" she asked.

"Yes."

Back to one-word sentences. "And he *likes* you."

Simon's lips thinned. "Yes." Then his eyes cut to the rearview mirror and held for a few moments. "What did the museum say when you asked for some time off?"

She looked in her side mirror. A string of cars and trucks jockeyed for position behind them on the highway. "I reached my boss on his cell and told him I got an offer to do some fieldwork that I couldn't refuse."

"Good one."

Then she turned back to him. "So why the aversion to Mexico?"

He looked at her and something flashed in his eyes. "Mosquitoes."

She crossed her arms. "You dislike an entire country because of mosquitoes?"

"That's right."

She waited. He didn't offer up an explanation, so she dove into dangerous waters. "From what I've seen so far, it's quite beautiful."

He frowned at that. "No better place on Earth to hide or get killed."

She blinked at the bitterness and certainty in his voice. "How many times have you been here?"

"Enough." And then silence.

He didn't want to elaborate, and that was going to drive her crazy. Not just because he kept his secrets, but because she really wanted to know what would cause a man like Simon to hate an entire nation.

She checked the glove compartment and found a road map. Matching the road signs to the map, it looked like they were heading south along the coast.

"I know the way," Simon told her.

She countered, "But I don't."

"You don't like not knowing where you're going, do you?"

She folded the map to the section she needed and laid it on her lap. "Would you?"

He shrugged. "That's what adventures are. Not knowing where you're going."

She leaned back and looked at him. "So how do you prepare for the unexpected?"

"That's part of the adventure, too."

"And how do you know you'll be able to handle the unexpected?"

"I'm good." He said it with supreme confidence.

Despite the fact that she found tomb raiders to be the lowest form of human beings, she was intrigued. "Does it pay well?"

He hesitated only a moment. "Very."

"So that's why it's worth the risk," she added.

He cast her a quick glance. "I didn't say that."

But you meant it, she thought. It was all about money. No one cared about the past. No one wanted to pay to save it. No one wanted to remember.

Snoring arose from the backseat, and they both turned around to find Paulie sound asleep amid the suitcases.

Simon chuckled for the first time since Boston. "That kid can sleep anywhere."

"He said it was a fine art."

Simon nodded, looking suddenly tired himself. "He's right."

Mancuso hadn't changed a bit since Simon last saw him. He was still wearing his trademark straw fedora and crisp white suit. Still short. Still smiling. And still trying to charm the pants off the women.

Simon watched him kiss both of Jillian's cheeks and felt a twinge of resentment when she laughed. What did he care? She could kiss whoever she wanted.

He yanked the suitcases out of the back of the Jeep and dropped them on the ground. Water trickled into a round marble fountain in the center of the circular driveway. The smell of lavender filled the air from the gardens. The ivory villa stood proud and solid as ever. The terra-cotta tile roof gleamed in the moonlight. Wide stone walkways welcomed all. The house hadn't changed a bit, either.

Mancuso shook Paulie's hand as they did the usual greeting stuff. And lastly he turned to Simon.

"Simon!" Mancuso said in a thick Mexican accent and clapped him on both shoulders, shaking him with amazing strength for a man in his seventies. "Good to see you. I heard you retired."

"Trying." He shook Mancuso's hand. "When are you going to get with the twenty-first century, hombre?"

Mancuso chuckled and swept his arms wide toward his sprawling hacienda. "And ruin all this? No. No. No. Technology is ugly. Wires and cables and things out of the roof. Ugly. A blight upon the Earth."

Paulie looked like he was going to croak on the spot.

"History is beautiful," Mancuso said, putting his hand to his heart in reverence. "With the grace and wisdom of a fine woman."

Then he winked at Simon, tucked Jillian's arm in his, and led her toward the arched doorway. She gave him a big smile, and they chatted all the way inside.

Loaded down with their luggage, Paulie fell in step beside Simon to follow them. They arrived at the cool entry and set the luggage down on the Saltillo tile floor. White stucco walls reached to the soaring plank ceilings with exposed rafters. Dark-stained shelves were crowded with Mancuso's art collection. Original paintings hung on the walls. Through the French doors, the ocean beckoned like an old friend.

"Mancuso's laying it on pretty thick," Paulie said with a frown.

Simon eyed him. "Jealous?"

Paulie looked back at him in disgust. "That's gross. Jillian is like a sister to me. Which, by the way, I've been meaning to talk to you about."

Huh. Simon crossed his arms and waited.

Paulie glanced around to see where she was before starting. "Jillian's a nice lady. She's not like, like—"

"Like me?" Simon prompted helpfully.

90   Samantha Graves

"Exactly," Paulie said. "If anything should happen to her—"

"No one's going to touch her."

"Like if someone takes *advantage* of her," Paulie overrode him in earnest, "I'd be obliged to do something about it."

Simon tried to control the grin that was working its way across his face. "Do something about it?"

Paulie puffed up his chest. "I might not be the biggest man in this room, but I have ways."

Ways. It was all Simon could do not to laugh at 150 pounds of Paulie playing big brother. "Thanks for the warning."

Paulie nodded a few times. "And don't forget it."

Jillian's laughter floated in from the kitchen, followed by the distinctive whirl of the blender. Mancuso's killer mango margaritas. It was going to be a long night.

"I won't," he said and hitched his head toward the interior. "But you might want to start worrying about Mancuso."

Paulie gave the kitchen a concerned look.

"Find anything on Franco?" Simon asked him.

Paulie nodded. "Your basic petty thug with a long list of minor convictions. Spent a few years in jail. Mostly for larceny, assault, and possession of stolen property."

"Looks like he's moved up to the big time," Simon noted.

"You think he's the ringleader?" Paulie asked.

Simon shook his head. "He didn't strike me as being particularly bright. Definitely a hired hand. But I'll take whatever you've got on him. What about *Lance?*"

Paulie smirked at the way he said the name. "Jealous?"

"Not in this lifetime."

"I'm still working on him. He just kind of disappeared."

Simon was beginning to wonder about good old up-standing Lance. Usually when a man disappeared, it was because he didn't want to be found.

Paulie said, "But don't worry. If he's still alive, I'll find him."

Simon eyed him. "Someday you need to tell me where you learned how to do all this."

Paulie grinned over his shoulder as he headed for the kitchen. "No, I don't."

CHAPTER
9

At midnight, Simon was nicely relaxed by a few margaritas, a couple of laughs, and some good Mexican food, and he was just getting into bed when Jackson's cell phone rang.

His pulse quickened as he riffled for the phone in his duffel bag. When he flipped it open and checked the incoming number, NO DATA was all it said.

He hit a button and said, "Hello."

"Took you long enough to answer, Jackson," a male voice said. It was being artificially distorted. Nice.

"Jackson doesn't live here anymore. And it would be helpful if you told me why."

There was a short pause on the other end. "Who is this?"

Simon smirked. "A friend of Jackson's. Now. I want to know if Celina is still alive."

The voice was not impressed. "What happened to Jackson?"

Simon frowned. This guy didn't know Jackson was

dead? "Someone killed him. For the second time, where's Celina?"

"How do you know her?"

Trick question. "I know a lot of things. Last time, before I hang up and you lose all the goodies you're looking for, let me talk to Celina."

The man covered the voice box of the phone for a moment, and Simon could hear him talking with someone else. That meant there were at least two of them. He waited, hoping the kidnappers hadn't already decided she wasn't worth the trouble. Celina could be a royal pain in the ass.

There was a clunking of the phone, and then Celina's voice. "Hello? Jackson, is that you?"

She sounded fragile and scared. Simon worked to keep his tone even. "It's me. Don't say my name."

Celina inhaled sharply when she heard his voice. "Oh, my God. How did you get into this mess? Where's Jackson?"

He closed his eyes. "He didn't make it."

"Oh, no—" She started sobbing.

Crap, he hated when she cried. "Listen, I'm going to get you out of this—"

She was becoming hysterical. "How? Do you *know* what they want?"

"Yeah, I know what they want. I'll get it."

"It's impossible. There's no way you can find—"

She was cut off. Simon heard her scream, and then the distorted voice came back on the line. "That's enough chitchat. You want to talk to her again, you'll pick up where Jackson left off. I'll give you the same deal I gave him. Find me the Archives of Man."

Simon asked, "And what do I do when I find them?"

"I'll give you instructions when you get close. Don't lose this phone. You wouldn't want to get your girl back missing any pieces." The caller disconnected.

"Shit." There was no way this was going to work. The kidnappers would never let Celina out alive. Simon ran a hand through his hair, the sound of her voice still fresh in his mind. She'd driven him crazy when they were married, nearly gotten him killed with her recklessness and greed. But he couldn't walk away and let her die, either.

He stared at the phone and the picture of Celina bound and gagged. Then he paged through the phone commands and deleted the photo and text messages. Tomorrow he'd give the phone to Paulie for a few hours and see if the whiz kid could trace that call.

Any relaxation Simon had gotten from the margaritas was long gone. He rolled his shoulders to work out the tension and walked through the quiet house to the kitchen.

Simon grabbed a glass out of the sink, rinsed it, and filled it with water. He was just about to take a drink when he noticed someone on the beach. Mancuso's beachfront was wide and private, but the moonlight outlined a slim silhouette. Every muscle in Simon's body went to ready mode.

Had someone followed them from the airport? He'd taken the long way out of Veracruz, hoping to lose anyone who might be on their tail. Maybe he'd missed one.

The person turned, and blond hair caught in the moonlight.

"Dammit," he muttered and slammed the glass to the counter. Was she *trying* to get herself kidnapped again?

Did she have any idea how dangerous it was for her to be out there alone in the middle of the fucking night? That was all he'd need—for her to disappear. Kiss Celina good-bye.

He slipped out the veranda doors that led to the beach, where she was standing looking up at the moon. A warm gulf breeze swept over him as he crouched through the low grass. Jillian stood a few inches into the surf, wearing a thin robe that wrapped around her thighs and fluttered in the breeze. No one around. No one to hear her scream if someone took her.

She never heard him come up behind her. He grabbed her around the waist and put his hand over her mouth. He was about to whisper, "This is how easy it would be to kidnap you" when she reacted.

Her elbow knifed his belly, and her head snapped back to bash him in the nose. Stars and agony shot through his head as he grabbed for his face. His eyes were closed when she delivered the knee to his groin. He went down in a heap of pain.

For a moment, his brain disconnected from his body, and then Jillian dropped down next to him in the sand. "Simon! What in God's name were you doing? I thought you were an attacker."

He rolled to his side and squinted at her. "Trying to teach you a lesson."

She threw her hands up. "What? That you're a big bully? I already know that. Are you all right?"

"No." Blood was dripping from his nose, he might never father children, and his ego was officially beyond repair.

"Oh, God, you're bleeding," Jillian said and touched his face.

"Just leave me alone for a minute—"

"I'm so sorry. I didn't mean to hurt you, but you came up behind me like that—"

He waved her off. "You didn't hurt me. And you shouldn't be out here alone."

"I know," she said. "I couldn't sleep."

"Try booze next time. Works for me," he said and rolled to his side. He wiped blood across his hand. "Where the hell did you learn to do that?"

She looked him over with worry and guilt. "I took a couple self-defense classes. I guess they worked."

The moon was behind her, making her loose hair glow. Her robe had opened, showing a deep V between smooth, pale breasts. If he wasn't in so much pain, he'd appreciate the view a whole lot more.

"Uh-n," he said and sat up. "Why didn't you use that on Franco?"

"He had a gun. That would have been stupid."

She helped him up, and he limped back to the house. "*I* could have had a gun."

"You had both hands on me," she pointed out as she followed behind.

True. And it had been fun for the split second that it lasted.

They made it to the kitchen, and Jillian flicked on the lights. Simon winced and settled on a stool. Jillian's face paled when she looked at him. She wet a cloth with cold water and pressed gently against his bleeding nose.

Pain shot through his head, and he gripped her wrist. "Easy."

Blue eyes met his, so close he could see the pupils dilate. Her breath was deep, and her lips parted slightly when she whispered, "I really am sorry."

He completely forgot about his throbbing nose and aching groin. And that was precisely why he got in trouble with women.

"My own fault for sneaking up on you," he said. He'd underestimated her again. Yancy would be laughing his ass off if he could see this.

Simon pried the cloth from her fingers and held it under his nose. "But it's not safe for you to wander off, babe. Not when we don't know who's after us."

For once, she didn't balk at the "babe" part. "I won't do it again."

Then she turned and looked at the sea through the windows. "It's just so beautiful. I've never seen an ocean like that before. I can't seem to take my eyes off it."

She turned back to him, and Simon's breath caught at the wistfulness in her face and the way it made her eyes shine bluer. He was so screwed.

"I know what you mean," he said.

Jillian sipped her coffee alone on the veranda and gazed out at the Gulf of Mexico. Impossibly blue water met the palest sky far in the distance. Terns screamed and dove over the white sand beach. Waves broke on the shore with a rhythm as old as time. A light breeze carried the sounds of an entire ocean. It was one of the nicest mornings she could ever remember.

Paulie shuffled through the double doors from the kitchen with a big mug and plunked himself down in the chair next to her. He looked groggy and disheveled, wearing a Grateful Dead T-shirt and jersey shorts covered with red chili peppers, which he'd obviously slept in.

"Morning," she said.

He opened one eye. "Lost an hour of sleep thanks to the time zones."

She laughed. "Is Mancuso up?"

Paulie yawned. "Passed him in his study. He's working on the lens."

"I hope he finds something," she said.

"Me, too. Would hate to think we flew down here for nothing." Paulie looked at her. "Are you sure Simon's telling you the whole story?"

She stared out at the sea. "I hope so. We're trusting him with our lives."

"Yeah, well, I don't think that's much motivation for a man like him."

A man like him. A man with secrets. A man with a past that could come back to haunt her. A man she could never entirely trust. The wrong man for her. And yet, she could still feel the warmth of his hands on her belly and her lips. There were times when he actually seemed like a nice guy. And then there were others...She shook her head. Men like him didn't fit well into normal society. Too cynical and too dangerous.

He can't be saved.

She blinked at the last thought. Why would she even think like that? Because her mother had tried to save her father, and look what happened. He'd left, escaping his responsibilities and abandoning her mother and two daughters to struggle financially and emotionally. That would never happen to her again. Simon told her he didn't rescue, and neither did she.

She looked up as Simon walked through the doors with a mug of coffee, and her body tensed automatically despite her newfound resolve.

He sat down, his gaze meeting hers over the coffee, and she winced at the dark circles under his eyes and the slightly swollen nose. Maybe no one else would notice.

Paulie squinted at him. "What happened to you?"

He stared at her. "Jillian."

Paulie turned to her and grinned. "Cool."

She felt awful about it, even if it was his own fault. He had tried to scare the crap out of her and succeeded. At least all that class training had paid off. For a brief moment, she'd felt powerful and strong. And *then* sick to her stomach.

Simon leaned back in his chair. "So, are there any other tricks you have up your sleeves that I should know about?"

She batted her eyelashes. "Live in fear."

A corner of his mouth curled. She had expected him to be angry or upset about last night. At the least, embarrassed. After all, he was a big bad tomb raider and she was, well, she wasn't.

"Any news on Lance?" Simon asked Paulie.

He shook his head. "It's weird. He totally vanished from Scottsdale three months ago. The gallery was abandoned, everything left in it. The gallery employees said he just called in one day and told them to lock the doors. Final paychecks came in the mail. That was the last anyone heard of him."

Jillian frowned. "Do you think something happened to him?"

Paulie shook his head. "I don't know. He seemed to tie

up all the loose ends. No one reported him missing. His bills are getting paid on time. It's almost like he took a vacation and planned to come back at some point."

Simon leaned back in his chair. "But no trace of where he went?"

"Nothing yet. I need to find a real Internet connection. My cell phone uplink is too slow here. I'm going into town today to see what I can find."

"Sounds like a plan." Simon's gaze moved to Jillian. "We're going to need some cooler clothes."

She couldn't argue with that. Already her jeans were sticking to her legs. "Does this mean sightseeing?"

"I'm not sure that's a good idea," he said, and she noted the edge in his voice. She could understand that, but to come to Mexico and not be able to see it just plain sucked.

"I thought you said Mexico was the perfect place to hide."

"Or get killed," he reminded her.

CHAPTER
10

The market in the center of the small Mexican town was crowded, noisy, and in full swing by 11:00 a.m. Jillian walked next to Simon between tightly spaced vendors selling everything from chilies to baskets to handcrafted silver jewelry. Canvas bags and flat woven bowls held foods she'd never seen before. Every vendor greeted them with beautifully bronzed, smiling faces that carried the integrity of their Mayan ancestors. Brightly colored blankets flapped in the midmorning breeze. The air smelled of cooking meat and tortillas. Voices rose above the tethered burros and caged chickens. Music wafted in and out through the alleyways.

In all, it was a menagerie of sights and sounds that Jillian did her best to absorb. This was fascinating, the way these people lived. Little had changed culturally for generations, and she didn't want to miss a thing. She'd seen enough remnants of the past to appreciate the present.

Simon took her hand, and they threaded between vendors waving their wares. He didn't seem at all interested,

looking past them as if scouting for something or someone. She had to remember why they were here and the
danger they could be in. But somehow it just didn't seem
real in this vibrant setting.

He finally stopped at one tent and spoke in Spanish to
a woman wearing a pure white loose blouse and a long
red embroidered skirt. She smiled and nodded at him, her
cheeks rounding on her wide face. Then she glanced at
Jillian and pulled a hat from the assortment attached to
the canvas ceiling and walls.

Simon handed it to her. "Try this on. You'll burn in
the sun."

It was plain straw with a wide brim that curved up
slightly. She pulled it over her head and looked back at
him. His eyes narrowed as they darkened and held hers.
Her breath caught for a fraction of a second at the way he
focused entirely on her. Times like this she could swear
he had his own second sight. What did he see when he
looked at her?

Then he turned away and paid the woman.

The hat did help to shield the midday heat as they wandered out of the market in search of clothing shops. The
streets narrowed, and low buildings were packed together
in a collage of pastels and whitewash. Slender alleys,
doorways, and windows dotted the adobe. Men pushed
carts that clattered across the cobblestone, laden with fat
canvas bags and firewood. Children laughed and raced
up and down the streets. Old women with sun-weathered
skin looked up from their basket weaving and smiled.

They turned a street corner, and he said, "Can you put
your hair up under that?"

She glanced at him. "I thought this was for the sun."

"And disguise. You aren't easy to hide, Jillian Talbot. Especially in Mexico."

She humphed. "And here I thought you were watching out for my well-being."

He gave her a quick glance. "Trust me, I am. Sunglasses and clothes are next."

She was tucking her hair up in the hat when a voice rose from behind them. Simon's head turned quickly. Jillian was about to look when he shoved her past him and into a nearby doorway entrance.

"Hey!" she said as she steadied herself.

He held her at arm's length and said, "Stay here until I come back for you."

Then he stepped back the way they'd just come and disappeared out of her line of sight around the doorway.

Not far away, Jillian heard a woman's deep voice say, "Simon. I thought that was you. How are you, love?"

Love? Jillian frowned. Who was that?

"Nice to see you, too, Alexis," Simon responded. "Been a while."

"Too long. Where are you keeping yourself?" Alexis said in a slow, thick, seductive accent.

"Just staying out of trouble," Simon replied.

Jillian pressed against the doorway and peered around the corner. Alexis had her back to Jillian, and Simon stood facing her. If he saw Jillian, he didn't show it. His eyes were glued to the gorgeous woman with the clingy blue dress, long powerful legs, and dark cascading hair. In fact, she looked a lot like Raven. Capable. Powerful. Confident.

Alexis took a step toward Simon and cooed, "Staying

out of trouble is no fun. Why don't you come to my place, and we'll catch up on old times?"

Old times, my ass, thought Jillian ruefully. As if reading her mind, Simon flicked his gaze to her. His eyes narrowed in warning.

Fine. She ducked back inside the doorway, pulled her straw hat over her eyes, and tried to figure out why she was so pissed. She didn't own Simon. Truth be told, he might be sexy but he wasn't her type. Not even close. Why should she care if some old flame was climbing all over him? She didn't.

Then she heard Simon speak Spanish and caught *"esta noche."* Tonight? Was he going to meet Alexis tonight? Disappointment settled in her bones, even as Jillian cursed herself for it.

Then Alexis made a bunch of flirting remarks that sounded fake and stupid. "Oh, please," Jillian murmured. If Simon fell for such an obvious come-on, he was a fool.

Not that she cared.

A few minutes later, Simon was hauling Jillian out of the doorway. "Let's go."

Jillian eyed him as he hurried her along. "Who was that?"

"An old friend," he said, scouting the area for any more familiar faces among the poverty-stricken struggling to survive another day. He didn't need to run into any other old friends at this point. Alexis had a reputation of being easy to buy, and he wanted to make damn sure he bought her before someone else did. Which meant he was coming back tonight, without Jillian, to see what she knew of Celina's last whereabouts, and then pay her handsomely to pretend she never saw him. At least he was pretty certain that Alexis hadn't seen Jillian.

"Funny, she didn't look that old," Jillian muttered. "Tomb raider?"

"Yup," he said, looking past the dilapidated buildings and busted-up cobblestone roads full of trash and waste. The town was going right to hell. Shoeless kids ran along the gutters. Old women hunched in the doorways of buildings that should have been condemned long ago. Some things never changed.

"Old lover?"

His mind took a quick detour, and he looked at Jillian, but her eyes were focused straight ahead.

"Yes. Very old," he said finally, surprising himself by the lousy way it made him feel to admit it.

"So, you're meeting her tonight?"

Simon stopped dead in his tracks. He'd purposely switched to Spanish so she wouldn't understand what he was saying to Alexis. Jillian turned to face him in silent question. Blue eyes peered out from under the hat with a quiet yet powerful sexiness he couldn't even put his finger on.

"How do you know that?"

She raised her chin. "I took a Spanish class. Nothing extensive, but enough to pick up a few words here and there."

How many damn classes had she taken? "And you didn't tell me?"

"Why should I?" she said coolly. "You have your secrets, and you aren't sharing."

The honesty and hurt in her face caught him off guard. He'd never even considered his secrets secret. They were just something he didn't talk about. And then there was Celina. A pang of guilt came and went. He should tell Jillian and Paulie exactly what they were up against. But something was stopping him, and he feared it was the clear blue beguiling eyes he was staring at.

He mentally shook himself. "I want to find out if Alexis knows anything about the legend."

Jillian nodded a few times, looking strangely impassive. "Of course. That's a great idea."

He narrowed his eyes at her flat response. "Right."

Then Jillian blinked once and turned away. "Right."

Kesel stood in the shadows of Carlos's office and listened to the dealer bargain with two grave robbers wearing ill-fitting clothes and several days' worth of dirt. This was Carlos's job—to screw looters out of their finds and then turn around and make a huge profit from collectors on the black market.

Although the office was small and ancient and pathetic, Kesel knew Carlos also owned a veritable mansion in a good Puebla neighborhood. His neighbors had no idea that Carlos made his money on the backs of poor, small-time grave robbers.

Five minutes later, a lopsided deal was struck, and the men handed over their treasure. They left with a small wad of cash and greed in their eyes.

Greed killed. Greed made a man sloppy. It was no way to do business, especially this kind of business. A tomb raider who gave in to greed was dancing with death.

Carlos waited until the door closed behind the men and waved Kesel forward. He pulled a chair up to the desk and inspected the fine tapestry the men had sold to Carlos. It was worth fifty times what Carlos had just laid out.

"Very nice," Kesel said. "This should bring a handsome profit."

Carlos huffed, his neat black mustache jumping in the process. Thick, neatly trimmed hair stuck out from under a tattered straw fedora. His sharp eyes were watchful as he took a long draw on his cigarette and then pointed at Kesel. "The archives would pay a hell of a lot more."

Kesel leaned back in his chair and laced his fingers over his stomach. That was the difference between him and Carlos. Carlos was in it for the money. Kesel was in it for revenge. No one fucked him over and lived to tell about it. Mistakes made doing business difficult. Money was nothing compared to honor. If that meant he had to play nice with a greedy, arrogant, ostentatious bastard like Carlos, he would.

Carlos stubbed out his cigarette. "So you think they're in Mexico already?"

"I know they are. They flew from Boston into Veracruz yesterday. Franco is watching Yancy in Boston."

"Elwood Yancy? He's still alive?" Carlos shook his head. "What good is it to watch him?"

Kesel said, "You never know when you might need incentive."

Carlos's eyes widened slightly when Kesel smiled at him. "What about Bonner and the woman?"

"The word is out that I'm looking for them in Mexico," said Kesel. "It won't take long to locate them."

Carlos squinted at him. "You think that will work?"

Kesel rubbed his fingers together. "Money talks."

Carlos gave a grunt and lit another cigarette. "And what do we do when we find them?"

"Nothing."

Carlos nearly swallowed the cigarette. He stared in disbelief through the haze at Kesel. "Nothing? Why would we do nothing?"

Kesel leveled his gaze at Carlos. "You want to find the archives?"

"Of course."

"The best way to do that is to let them find it for us. Then when they get close, we step in."

Carlos frowned in thought and nodded. "Yes. Yes, that's good. But what if Celina beats us to them?"

Kesel smiled. He was counting on that. In fact, that was all he cared about. He had a reputation to uphold. No one was going to steal what was rightfully his. "She won't make a move until the treasure is in hand. And once she does, I'll be waiting."

Carlos watched him warily. "You're a scary enemy to have, Kesel."

He let that hang in the air like so much smoke. "Remember that next time you try to screw me on a deal, Carlos."

By the time they got back to Mancuso's house, Jillian was exhausted from the shopping, the heat, and her stubborn curiosity about Alexis. She headed straight for her bedroom, dumped the new clothes on the bed, and was about to lie down when someone knocked lightly on her door.

She opened it to find Paulie standing there.

"Are you alone?" he said, looking antsy.

Trouble. "Yes. What's wrong?"

He glanced down the hallway and scooted inside, closing the door behind him. "We got a problem."

Her stomach twisted in dread. "Is it Lance?"

Paulie looked confused for a moment. "Lance. No, but I have a phone number for him for you. He's here in Mexico."

"What's he doing in Mexico?" she asked.

Paulie waved her off. "Forget Lance. Bigger problems here. Take a look at this."

He handed her an open cell phone screen. It took Jillian a moment to realize that she was looking at a woman in a chair with a gag around her mouth and her hands tied behind her back. She appeared terrified.

"Oh, my God. Who is she?"

"Someone named Celina. Someone being held for ransom."

"That's terrible." Then she noted the strange look on his face. "What does this have to do with us?"

Paulie took the phone from her. He punched in a few numbers and shoved the phone back to her. "Read the text message that came with it."

Jillian skimmed the short note.

> *Jackson, we have Celina...will kill her...find the Archives of Man...contact is Jillian Talbot... Manhattan...find her, use the lens, get the treasure...you have ten days.*

Chills ran through her as her mind began to connect the dots. Simon had the lens. He knew her name, had her photograph. And the name Jackson, he'd asked her about him. He had convinced her that she was in danger and had dragged her to Mexico for her own good. Because the bad guys were after them. Because they needed a treasure to negotiate with...

And she'd believed him.

Her hand started trembling. "Whose phone is this?"

Paulie shoved his hands in his shorts pockets and gave her a sympathetic look. "Simon's."

"You lied to me."

Simon glanced up from the center island in the kitchen to find Jillian standing in front of him and Paulie hanging in the background.

Lied to her? Now, there was a mighty wide opening. He decided to play it cool until he knew exactly which lie she'd figured out. He put down the mango he was peeling and wiped his hands on a towel. "How so?"

She held out the cell phone, and he stilled when he saw Celina's picture. Shit. Didn't he delete that? Then he looked at Paulie, who glared back. He must have retrieved it. Damn geeks.

"Who is Celina?" Jillian asked. Her face was flushed, her eyes wide, and the cell phone in her hand shook badly. He couldn't tell if she was going to cry or murder him. He noted the butcher block full of knives and discreetly slid it out of reach.

"My ex-wife."

Jillian lowered the phone with the careful control of a woman on the edge. "She's what this is all about. You don't give a damn about me or Paulie or Elwood or anyone else. You need to find the treasure for *her*."

He rubbed the back of his neck. "What was I supposed

to say to you? 'Hey, Jillian, would you mind terribly putting your life on the line to save a woman you never met?'"

"You could have told me the truth," she said. "You could have been decent and told me exactly what was at stake. You could have—" She stopped abruptly. "Trusted me."

He squinted at her. "Trust you? Babe, you're not the one I'm worried about."

She didn't look at all appeased by his confession. "And Jackson? Who is he?"

Simon braced his arms against the island. She'd read the text, too. The game was up. He might as well tell her the rest. "Celina's current husband. He's dead. Murdered." He looked her in the eye. "Because he was carrying the lens and coming for you. He was supposed to find it in return for Celina."

She blinked a few times. "Murdered. By who?"

"A man named Kesel. A mercenary and an assassin. Apparently, we aren't the only ones looking for this treasure. There are at least two other parties."

Paulie looked at the ceiling and swore. Jillian just stared at Simon like he was the lowliest man she'd ever laid eyes on, which he was.

"The Archives of Man is the legend we're after?" she asked.

"Yes."

"Which you knew about back at Elwood's?"

Simon watched her. "Yes. Some of it. Not all. We still need Mancuso for the rest."

"I see." She blinked a few times. "And did you ever consider the fact that I might not be able to help you? That I might not be able to find these archives? Did it ever occur to you what that would do to me?" Her voice broke on that last sentence, and he felt emotion build in his chest.

"No," he said honestly.

She didn't move, didn't flinch. Emotions warred across her face, and Simon braced himself for the inevitable explosion of anger.

"Ask me," she said softly.

He shook his head because he couldn't have heard her right. "To what? To help me? It's a little late—"

"Ask. Me," she repeated, slowly this time. Desperately, as if everything hinged on that one small request.

He hung his head. It served him right for holding out on her. He'd brought her into this; he owed her the chance to give him hell before getting out. He'd just have to find another way to get Celina back.

"Jillian Talbot, will you help me save a woman you never met before?"

Silence stretched between them.

He lifted his head to find tears rolling down her face. He held his breath, because he knew what her answer would be.

She handed him the cell phone and whispered, "Yes."

Then she walked away, leaving him rocked to his soul.

CHAPTER
11

By the fourth time she'd licked the salt from her hand, downed the shot of tequila, and bitten into the lime, Jillian decided that she really loved Mexico. It just required a little coordination.

She slid her empty shot glass across the island to Paulie, who was pouring. Mancuso laughed at something she missed, but she joined in, anyway. He'd asked her to marry him six times. Although the last five probably didn't count.

Paulie poured her another one, spilling a good portion of it on the counter. "So what are we drinking to this round?"

Mancuso raised his glass. "Beautiful women."

"We already drank to them," Paulie said and slid her shot glass back. "I'm thinking you got more tequila in your cupboard than there are women in Mexico. Let's see." He lifted his glass. "To ugly women. No one drinks to them."

Jillian half laughed, half choked. "Paulie, that's terrible. You can't do that."

"Okay," he said. "To ugly men!"

Mancuso and Paulie slammed their shot glasses together, gave a well-practiced, synchronized manly grunt, and drank their tequila straight up.

She shook her head and dutifully licked her fist, sprinkled it with salt, and picked up a lime wedge. *Lick, swallow, suck.* After the tequila burned in her throat, she burst out laughing at the little jingle she'd made up. It sounded like something Raven would think, except *she* wouldn't be afraid to say it out loud.

By the time they had drunk to the Yankees and the Internet and reruns of *I Love Lucy,* Jillian was feeling warm and fuzzy and strangely free. So what that Simon had lied to her? Would she have done the same thing in his place? What if it was her sister who had been kidnapped? She'd do anything to save her. Anything. Lie, cheat, whatever it took.

Besides, she wasn't entirely surprised. Simon didn't look at life the same way she did, didn't play by anyone's rules. Lying and cheating were a natural part of his world, and he was clearly beyond her help or anyone else's. Besides, how did you save a man who didn't want to be saved? Her mother had tried that. Didn't work. Never did.

"Can't save him," she said, not realizing she'd said it aloud until Mancuso turned to her.

"Can't save who?"

She sighed. "Simon."

Paulie gave a snort. "Why would you want to? It's not

like he'd save you unless there was somethin' in it for him. He doesn't deserve you."

"What could I do? Let a woman die?"

Paulie shrugged. "Dangerous business here. No one would blame ya."

I would, she thought. How could she live with herself?

Mancuso said, "Simon is good man. He just lose his faith."

Jillian blinked at him. "How?"

The old gentleman leaned in a little. "He didn't tell you about his time in prison?"

Paulie lifted a shot to his lips. "Now, *there's* a big surprise."

"What happened?" she asked, ignoring Paulie.

Mancuso stared at his empty shot glass. "He was betrayed. And he paid a terrible price."

She leaned closer, hanging on every word. "Who betrayed him? What did he do?"

"Nothing worth repeating."

Jillian squinted at Mancuso, because his lips hadn't moved. Huh. That hadn't sounded like his voice, either. Then she looked up to find Simon standing in the doorway with a slightly amused expression.

"We were just talking about you," she blurted out.

He shoved off the doorframe and entered the kitchen. "So I heard."

Jillian sighed inside as she watched him move. Just move. Everything he did was so powerful and sure. God, he was a beautiful man. Too bad he was beyond saving, really. Maybe she could try mouth-to-mouth.

She giggled at the thought, and Simon eyed her. Then

he slapped Mancuso on the back. "I think it's bedtime, amigo."

Mancuso grinned wide and slid off the stool. *"Si."* He teetered in place for a few moments before swerving off to his room, babbling in Spanish.

Jillian turned to Paulie and noticed that his head was on the counter. His cheek was squished up, and he was snoring.

"Humph," she said and turned to smile at Simon. "Hi."

"Hi," he said and pulled up Mancuso's vacated stool next to her. Even drunk, she was uniquely intelligent, classy, and beautiful. He never thought he'd appreciate such a combination. He'd just spent the night spurning Alexis's overt seduction, and the whole time, all he could think about was getting back to Jillian. Her "yes" to his question had haunted his every moment with Alexis, reducing the woman to nothing but talk.

He confiscated Jillian's shot glass. "I leave you alone with the boys and this is what happens."

She put her elbow on the counter and cupped her chin, rocking back and forth. Her eyes were hooded and sexy. "Your fault."

He raised an eyebrow. "Is this about Celina?"

She shook her head. "No. I understand why you did what you did. Do you love her?"

"I thought I did once, a long time ago. Doesn't mean I don't care about her." He poured himself a shot of tequila and downed it.

The alcohol burned down his throat, purging the lingering scent of Alexis's perfume. He'd wasted a few hours trying to get info from her when all she was interested in was rekindling a one-night stand.

"What about Alexis?"

Simon looked over at Jillian, who was watching him with sudden clarity. "I definitely don't love Alexis."

Jillian's eyebrows went up. "So you didn't sleep with her tonight?"

He frowned. "What kind of guy do you think I am?"

She didn't answer for a moment, and he was sorry he'd asked the question.

"I think you are a good man."

He laughed and shook his head. "Babe, you can't blindly trust everyone." *Especially me,* he added silently. "It'll get you killed."

"Maybe. Think I'm right on this one, though." Then she slid off her chair and gripped his shoulders for support. He put his hands around her waist to steady her. Heat seeped into his fingers through the gauzy white blouse. Tequila had nothing on her.

She leaned forward and whispered, "I might need some fresh air."

She was close enough to kiss, and for a split second he considered doing just that. Then he remembered what he was already costing her.

"Come on," he said instead and led her outside onto the veranda. A star-studded night sky loomed low over gentle waves. The full moon brightened the sand and laid down a long white streak across the gulf. The day's steamy heat lingered in the air like a dewy caress. Beside him, Jillian raised her face to the light breeze, her long hair floating around her shoulders.

Why did she agree to help him? After he'd lied to her?

Dragged her to Mexico? Was it to save herself? After all, the bad guys were still after her. Maybe she was afraid of Kesel—and she should be. *He* was afraid of Kesel.

Simon scanned the beach, looking for activity. All was quiet. Just the night to watch over them.

"This is the most beautiful place on Earth," she said, her eyes closed, her lips barely parted.

Tonight it is, Simon thought. "How about a walk?"

She turned to him. "Is it safe?"

"It is with me," he said and took her hand. He laced his fingers in hers and helped her through the sand. She lost her footing a few times and laughed as she stumbled. A deep, throaty, relaxed laugh that made him smile and wish for more.

When they reached the beach, she raced ahead of him to the water's edge, where she raised her arms to the moon as if absorbing it into her skin. Then she spun around in a circle and started dancing to a beat only she could hear. Her hips swayed, and she hummed a catchy tune.

He knew he should be watching the beach, but frankly, he couldn't pull himself away from her uninhibited exuberance.

Then she stopped, lifted her blouse over her head, and flung it into the breeze. It drifted away like a surreal dream. A white bra hugged her breasts and glowed in the moonlight. Before he could say anything, she unzipped her shorts and kicked them off, revealing matching white panties.

His mouth went dry. She had the body of a goddess— long, lean, soft in all the right places. Without looking back, she rushed into the water, laughing and kicking the waves as they crested. Then all he could see was her white panties as she dove into the deeper waves.

"I'll be damned," he said. Underneath that cool curator exterior, Jillian Talbot was a wild woman.

She surfaced and waved an arm. "Afraid of a little water, Simon?"

He grinned. He couldn't very well let her drown. It took him three seconds to shed everything but his shorts and less than a minute to reach her.

The salt water stung his eyes as she splashed him in the deep waves. He planted his feet in the sandy bottom and grabbed for her. She screamed playfully and then draped her arms around his neck when he pulled her close.

Water dripped from her eyelashes and lips as she held him tight. Her body melded to his, and he was glad he'd left his shorts on, because things were getting real interesting below the surface. To his surprise, she rubbed her cheek against his, breathing softly in his ear.

She pressed her lips to his neck, and he groaned at the sensation. She traced his jawline, and he shuddered.

"Jillian—"

Soft lips grazed his.

"Just once," she whispered, and then she kissed him. He inhaled at the jolt of electricity that shot through him. He took her mouth with an urgency that staggered him, releasing all the pent-up energy he didn't realize he was holding on to. She answered by running her tongue along his lips. He opened, tasting tequila and salt.

She moaned and wrapped her legs around his waist. They rocked together in the surge, and he realized he was very close to the point of no return. As much as that appealed to him, Jillian was not, well, Jillian. He didn't want to make love to the tequila. He wanted to make love to the woman. The real woman. That one thought was enough to give him the sanity to stop.

With every ounce of self-control he possessed, he broke off the kiss and pulled back to breathe.

Jillian let out a moan that went straight to his aching groin and tucked her head to his shoulder. "I knew it. I knew you'd be like that."

He was having a hard time hearing her through the pounding of blood in his ears. Just keep breathing, he kept telling himself. But it wasn't easy with her bare skin pressed to his. His body was seriously confused.

Suddenly, she lifted her head, pushed free, and dove under the water, leaving him to wonder what had happened.

After a moment, he realized she hadn't come up. Silent waves rolled past him, and he scanned the water. A few more seconds ticked by. His heart seized up. *No.*

"Jillian!"

He started thrashing through the water, searching for her. Where was she? How drunk was she? Drunk enough to drown? "Jillian!"

Finally, he heard a big splash behind him and turned to find her treading water twenty feet away. Blind anger overtook panic as he swam to her. "Are you trying to kill me?"

She smiled back in triumph. "You were worried."

He gripped her arm and started towing her toward shore. "Hell, yes, I was worried. Don't ever do that again."

They staggered out of the surf and picked up their clothes. Simon's head had cleared from the kiss with lightning speed. He scanned the beach. All clear. One kiss and he'd totally lost his mind. What the hell was wrong with him?

"What was that, some kind of test?" he said. "Because it wasn't funny."

"I can see that," she said, clutching her clothes as she studied him. "I'm sorry. Didn't think you'd get so upset."

She walked by him a few paces and then stopped dead. He walked up beside her as she stared toward the south.

She asked, "What's that blue light?"

He scanned the horizon and saw nothing. "What light?"

She blinked a few times. "You don't see it?"

He frowned. He was going to have a word with Mancuso tomorrow about getting his girl plastered. "No, but then again, I didn't drink half a bottle of tequila tonight, either. Come on."

Once they reached the house, Simon turned on the outside shower and drew her beneath the water to rinse off the salt. He ran his fingers through her hair, trying to ignore the fact that her white bra and panties had become essentially see-through. He didn't need to torture himself any more tonight.

He grabbed a towel from a hook and handed it to her to dry off while he stepped under the spray. He braced against the shower wall and took a moment to get a grip on himself. He hadn't been that scared in a very long time. All the shit he'd been through, nothing had gripped him with the sheer terror he'd felt when he'd lost her. She was making him crazy.

By the time he turned off the water, he was almost back to normal.

Jillian held her towel over her breasts and watched him

as he dried off. "So who were you saving out there? Me or Celina?"

He dragged the towel across his neck. "What kind of question is that, Jillian?"

"I need to know."

Simon hung the towel back up and turned to her. She looked tired suddenly, and fragile in the moonlight. Like she could break with one touch. The last of his anger subsided, replaced by an honesty he didn't want to own.

"You," he said.

A small smile touched her lips. For the first time, he realized how much trouble he was in. They gazed at each other, and time stood still except for the waves surging to the shore.

"We'll save her, Simon."

He closed his eyes as the emotion hit him. Jillian was the last person who should be telling him it would be okay. No matter what happened, he vowed he'd get her through this in one piece. Because one thing was crystal clear—she had no idea how bad this could get or she wouldn't be so sure about the outcome.

"I hope so."

CHAPTER
12

Kesel's cell phone rang. He walked across his Puebla hotel room to answer it. He didn't recognize the phone number, but that didn't matter. This was the fifth phone he'd owned this year, so it was either a wrong number or an informant.

City noise filtered through his fifth-story window as he gazed out over the rooftops and said, "Hello."

"Hello, love. This is Alexis," the caller said.

Kesel cracked a smile at the sultry voice. Alexis was on his short list of informants and one of the best, because no one suspected what lurked under that gorgeous facade. "To what do I owe this pleasure?"

She gave a laugh. "I just wanted to hear your sexy voice."

"You have something for me?" he asked, done with foreplay.

"Of course. Whatever you want. All you have to do is ask."

He never doubted that. Alexis was a woman with an

insatiable sexual appetite and amazing stamina. Unfortunately, he couldn't be distracted at the moment. Business first.

"I heard you were looking for someone," she said. "I might know where he is."

For the right price, he finished for her. "How long ago did you see him?"

"Last night, but I know they are still here."

They. Good. Kesel said, "I'd be willing to meet you to discuss your terms."

She made an *mm-m* sound. "I thought you might. Alvarado. Call me when you get into the city. Bring your checkbook and your sexy body."

Alvarado. It would take him most of the day to drive there. "I'll call you when I arrive. Don't lose them."

"I won't. But don't make me wait too long." She hung up.

Kesel memorized her number and closed the phone. He grabbed his suitcase. She knew how badly he wanted Bonner now, and if he was late, she'd sell her info to the highest bidder. But if they were gone by the time he reached her, Alexis would find out that her insatiable appetite wouldn't be enough to save her.

Jillian awoke the next morning in a bed that was spinning. She opened her eyes, which was her first mistake, and closed them to the merciless morning sunlight. The second mistake was moving anything below the neck. And the third was trying to remember why she felt like she'd been dragged through the wringer.

She covered her eyes and moaned as her mind slid into

gear and scraps of last night came back. Paulie and Mancuso. The tequila. The laughing. The beach. Simon.

"Oh, God," she said with a groan.

Simon. What had she said? What had she *done?* She
vaguely recalled stripping on the beach and kissing him
in the water, which was definitely the highlight of her
life—drunk or sober.

Of course, *then* she'd pretended she was dead, which
was just mean, even if he did deserve it. And then he'd
gotten mad and put her to bed.

She opened one eye tentatively. Alone. She lifted the
sheet. Still wearing her underwear. A good sign. At least
she hadn't hauled him into bed with her. In fact, it was a
damn miracle, considering he was one hell of a kisser.

She closed her eyes and gave a little sigh. She recalled
Simon's hard body, which felt as good as it looked. And
the incredible way he'd made her feel without even trying. The way he tasted. The rush of blood through her
veins. That much she remembered. He'd been right there
with her, and then he'd stopped.

She frowned, trying to remember. Yes, he was the one
who broke off the kiss. Why? A weird kind of disappointment settled over her. She should be relieved, so why did
she feel disappointed?

"Get over yourself, Jillian," she said aloud. Besides, it
was time to face reality.

Never again, she vowed as she sat up on the side of the
bed and adjusted to vertical. Never drinking again. Never
touching alcohol. Ever.

Slowly, she dragged herself into the bathroom. Ten
minutes in the shower and three big glasses of water did

wonders, but she still looked like hell in the mirror. At least the headache was down to a dull roar.

Tequila was the devil. It was as simple as that.

She dressed in a blue tank top and shorts and headed for some strong Mexican coffee.

Of course, Simon was there, standing barefoot in the kitchen, looking fully rested and *not* hung over. Better than good, in fact, in a white collared shirt, loosely buttoned, and khaki shorts. Her dehydrated brain registered the muscled arms and powerful legs. If she was feeling better, she'd have come up with some kind of great fantasy. Right now, she just wanted to sit.

Simon didn't say a word, just handed her a big cup of coffee when she pulled up a stool.

"Thank you," she murmured and tried to act like she hadn't made a complete fool of herself last night. Should she apologize for throwing herself at him? For playing dead? For whatever else she'd said or done? Like a blanket apology for the whole night.

"Paulie still sleeping?" she said by way of focusing attention away from herself.

"Yup."

An awkward silence followed, and Jillian noted that Simon was failing badly at hiding a smile. Damn.

"So," he said as he leaned back against the counter and studied her. "Nice underwear."

So much for distracting him. "Glad you liked it."

He nodded. "I *really* liked it when it got wet."

Her eyes widened. Oh, crap. "Good thing it was dark."

He grinned behind his mug. "Not *that* dark."

She felt her face flush. *Just kill me now.*

Then Simon turned serious as he swirled his coffee. "How much of last night do you remember?"

Please, kill me now. "A little."

"Do you remember the blue light?"

She blinked at him as a scrap of memory floated by. The strange light in the sky. "Yes. It was coming from the south."

"I didn't see any light," he said, straight-faced.

She stilled. "You didn't?"

He shook his head, but his gaze stayed on her for a long time.

She gave him a weak smile and mumbled into her coffee cup. "Maybe it was the tequila."

He smiled a smile that didn't quite reach his eyes. "Maybe." Then he hitched his head to the right. "Mancuso has something for us."

Thank God. She couldn't handle any more humiliation today, and the day had just begun. She practically leapt off the stool and ran to Mancuso's den. He stood when she walked in, looking no worse for wear, in his white linen suit with a red silk hanky in the pocket.

He gave her a kiss on each cheek and peered past her to Simon. "I asked her to marry me, you know."

Jillian added, "Six times. He's very focused."

Simon sat in a chair across the table. "Especially when it comes to women."

Mancuso clasped his chest. "*Si, si.* My weakness."

She took a seat next to Simon as they gathered around the pile of papers and the lens on Mancuso's desk. A thick, worn tome filled with yellowed, dog-eared pages lay open in front of them.

Jillian noted how Mancuso became serious as he turned the book to face them.

"This is the legend," he told them.

A hand-drawn black-and-white picture showed an ancient people arriving by boats on the virgin shores of what must be Mexico. Proud and regal, they displayed classic Olmec features—wide-set eyes, generous lips, brown skin.

Mancuso tapped a man standing on the beach, amid the boats and people. "The high priest."

He was the only one who seemed aware of the artist. His head was shaved and so were his eyebrows. His feet were bare, and he wore a simple white robe with a blue sash at the waist. He held scrolls tightly in his arms.

But it was his eyes that mesmerized her. It seemed as though he was staring right at her. Right through her.

Mancuso said, "Legend is told that members of a highly advanced ancient civilization landed on Mexican shores fifteen thousand years ago to escape the unrest and massive climatic change in their homeland."

She eyed him. "Sounds a lot like Atlantis."

"Perhaps it is," Mancuso said with a broad smile.

Maybe he was still drunk from last night. "There is no proof that Atlantis ever existed."

"Doesn't stop people from believing it," Simon pointed out.

"This is true," Mancuso agreed. "The ancients brought with them the entire legacy of their world—art, text, medicine, laws, ancient technology, weapons."

She studied the picture again. Sure enough, large pots and crates filled the boats and littered the beach.

Mancuso continued, "They were the forbearers of

Central American civilization and possibly the cradle of humankind."

She stared at him. Now he had her attention. Forget Pre-Columbian or Pre-Classic. This could be a root civilization. The answer to all the rising discrepancies that archaeologists and historians struggled with for how ancient man could have such developed technology.

"What happened to them?" she asked.

Simon answered. "The same thing that happens to most civilizations. Given the freedom to rebuild, they naturally blew it and began fighting among themselves."

She realized suddenly that he already knew this. Elwood must have told him, and Simon never told her. Part of her hardened. He'd lied to her about more than Celina. Was everything a lie? What about last night?

Mancuso broke into her thoughts. "Precisely. Just before they decimated their numbers to the point of extinction, the priests hid their archives in Mexico. According to the legend, a Seer will arise before self-destruction threatens mankind anew. Before we die out and start over again."

She felt like the air had been sucked from her lungs. His words echoed in her mind until they settled. No. This couldn't be. Not her.

"This Seer will bring forth the archives. They will be our one chance to break the cycle of death and rebirth that humankind has endured for thousands upon thousands of years," Mancuso said, his eyes locked on hers. "And to enter into a great age of peace."

I don't want this, she thought fiercely. *I don't want to be the one.* This was too much. The responsibility, the weight—

Mancuso put his hand over hers. "Are you the Seer?"

She could barely speak. "I don't know."

He pressed his lips together, a look of concern on his face. "Then may God be with you."

Simon stood on the patio and watched Jillian pace anxiously. She was beside herself, and he knew that it wasn't all from the legend. She was tied to that lens in some way he couldn't figure. Some way that went deep to her soul. They were linked, and he was beginning to worry what would happen once she and the lens were separated forever.

"There has to be another way," she said. "Something else we can give the kidnappers in exchange for Celina."

He crossed his arms over his chest. "They were pretty specific. The Archives of Man."

She shook her head a few times. "This isn't just a turquoise cup, Simon. If this is true, there is an entire civilization in those archives. One we know nothing about. Do you have any idea how historically significant this could be?"

"Do you have any idea how historically dead we'll be if we don't hand it over? Forget Celina for a minute. These guys know about you and the lens. Kesel knows about this. It's only a matter of time before someone else comes looking for us."

She stopped in front of him. "So we just hand it over to them and all this goes away?"

He shrugged. "If the legend is true, and it's one lens and one Seer, then yes. You should be safe. They would have no further use for you."

Her eyes narrowed as she studied him. "You knew all

this in Boston. You knew what you were asking me to do then."

Simon took a deep breath. He couldn't lie to her anymore. "Most of it."

The look of betrayal on her face made him feel like crap. He knew betrayal, had experienced it so often that it had become a part of him. And now he'd done it to her. Somehow, that felt worse than being the one betrayed.

"I know I lied to you, but it doesn't change the situation. This is our only hope. We use it as our way out—as Celina's way out—or we all die."

Her eyes closed. "You don't understand, Simon. I was chosen to find this. To give it to the world, not to a bunch of thieves."

Like me, he finished silently. Simon clenched his jaw. "How many lives is that worth to you?"

He hated saying it as much as he hated seeing her flinch. This would tear her apart, but there was nothing he could do about it.

"The world has gotten along just fine for the past fifteen thousand years, Jillian. I doubt one cache of ancient wisdom is going to change anything," he added softly.

"You say that because you have no faith," she said.

He blinked at the certainty in her statement.

"This is more than knowledge," she continued, her voice cracking a little. "There's a danger here. Something in the wrong hands—" She stopped and shook her head. "I don't know."

She looked away, out at the waves crashing in the midday sun. Away from him. She was shutting him out; he could feel it even where he stood. In truth, it was better this way, anyway. At least for her.

When she turned back, her entire expression had changed. The warm blue eyes were gone as she looked at him. A cool, detached gaze met his. "Where do we start?"

He should have felt relieved, but there was something in her eyes that set him on edge. "Mancuso said we should follow the Olmec ruins. The three major sites are Tres Zapotes, San Lorenzo, and La Venta. He thinks those would be our best chance of finding something."

She nodded, but her mind was elsewhere, and that bothered him more than he cared to admit.

"We need to leave soon if we want to see Tres Zapotes today. If we find nothing there, we'll spend the night in Catemaco and then head on to San Lorenzo," he said.

"I'll call the museum and ask for a few more days," she said.

Simon watched her. "That might be a good idea. As for Paulie—"

"Paulie stays here," she cut in sharply, surprising him with her firmness. "He can't do anything for us, and I don't want him in the line of fire."

There was something else at play here. "You don't think we'll make it."

Her gaze flickered from his, giving her away. "He said he tapped into a solid wireless connection here. If we need him, he's just a phone call away."

"Fair enough." Simon handed her a piece of paper. "Paulie found Lance's phone number. We need to call him and set up a meeting, if possible."

If he hadn't been paying attention, he might have missed her wince. "We?"

"I want to be there."

"I'd rather you weren't," she said. "Besides, what difference does it make now whether or not he told anyone?"

"Depends on who he told." He waited for her reaction.

She swallowed. "I can ask him that on the phone."

"We need to talk to him in person," Simon pressed. He wasn't leaving any lead unchecked. Besides, Simon wanted to see who Jillian thought would be the perfect man for her. Because it was pretty obvious she'd never gotten over Lance.

Her eyes cut to his. "We already have a mission. This would only take us out of our way."

"If he's close to Tres Zapotes tomorrow, it'll be worth it." *And it'd be a hell of a coincidence,* he added silently. *Which would move Lance to the top of the hit list.*

"And if not?"

"Then find out where he is," Simon told her. "And ask him—point-blank—who he told."

Her expression strained. "*If* he told anyone."

"Right."

She looked at him, and he could see the sadness and regret in her eyes. He wanted to kill Lance for whatever it was he had done to her. Maybe that was the *real* reason he was hoping Lance was close by.

"Okay," she said and then she stared out over the ocean one more time before going inside.

Simon dropped his head back and closed his eyes. How did he get himself in this much trouble? All he wanted was to live a quiet life, have a few meaningless relationships, and leave all this crap behind. Mow his lawn. Get a dog. Read a damn book.

What he didn't want to do was get tangled up with a woman who would challenge him every step of the way without so much as raising her voice. Who could make him feel like shit every time he hurt her. Who could make him *feel*, period.

Footsteps brought him around. Mancuso walked up and handed him a few sheets of paper. "Here are the glyph translations."

Simon scanned the images and the text Mancuso had written beside them—"moon," "shut eye," "simple circle," "hand," "new sun." A bunch of lines all linked together.

"Not much to go on," Simon pointed out.

Mancuso stepped up to the railing overlooking the beach and gave a sigh. "*Si.* It was the best I could do. This is an unknown script. I could not decipher the lines. Perhaps they will mean more when you take the lens to the sites."

Simon folded the papers and put them in his shirt pocket. "Any idea what we're looking for?"

Mancuso turned to him, a rare frown on his face. "What Jillian is looking for. You will see nothing. But if she can view the past—" He paused. "You know what early civilizations were like. Human sacrifice. War. Atrocities."

He didn't even want to consider what that would do to Jillian. "I don't want her here, either, but we have no choice. Celina's in trouble. I can't walk away from that."

The old man nodded and clapped Simon on the back. "You never could. That is why you are a good man."

Right, he thought. *That's why I'm dragging an innocent woman through Mexico. That's why I'm breaking her soul every step of the way.*

"I won't let anything happen to Jillian," he said after a few moments of silence.

"That might be difficult. This is much bigger than you can imagine," Mancuso said. "Many would kill for this. I have guns and ammunition in the house. Anything you need is yours."

"Thank you."

Mancuso turned to look at him, his old eyes appearing more weary than usual, and Mancuso had seen his fair share of pain and struggle. "Trust no one, Simon."

"I never do."

"Only Jillian."

An uneasy feeling swept over Simon, and he shook it off. It was a feeling he'd experienced many times just before everything went to hell.

"I don't have much of a choice there."

CHAPTER
13

Jillian sat on her bed and stared at Lance's phone number. The map of Mexico was stretched out on the bed with the locations of the three ruins circled. Her fingers practiced the buttons on her cell phone.

The numbers blurred. She'd trusted Simon. Last night he told her he was saving *her,* not Celina. Was she just an idiot? Apparently so.

He can't be saved.

She closed her eyes.

I wish he could.

But she wasn't the one to save him. She couldn't. It would hurt too much. He knew what he was asking of her. He knew what would happen to this treasure, this gift to mankind, and the burden that placed upon her. The choice between one life or billions. It wasn't fair.

It's not his fault, this choice.

She bit her lip. In her heart, she knew that. That's not what hurt. For a precious few moments, she'd thought perhaps she'd finally found someone who understood her.

How lonely she felt and how different. But he was only using her. He didn't understand at all.

For the first time, she realized that Raven was right. The gifts they possessed were a curse. Raven had been lucky enough to find a man who accepted and supported her. Understood that her gift was a part of her that couldn't be ignored or shamed or tossed aside.

Jillian's fingers stilled on the phone as she thought about calling her sister. But even if she wanted to bring Raven into this, it would be pointless. Her sister's gift was touch, not sight. Raven couldn't help her out of this. Not this time. She was on her own.

She took a deep breath and punched in Lance's phone number. He answered on the fourth ring. "Hello?"

The sound of his voice brought back a lot of painful memories, but it was all relative now, and she shoved past it. "Lance? It's Jillian."

There was a long pause. "Jillian? My God, honey. How are you?"

She wanted to laugh. *I'm the Seer for man's salvation. How you doing?* "Fine, thank you. How are you?"

"Great. It's so nice to hear your voice."

All you had to do was call, she thought. "I heard you left Arizona in a big hurry. I got worried."

He laughed, deep and soft, like old times, and her chest tightened. "Always looking out for me. No problems. Believe it or not, I'm in Mexico. I'm surprised you were able to track me down. I changed phones when I got down here."

Jillian stilled. "Just did a little detective work." She continued before he could ask for details. "So what are you doing in Mexico?"

"An archaeological crew is excavating a new site, and they wanted an expert on hand. It's a real small project but worthwhile. This could be an important discovery, and I want to make sure the pieces find a good home with the Mexican people."

Despite what had happened between them, she respected his commitment and integrity to the art world. That was a part of him that would never change. "They're lucky to have you on their side."

"This is their heritage. I'm just happy to be a part of it. So how's Manhattan?"

"Actually," she said. "I'm in Mexico myself. On vacation."

"You're kidding? Where?"

She hesitated and glanced at the door. "South of Veracruz."

"I'm not very far from you at all. We should get together."

Damn. Jillian stared at the door. *I hate you, Simon.*

Lance added, "I'd really like to see you again, Jillian. I've been thinking about you a lot lately."

She closed her eyes. This was stupid. Just ask him. *Did you tell anyone about my second sight? Did you share the most important thing I have? Did you betray me?*

"Just give me a place, Jillian, and I'll be there for you."

I'll be there for you. Right. She was getting really sick of hearing that and finding out it meant nothing. Still, she wanted to believe that he would. She was pathetic. "Okay."

She scanned the map. "What about Catemaco Lake? Tomorrow?"

"I'm just a few hours south of there. How about we meet for lunch at two p.m.? There's a small café on the edge of Parque de los Niños."

"That's perfect," she said.

"I can't wait to see you, Jillian."

She closed her eyes and lied. "Me, too. Bye."

After he said good-bye and disconnected, she tossed the phone on the bed and lay back to close her eyes.

That went well.

Except, of course, for the part where she *didn't* want to see Lance again. And the part where she was going to have to find out he might have betrayed her, in living color, with Simon there to enjoy the show. *And* the part where Lance stomped all over her heart again.

Other than that, things were just ducky.

It was midafternoon before they had packed their bags and bought or borrowed enough supplies for a trip into the great unknown. *Put on your seat belt, Jillian.*

"I don't like it," Paulie said for the tenth time as they loaded the Jeep. "Raven told me to watch over you—"

Jillian cut him off. "Paulie, you don't understand. This is about me. Not you. And certainly not Raven." She tapped her chest. "Me. My responsibility."

He shook his head in wonder. "Jesus, you two are like clones. Never met such a stubborn pair. You must have some real knockdown, drag-out fights."

She pressed her lips together. "Actually, Raven always got her way." *Because I let her. Because it was easier.*

Paulie glanced at Simon and Mancuso, who were just coming out of the house with the rest of the gear. "Fine. I'll stay here. But if you need me, all you have to do is call. I pre-programmed my contact info into your cell phone."

She nodded. "Got it."

He handed her a wad of money. "I hit the ATM machine yesterday. You might need more cash."

She was going to owe everyone after this trip. "Thank you."

Simon and Mancuso walked by them to put the suitcases in the back.

Paulie leaned in and whispered, "And stick close to Simon. He might be a dick, but I don't think he'd let you get killed, 'cause, you know, he needs you."

Jillian smiled at Paulie. "Gee, what a nice thing to say."

Paulie shrugged. "Sorry, but it's true. And call me every day."

Okay, now he was beginning to sound like her father. "If I can. I don't know where we will end up."

He threw up his hands. "*The point is* if you don't call me, then I'll know something is wrong and I can find you using the GPS tracker."

She narrowed her eyes in warning. "Unless I throw the cell phone in the gulf on the way to Tres Zapotes."

Paulie rolled his eyes. "Fine. I swear, you're clones."

She grinned and gave him a fierce hug. "Be careful. Just because you aren't coming with us doesn't mean you're in the clear."

"Don't I know it."

She stepped back and noticed Simon watching them. A flicker of something came and went on his face as he closed up the Jeep and headed toward them.

He shook Paulie's hand. "Take care of Mancuso."

"Take care of Jillian," he returned.

Some silent male understanding passed between them, and Jillian shook her head. She turned to face Mancuso. He removed his hat with elegant flair and gave her a soft kiss on each cheek. His hands remained on her shoulders while he said, "Be careful, Jillian."

She gave him a smile. "I will. Thank you for everything."

He nodded and shook Simon's hand as she climbed into the Jeep. Simon got into the driver's seat, and they pulled out of the driveway.

Jillian looked back to wave to them and saw Mancuso make the Sign of the Cross.

Through the binoculars, Kesel watched the white Jeep head east. He easily picked out Bonner, and the blonde must be Jillian Talbot. A skinny kid and an old man waved from the driveway. He'd need to find out who they were. The kid definitely wasn't a local.

"I told you," Alexis said from the passenger seat of his rental.

Kesel watched the Jeep until it disappeared out of sight and lowered the binoculars. "You'll get your payment in full."

Her perfume wafted over him as she leaned close. He noticed new fine wrinkles around her eyes when she smiled. Her hand went to his chest, fingers slipping between the buttons of his shirt to the skin beneath.

"Is that all?" she asked.

He gave her a patient smile. "I need you to do something else for me."

She raised one penciled eyebrow. "Anything."

"See what's going on inside that hacienda." He hitched

his head toward the house Bonner had just vacated. "I want names, details, backgrounds, and anything else you can uncover."

Alexis's other hand traced a line down to his chest. "Uncover?"

He realized there was no hurry. Not with the GPS unit he'd put on Bonner's Jeep. All he had to do was follow the dot on the dashboard screen.

"I know that's your specialty," he said and kissed her hard.

Simon's attention was split between the traffic on MEX 180 and Jillian. She'd been quiet since they left Mancuso's. He knew part of it was the legend, but part of it was the iron grip she held on her thoughts and on her every move. He'd seen her cut loose, throw caution—and her clothes—to the wind. Somewhere under all that sleek reserve lay a tiger in wait. What would it take for him to see that again? Probably more than he was willing to give.

"Know any good road games?"

She looked up from the map that was permanently attached to her lap and stared at him in surprise. "Excuse me?"

He knew that'd get her attention. "Road games. For long trips. Didn't you ever do that when you were a kid?"

"No."

It was his turn to be surprised. "Never?"

"We didn't travel," she said simply. "My father wasn't home much."

Huh. "Where'd you grow up?"

"Yonkers."

"College?"

"Columbia U."

"So you've never been outside New York City?"

She frowned at him. "I've been to a few conferences and museums."

That explained a lot. "So why do you have a passport?"

"My sister insisted."

He nodded. "Your sister is smart."

"She is," Jillian said with total sincerity and love. "What about you? Any siblings to drive you crazy?"

His grip tightened on the steering wheel. "Just me."

"An only child? No wonder you're so used to getting your way," she said.

"Foster child."

There was a short, potent silence during which Simon concentrated on the road. Then Jillian said, "I'm sorry. I didn't realize."

He shrugged. "Forget it. Whoever my parents were, they weren't ready for a kid."

The horrified look on her face said it all. Just what he needed, a little pity to add to the mix. Time to change the subject and never return. "Did you get a hold of Lance?"

She nodded, looking slightly distracted. "Uh, yes. He said he was a few hours south of us. We're going to meet him at a café in Catemaco tomorrow at two p.m."

Son of a bitch. He *was* close. "Did he say what he was doing here in Mexico?"

"Working on a new excavation in Oaxaca."

Simon made a mental note to ask Lance exactly where.

"I'd really rather meet him alone," Jillian said.

"I'd rather you didn't."

"If he's betrayed me, I'd prefer you weren't there to see it."

If he's betrayed you, I'm going to kill him with my bare hands. "I need to meet him."

"Fine." There was a sound of defeat in her voice that he didn't care for. Why didn't she just tell Lance off? He'd obviously hurt her and deserved it.

Just give me a reason, Lance.

It had gotten quiet again, and Simon cleared his throat. "So, road games. Ever play Horny?"

Her eyes widened. "*Horny?* You know a game called Horny? I can't wait to hear this."

He tried to keep a straight face. "Every time someone blows a horn, one of us has to remove a piece of clothing."

"I see," she said, acting fascinated. "And how do we decide which one of us that would be?"

He checked the rearview mirror. "If the horn beeps on my side, I strip. If it beeps on your side, you strip."

Jillian laughed for the first time in too long, and Simon grinned. He liked hearing her laugh. He liked being the one to make her laugh even more.

"Why do I have the feeling this game is illegal at sixty miles an hour?" she finally said.

"Not in Mexico, it's not."

"You're serious," she sputtered, looking somewhere between terrified and intrigued.

He swerved the Jeep into the right lane, and the driver beside her lay on the horn.

Jillian grabbed the side bar. "That's not fair!"

He leaned back in his seat in sweet victory. "You're up first, babe."

CHAPTER
14

Fortunately, it took them only about an hour to reach Santiago Tuxtla, because Jillian was really worried that Simon was going to get pulled over for reckless driving. And although she had not succumbed to the game, she was sorely tempted to get another peek at what lay under Simon's shirt. And with that, he'd managed to keep her mind off reality for a while.

The old colonial town nestled comfortably in a valley of low volcanic hills that had formed long ago. White church steeples speared through the trees. Pink buildings lined up in an orderly fashion along the main thoroughfare. She was beginning to really love this place. It was so wise and relaxed and at peace with itself.

Too bad it was lost on Simon. She doubted there was anything about Mexico that he found appealing.

He was betrayed, Mancuso had told her. How? Why? She ached to know, but Simon would never tell her. She was shocked he'd told her he was a foster child. And at the same time, she was grateful, humbled even. She wondered how many others knew that about him.

They drove through the picturesque countryside of green rolling hills. The road narrowed, and traffic slowed behind buses, trucks, and cows. Modest houses and shops interrupted the green backdrop and leggy trees. By the time they passed the next town, the road had become a minefield of potholes, and Jillian's stomach was in knots.

What if nothing happened? What if they got there and she couldn't see anything? Part of her wanted to make it work, to save Celina. Part of her wished it wouldn't. Would it be better to have the choice taken away from her rather than have to make it herself?

The town of Tres Zapotes was small and pleasant, but Jillian didn't pay it much attention. She was focused on the end of the road and the small museum near the excavation site. Her hands were shaking by the time Simon parked the Jeep. All she could see was green grass, chain-link fences, and buildings. Where were the ruins?

A warm hand touched hers, and she turned to Simon. "You okay?"

"Fine," she said, but it didn't sound like her voice.

He studied her face for a moment, and then he reached in the back for a pack. "Let's see what this magic looking glass can do."

She exited the Jeep and was immediately assaulted with the sultry afternoon heat of Mexico. Then Simon came around the Jeep armed with mosquito spray, and she burst out laughing. "You really don't like mosquitoes, do you?"

He grinned and sprayed her down. "Spoken like a woman who's never contracted malaria."

She dutifully turned around so he could get her back, which was more erotic than it ever should be. The spray cooled her legs and sent shivers up her spine. God, she was pathetic. Then he handed her the can. "Do me."

She froze as she looked into his eyes. They had changed somehow. Warmer now. Less distrustful. Sexier. *Get a grip, Jillian.* Either the heat was getting to her or the "heat" was getting to her.

"Jillian?"

"Sorry." She blinked and started with his front—spraying his arms and chest and bare legs—and then walked around him to do the back.

The spray shimmered across long, thick thigh muscles. What a body he had. He probably didn't even realize what he did to women. What would it feel like to have those legs tangled with hers? To run her hands across his warm skin? She wished she hadn't been so drunk in the water back at Mancuso's.

It occurred to her that the bug spray was running in rivers down his legs and pooling in his walking shoes while she was lost in her fantasy.

He was watching her when she came around front and handed him the can. "Done."

He smiled as he took it and put it back in the pack.

Oh, damn, she thought. He knew. Stupid fantasies. Had to be the heat.

She walked down a dirt path to the museum entrance before he could read any more of her mind. On the way, Simon took her hand and slipped the lens into it.

"Just try not to be too obvious," he said quietly. "I'll screen you."

Visitors were wandering the spacious grounds once they got inside the gate. A short distance away stood an outdoor museum courtyard. As much as she wanted to see the artifacts within, she needed to know if the lens worked first.

She stopped on the grass and scanned the area. There were no signs of ruins. Had they been ravaged, or had they simply sunk back into the earth from which they came? She concentrated, but nothing came through her naked second vision. Disappointment marred anticipation.

The glass was smooth and cool in her hand. *Now or never.*

After glancing around to make sure no one was looking, she lifted the lens to eye level and swept the yard, pausing on one of the giant Olmec heads placed near the boundary.

Figures emerged slowly, chiseling and rubbing the stone—two men in loincloths and wearing beads around their necks. Their heads were tanned and shaved, lips full, and bodies strong. Mancuso's drawing had been eerily accurate. *How was that possible?* She watched the men engaged wholly in their work, the past in the making. No one had ever seen their smiles or how they moved or worked. This was a gift just for her.

"Anything?" Simon asked, interrupting her vision.

She put the lens down abruptly and looked around. Simon's big body blocked her from the museum, and none of the other incoming visitors seemed to be paying attention to them.

"I saw the stonecutters, but nothing else," she replied

softly and raised the lens to scope out the rest of the visible yard. "Either there's nothing left of the site, or this isn't the exact location of the Olmec occupation."

Then the lens picked up something in the corner of the yard, and she froze in disbelief. It couldn't be.

The high priest from Mancuso's book was watching her. A low buzz filled her ears, and suddenly she was pulled into a surreal vacuum as the rest of the site fell away. The priest seemed to draw her closer until she could see the whites of his eyes.

He began to speak, but she couldn't make out the words, only his low intonation. She shook her head. *I don't understand you.*

He lifted his arm to point to the left. She moved the lens in the direction he indicated, but nothing was there. And when she moved it back, he was gone.

"Jillian, talk to me."

Simon's harsh whisper shook her back to the present with a dizzying rush. She lowered the lens as she swayed on her feet. He grabbed her, and she leaned into him. The heat and the humidity swamped her senses.

"What happened?" he said in her ear after a few moments.

She closed her eyes and absorbed his strength until the ground stopped spinning.

"It was Mancuso's priest. He tried to talk to me, but I didn't understand. Then he pointed to something, but I couldn't see it, and then he was gone."

She didn't need to see Simon's face to sense his disappointment.

"What if I'm not the right person, Simon?" she said against his shirt.

"You are. This just isn't the right place."

She wanted to believe him, and the priest was a good sign that they were at least on the right path. But the clock inside her head kept ticking away. How many sites would they visit before finding the answers? Time would be their enemy.

She stepped back and fixed her mussed hair. "I'm okay now."

His eyes stayed on her a few seconds longer. "Well, we're here. Might as well check out the museum."

She almost fainted all over again. "Sightseeing? Like real tourists? Won't that ruin your image?"

He smirked and headed toward the outdoor courtyard. "I know you have a thing for museums."

They stood under the peaked roofs and stared at a bunch of old rocks.

Jillian fell silent, her whole being focused on the stone heads and boulders housed on the patio underneath. She stopped at the first one and almost swooned—over the giant Olmec head, he hoped.

She didn't seem to realize that she'd gone into a complete trance in the yard. All the blood had drained from her face. Her eyes had glazed over, unblinking and unseeing. Her body had turned stiff, like death. For a moment, he had been afraid she wouldn't come back at all. Did that happen every time? Did it always take that much out of her? It had never occurred to him what effect the lens would have on her.

She'll be all right, he told himself. She had to be.

He watched her circle the other artifacts, her eyes now clear and bright. Blond hair curled around her face in the humidity. Color rose in her cheeks and lips. And when she smiled at him over the Olmec head, he realized how much he liked looking at her face. He'd even play tourist for that privilege.

They moved through the outdoor exhibits with Jillian studying every fragment of rock. Aside from the heads, the rest were touted as thrones, altars, and stelae. But to him they were simply stones that could be anything, given enough imagination. *Archaeologists.*

Inside, the museum was small and unpretentious but well attended. And filled with more rocks. Jillian stopped in front of a small exhibit of bowls and masks. He'd had enough of rocks for the day and was about to suggest they leave, when she whispered, "Look at that cup. Someone crafted that thousands of years ago."

She looked around, and her expression dimmed. "Such a small collection. So little left of an ancient race."

"Some races leave nothing behind," he noted.

Jillian eyed him. "Maybe that's because someone's stolen it."

He lifted an eyebrow. "And maybe a cup is just a cup."

Fire lit in her eyes. "It is a glimpse into the past. Into humanity. Where we came from."

He grinned. "Or maybe they just wanted a cup to drink from. Doesn't tell you a damn thing about them. You don't know what they drank or why. It might as well still be in the ground."

Her voice rose. "Is that how you justify what you've done?"

A few people glanced in their direction.

He narrowed his eyes at her. Was she trying to pick a

fight? "And who are you to tell me I'm wrong? Some of my best customers were museums."

Her eyes widened. "I would never—"

"You've worked with stolen goods, and you know it. How many pieces have 'unknown origin' on the provenance? It's easy enough to forget that when it's in your hands, isn't it?"

He was aware of the stares they were getting, but he didn't care. This was one battle he was tired of fighting. It would end here.

She was fairly trembling with anger, and her words were clipped. "It doesn't make what you do right."

"Unless it goes to a museum," he countered. "And then it's okay because you don't care how it got there or whose backyard you took it from."

"Our pieces come from all over the world," she said.

"Exactly. And how do you justify putting your name on something from outside New York? Or the U.S.? Or North America? You don't own those."

"If we didn't have artifacts from other countries, how would we learn and appreciate their cultures? How would we get to view the beauty and art of ancient peoples?"

Simon countered, "And what about the people who watch artifacts being dug up in their villages by archaeologists? They take everything away to their museums, your museum, and those village people get nothing."

A small Mexican man wearing a museum patch on his lapel approached. "Excuse me, but I'm going to have to ask you to keep your voices down."

Jillian completely ignored him. "This is irreplaceable history. Would you rather that it wind up in some collector's closet where no one can see it, or used to buy drugs? Would that be better?"

"*Por favor,* senorita—" the man said.

"Maybe it would," Simon told her over the man's voice. He pointed to the cup. "Because a thousand years from now, I won't give a shit if someone finds that I once owned a fucking coffee mug."

Jillian said, "You don't know that. Someone might want that knowledge. Respect it, even."

"I'm going to have to ask you to leave," the man said, looking a little nervous.

Simon crossed his arms. "Like you? Not everyone has your vision, Jillian. Trust me, no one will care."

She went very still, and her eyes burned into his. Then she spun on her heel and stormed out of the museum.

Oh, no, you don't, he thought and went after her. Every time they started this conversation, she bailed. Not this time. He caught up with her halfway back to the Jeep.

"We finish this here and now. No more running. No more guilt trips. Everything on the table," he said and pulled her to a stop. She rounded on him with so much fury in her eyes that he almost stepped back.

"You think this is funny?" she said and threw her arms out to encompass the yard. "You think the past means nothing? That history is worthless? Because if you do, then you think I'm worthless."

She was mad as hell. He'd never seen her like this, so out of control. "That makes no sense, Jillian."

"It makes perfect sense," she said, and took a step forward until she was toe-to-toe with him. "That's why you don't care about humanity or what it took for us to get this far. You have no faith in man." She jabbed a finger in the center of his chest with a sharp fingernail to make her point.

"Hey, that hurt." He rubbed the spot. "Faith in man? Have you taken a good look at man lately?"

"The only time you care about the past is when you can use it for your own selfish gain."

He'd wanted a fight. He got one.

"Trust me," he said softly. "If Celina's life wasn't on the line, I wouldn't touch another one of your precious trinkets. From where I stand, they have never caused anything but pain."

She glared at him and said, "You have no idea what pain is. You don't know some of the horrible, horrible things people have done with objects. But there is still beauty underneath all of that. You just don't want to see it." Her lip trembled when she finished, and she bit her lip to stop it. "Are we done now?"

He blew out a breath. Yeah, they were done. There would be no agreeing on this point. "We're done."

She glared at him. "Good."

Simon walked behind her back to the Jeep. He was crazy to think anything he'd said would sink into that stubborn head of hers. What did he care? Once this was over, she'd be back at work, huddled over something that mattered only to her. Consumed by the past.

When they reached the Jeep, he scanned the parking lot for any familiar cars as he unlocked the doors. One blue pickup truck caught his eye. Had he seen that recently? He committed the license plate to memory, just in case.

Jillian said, "I would care, you know."

He looked over the hood of the Jeep, and her gaze met his.

"I would care that you owned a coffee mug. I wouldn't let you be forgotten," she said and climbed into the passenger side and shut the door.

Not forgotten? It took a moment for her words to register. *Because she would be able to see him.* It occurred to him that the past was more than just the passing of time to her. She saw it like no one else, was bound to it in a way that no one could ever understand. Felt responsible for respecting it, for keeping it sacred, for remembering it.

If you think history is worthless, then you think I'm worthless.

Now he understood what she meant. The question was, did *she* understand? Because no one could live in the past all the time. No one could carry that burden for the whole of mankind, not even Jillian. She'd have no future.

CHAPTER
15

Donovan took a puff of his Cuban Cohiba cigar, careful to not let the long ash tip drop on his new linen suit. "Are you sure they are here in Mexico?"

The woman on the other end of the line said, "Positive. They came in through Veracruz and are making their way across the country. Right now, they are near Catemaco."

Donovan balanced the cigar between his fingers and studied the tight wrap as he exhaled. "Do you think they're on the trail of the archives?"

"I know Bonner. He has a plan. Nothing will get in his way."

"And you think he's capable of finding this cache?"

"If anyone can, he can. You'll have treasure worth more than you could ever imagine."

Donovan swung his feet off the mahogany desk and walked across the marble between the expensive furniture and tropical plants to the penthouse balcony. He leaned against the thick glass railing.

The beach below was covered with half-naked brown-skinned beauties, white lounge chairs, and grass umbrellas. He loved Acapulco in the summer.

"Half of the treasure," he said.

"That was the deal," she replied, her voice hardening ever so slightly. "I find the treasure, and you clean up the mess."

Donovan smiled. That was a mighty big price for cleanup, and he knew why. She'd screwed everyone from heaven to hell. He wouldn't trust her until he had the treasure in hand. "That was the deal. By the time I'm done, you won't have any worries."

"I better not, Mr. Donovan. I want a clean start."

He savored the cigar. "You will. And you'll keep me posted as to their progress?"

"Of course. I'll contact you as soon as they find the location. You have men ready to move in?"

Donovan tapped the cigar on the railing and the ashes scattered into the wind. "Of course."

"Good. It's nice doing business with you, Mr. Donovan."

He smiled. "Perhaps we will work together again sometime."

She laughed. "I don't think so. This is my chance to get out of this business, and I'm never coming back."

"Pity. Your skills are valuable."

"I know," she said and disconnected.

Donovan closed the phone and watched the sun glisten across azure water. Boats and yachts dotted the bay. A rich man's paradise, to be sure. This deal could bring him not only money but also a glory he longed for. No one was going to top this. He would be the best of the best, go down in history, even. All he had to do was keep it together for a few more days.

He took a puff and pressed a preset on his phone. While it dialed a long number, he watched the women walk along the shore topless.

"Hello."

Donovan said, "It's a go. Put me through to Walsh."

Catemaco Lake was absolutely lovely, Jillian decided as the crater lake stretched like glass to the volcanic edges. Late afternoon sun kissed the shallow waves, and giant herons careened overhead. White tourist boats with blue-striped canopies chugged along the shores. Small sailboats zipped over the dark blue water.

The makeshift stands by the side of the highway increased in number as they neared the city of Catemaco. Some folks waved as they passed. Jillian smiled at the love for life and the energy the people of Mexico seemed to exude from their souls.

"We need to find a place to stay. Any preferences?" Simon asked.

"Separate rooms would be perfect," she answered.

He glanced at her, but she pretended not to notice.

"I'll see what I can do," he said, tight-lipped.

The city itself stood majestic and proud tucked in the jungle and hills. Colonial buildings gleamed above the palms and deciduous trees. Graceful arches adorned every storefront and stucco facade.

The city was lively with scattered marching bands and celebrations in the squares. Clowns wielding balloons entertained the children, and families wandered up and down the streets.

Simon stopped at three hotels and each time came out shaking his head. They wound up in the southern part of the city in a small hotel with peeling paint, broken tile floors in the lobby and no elevator to the upper floors. Her room was on the small side but clean and bright, with a third-floor view of rooftops and the mountains to the south.

She stepped out on the balcony and took in the scenery. The sun was dipping lower in the sky and promised a gorgeous sunset.

"Nice view."

Simon's voice surprised her, and she spun around to find him in her room with his bag.

She narrowed her eyes. "Don't tell me."

He smiled and dropped his bag. "Only room available. The circus must be in town."

Her gaze cut to the lone full-size bed that would barely accommodate Simon. Perfect.

"Still mad at me?" he asked. He watched her with wary eyes. Although he looked relaxed in the cotton shirt and shorts, there was a tension in his face that betrayed his true feelings.

You can't save him.

"I guess we just come from different worlds," she said.

A corner of his mouth curled. "Right." But he didn't sound like he agreed. "Come on. I'll buy you dinner."

She pulled on her hat. "Is it safe to walk around?"

"It is with me," he said. She realized that she believed him.

As they wandered out onto the street, Jillian absorbed the sounds and smells. Tiny markets and stalls sold crosses and magic amulets, side by side.

As they walked, Simon explained that Catemaco was

well known as a spiritual haven for wizards and witch doctors offering spells and cures for anything that ails. Signs everywhere offered readings and incantations while boys on bicycles did their best to steer them into the shops. Simon discouraged them with one look.

At one stall, a unique necklace on a table caught Jillian's eye—a long, clear crystal wrapped on one end in intricate gold filigree and suspended on a gold chain. She stopped and picked it up. The facets seemed to drink in sunlight, spotlighting everything they lit upon. Colors flashed and merged and pooled back to white.

"Beautiful," she murmured.

The crystal spun slowly, feeling far heavier than it looked, and Jillian was mesmerized. The seller minding the booth said something in Spanish to her.

Jillian blinked. The woman had beautiful brown skin, a wide forehead topped with white-streaked hair pulled back into a ponytail. She looked familiar somehow.

"Por favor?" Jillian said.

Simon leaned in. "She said the crystal is very old. Very special. The only one she has."

"Si," Jillian said with a nod. *"Muy bueno."*

The seller smiled, revealing straight white teeth set brightly against her brown skin. Then everything got very quiet, and Jillian couldn't take her eyes off the woman. A familiar dissociation threatened, and fear prickled down Jillian's spine.

"You are the one," the woman said to her in perfect English.

Jillian swayed on her feet. "What?"

The old woman pointed to Jillian's eyes. "You can do this. Don't be afraid."

The words hung in her ears until the sounds of Catemaco rushed back over her, drowning her senses as she fought to get a grip. She didn't even realize Simon had taken the necklace from her until the seller handed it back to him in a bag. Jillian stared at the woman, but she'd already busied herself with another customer as if nothing had happened. As if they hadn't been the only two people in the world a moment ago.

Jillian closed her eyes and rubbed her forehead. What was happening to her? Was she hallucinating now?

She opened her eyes when Simon removed her hat and lowered the necklace over her head. It settled perfectly between her breasts, exposed by the low tank top.

Her fingers traced the length of the crystal, feeling a strange warmth. It was the same feeling she got whenever she worked with an artifact with positive memories. In this case, a gift from Simon.

Something old.

Something from the past.

For her.

She inhaled at the insight. *He knew.*

When she looked up at Simon, his eyes were dark and intense. A shudder went through her at the concentration of his focus. Blood flowed to key parts of her body in dangerous anticipation. For the first time in her life, she felt truly understood by a man. Now she knew why her mother tried to save her father. Why a woman would risk that. But she couldn't. It would hurt too much.

"Thank you, Simon," she said softly.

He gave her a smile and replaced the hat on her head. "You're welcome." Then he laced his fingers in hers and led her through the city.

*   *   *

The blue truck was parked across and down the street from the hotel when they returned from dinner. At 10:00 p.m. the streetlights were few and far between, but Simon knew it was the same truck he'd seen at the museum.

"Shit," Simon muttered. This was going to be a crappy end to an otherwise excellent day.

"What is it?" Jillian asked.

He gazed at her upturned face, still flushed from a night of laughing and dancing and enjoying life. His eyes lingered on the crystal cradled between her breasts. Damn lucky gem.

He ushered her inside their hotel lobby and handed her the key to the room. "Go to the room and lock it. Don't let anyone in but me."

Her eyes widened. "What's wrong?"

"Something just came up that I need to handle. Go."

She eyed him with uncertainty and then headed to the stairs. He waited until she was out of sight before ducking out the side exit of the building into the dark alley. Not the smartest thing to do in Mexico at night. Every one of his senses was on high alert. He wished he'd had time to get the gun he'd borrowed from Mancuso.

He ran down the alley to the next street over behind the hotel and then took the next alley back. When he came out again half a block down from the hotel, he had a good view of the other side of the street. He waited.

Ten minutes passed with no movement before his night eyes picked up a small flame and a man lighting his cigarette in a closed and darkened storefront entry. The flame went out, but the cigarette glow gave him away long enough for Simon to make his way down and across the street. He came up behind the man.

Simon reached out, grabbed him by the throat, and slammed him against the hard stucco. The man flailed as Simon pulled him forward and banged him against the wall again. There was an unmistakable crunch when man met wall.

He was Mexican, about twenty-five years old, with a heavy mustache and thick black hair. He grabbed at the hand that was around his throat while Simon riffled through his shirt for a gun or a knife. It was his lucky night. He found neither. He let go of the man's throat and punched him in the stomach.

The man doubled over with a groan. Simon pulled him up by his shirt and pinned him to the wall.

"Where is Celina?" Simon asked.

The man's eyes widened like he recognized the name, but he shook his head.

You bastard, Simon thought. *You know.*

Simon yanked him back and slammed him to the wall harder. His head bounced, and his eyes rolled back for a moment.

"I don't know about you, but I could do this all night," Simon whispered, his anger growing. "You can tell me who you work for and where Celina is, or you can have the world's biggest headache tomorrow."

The man's eyes rolled down again, and he shook his head. "No, gringo. No."

It would be so simple. Just a few fucking words and all this would end—for him, for Jillian, and for Celina. A location, that's all he needed. Rage pumped through his body, clouding his mind. Simon was about to slam him again when he heard Jillian's voice.

"That's enough, Simon."

He snapped his head around to find her standing a few feet away, silhouetted in the hotel's neon lights.

"Go back to the room, Jillian."

"You have to stop."

He tightened his grip on the Mexican. "You handle the old stuff. Let me handle the interrogations."

"Let him go."

That was when Simon noticed the Glock in her hand at her side. He swore aloud.

"He's been following us, Jillian. He's working for the man who kidnapped Celina. He knows something."

She didn't seem moved. "Are you going to kill him for that?"

He narrowed his eyes at her, and then back at the man, who looked far more scared than bright. He was as much a pawn in this mess as Simon was. But that didn't mean he was getting away without a little pain.

Simon leaned into him and said softly, "You tell your boss to back off, or he'll never get what he wants. Because if Celina doesn't make it through this, I'm coming after him. If I see *you* again, one of us is going to die."

The man's eyes widened, and then he nodded emphatically. Simon shoved him toward the street, and he stumbled to his pickup truck, got inside, and peeled out.

Simon watched his taillights disappear around the corner. His head seemed to clear, but his body was still wound tight from frustration and adrenaline. "Don't say it."

"I wasn't going to," Jillian replied as she stepped

up and handed him the gun. "I just came out because I thought you might need this."

The safety was off. He eyed her. Her expression was hooded in the darkness. "Were you planning on shooting him or me?"

She turned and answered over her shoulder as she walked away. "I hadn't made up my mind."

Simon woke from a restless sleep to find himself lying on the hard floor of a hotel room. Not the first time, but still, it took him a moment to figure out where he was. Sweat covered his body in the humid, still air. He sat up and rolled his shoulders. He was getting too damn old to sleep on the floor.

Then he noticed that the bed was empty. He got to his feet and checked the bathroom. No sign of her. The room was still locked from the inside. The panic building in his belly subsided when he saw her on the balcony.

He was powerless to fight the relief that poured through him. She'd gotten to him, and there was nothing he could do to change that. He pushed the double doors open and joined her behind the wrought-iron railing. Sultry heat blanketed his skin. Jillian didn't seem to notice as the breeze molded her camisole and shorts to her body. And she didn't notice him noticing.

She just stood stock-still and stared at the mountaintops to the south. In fact, she looked a lot like she had back in Tres Zapotes. A chill came over him despite the heat.

"Jillian?"

"Do you see it?" she asked him.

He followed her gaze but saw only a sleeping city dotted with streetlights and neon signs. "See what?"

"The blue light coming from behind those mountains."

He shook his head as he watched her. "No, sorry."

Her voice wavered. "Did you hear the old woman talk to me in English?"

He stilled. "Must have missed that."

"You couldn't have. You were right there."

Slowly, she turned her head to face him. A tear rolled down her face. "I think I'm losing my mind, Simon."

His chest tightened at the heartfelt confession. He didn't usually hear those. "It's just stress—"

"I can't tell the present from the past anymore," she continued, rubbing her bare arms even though it was sweltering. "That woman talked to me, clear as day. In perfect English. But it didn't happen. I only imagined it. What else am I imagining? What's real? What's not?"

She looked so scared, and so very alone inside her mind. Simon reached out and pulled her to him. Her body was rigid and trembling as she buried her head in his chest. He closed his eyes and whispered into her hair, "This is real."

A shudder racked her, and he held her tighter. He inhaled her scent, felt the silky weight of her hair as he wrapped his fingers around the nape of her neck and rubbed the tense muscles.

"This is real," he whispered.

She relented ever so slightly. He was becoming very aware of the steamy heat building where their bare skin touched. His fingers caressed her slender neck. With his other hand, he explored the hollow of her back through the fabric.

He felt her arms wrap around him, palms spread across his back, and inhaled at the surge of blood through his veins. His cock thickened against her belly, and he didn't have the willpower to fight it. Hell, he didn't have the willpower to stop touching her, period. He should step away now, before he took advantage of her any more than he already had.

She raised her head, eyes hooded and glazed, and kissed his bare shoulder. A shock wave rippled through every fiber of his being, and he knew he was in major trouble.

He closed his eyes and felt more kisses across his shoulder and neck. When she reached his jawline, he bent to capture her lips. She moaned a little, sending shivers across his muscles. He delved between her lips, tasting forbidden fruit.

Somewhere in the back of his mind, he knew he should warn her that he'd been out of the country for the last few months. That his reservoir of self-control was just about dry. That he wanted her more than he had ever wanted another woman before.

"I need this to be real," she murmured against his lips.

His cock ached. This was as real as it got.

She rocked against him, pressing her stomach into the hard ridge between them and drawing a low growl from his throat. Her fingers traced the muscles of his back, exploring every inch. She had no idea what she was playing with. No idea how sexy and desirable she was, or how hungry he was. Another minute of this and she'd be very disappointed in reality.

He gathered his control and kissed her deeply. Her skin

was smooth under his hands, so soft he could hardly tell where the silk ended and she began. Under the camisole, he bridged her stomach with his hands and moved up to cup two perfect breasts.

She inhaled and her head fell back, eyes closed at the sensations he was stirring. The look of peace and ecstasy on her face nearly eclipsed the weight of her breasts in his palms and the tight nipples that cried out for attention. He lowered his head and wrapped his lips around one nipple through the fabric.

"Simon," she breathed.

The sound of his name on her lips shattered what was left of his best intentions for foreplay. With a single move, he picked her up in his arms and carried her into the room. She had her camisole over her head before her feet touched the floor. The bed creaked under their weight as he laid her down and settled on top of her.

Her bare breasts pressed against his bare chest, her fingers explored his chest and arms, her lips kissed every part of him. He wrapped her face in his hands and lowered his lips to hers. His knee slid between her legs, and she opened for him. The sweet invitation was more than he could have dreamed, more than he deserved.

She burned under him, giving as hard and fast as he did. Her calf skimmed the back of his thigh. Her fingers gripped and caressed and burned a trail across his skin.

If she was losing her mind, then so was he. He didn't remember shedding his shorts or stripping off hers. He couldn't recall the few seconds it took to find a condom. All that registered was how tight and right she felt when he eased into her. Heat and passion consumed every inch of his body and soul. Her voice and her name filled his mind as they rocked together for an eternity.

He didn't want to stop, didn't want to lose the wonder, softness and magic he'd found. Sharp little nails dug into his back as she threw her head back and tightened beneath him in orgasm.

And then he lost himself in her and to her, in a frenzy of passion that built until he thought he'd burst into flames. The climax roared through him, ripping him apart.

Simon collapsed on the bed beside her, both of them soaked and breathing hard. Despite his pounding heart, he closed his eyes, on the verge of peaceful slumber.

"*That* was real," Jillian whispered.

He roused a moment to kiss her damp hair. That was real.

CHAPTER
16

After Bonner had carried Jillian inside, Kesel set the night-vision binoculars down on the seat next to him.

This was an interesting development. Bonner had found himself a woman, which in itself was not surprising. But for a man who was careful not to get too close to anyone, it was an advantage Kesel would use when the time was right. Sooner or later, he and Bonner would meet again, and when they did, the outcome would be different.

Kesel flipped open his cell phone and placed a call. A sleepy voice answered in Spanish, saying, "I should have known it was you, Kesel. What do you want?"

"Is that any way to talk to the man doing all your dirty work?"

Carlos yawned loudly. "Don't give me that. You live for dirty work. So why are you calling me in the middle of the night?"

Kesel eyed Bonner's Jeep sitting half a block away. "Just checking to see if you double-crossed me."

There was a long pause before Carlos came back. "That's bullshit. We're in this together. Why would I screw you?"

"For a priceless treasure?"

Carlos gave a short laugh. "I don't need you to find it. There are plenty of other raiders I could have called. Besides, you will get there first. I'm trusting *you*. If anyone is going to get screwed, it's me."

Greed drove Carlos's every move. He wouldn't jeopardize the operation for anything. But Kesel didn't give a damn about treasure. The earth was full of it. Like fear, money could be earned. Pride couldn't.

"Keep that in mind," Kesel replied. "I don't want anyone getting in my way." He opened the man's wallet and read the name on his license. "Including Raul Vega."

"Who the fuck is that?"

An honest response. The man Kesel had caught following Bonner wasn't working for Carlos. Kesel wouldn't worry so much if his wallet hadn't contained so much money, more than enough for your average local. Other than that, though, Raul was clean. If Kesel wanted more on him or who he'd been working for, he was going to have to dig.

"He's a man who got in my way. I'm going to send his information to you. Find out what you can about him."

"Trouble?"

"Nothing I can't handle."

Carlos sighed. "What's the status?"

Kesel scanned the street. "They're moving, and they seem to have a plan. That's all I can tell you. But I did give them a little incentive to speed things up. A dead body has a way of making one contemplate his own mortality."

"I don't want to know," Carlos said. "But you better call me in when things get interesting. We had a deal. I put you on their trail, you get Celina and your precious lens back, I get treasure."

That was the deal. Didn't necessarily mean it was going to happen exactly that way. "Of course."

Then Kesel disconnected and tossed the phone next to the binoculars. He pushed the back of the seat down so he could sleep. He didn't want to miss all the excitement tomorrow morning.

Jillian awoke from a deep sleep with the slow realization that someone was breathing in her ear. She opened her eyes. She was facing a wall awash in sunlight. Simon's big, hot body pressed against her back, his arm draped over her waist, hand curled around her breast like he owned it.

Which, actually, he did.

Oh, God. She was in so much trouble. How could she let this happen? A tomb raider, of all people. A man who had defiled everything she held dear.

And she couldn't even blame him. She was the one who'd seduced him. She reached up and touched her tender lips, which still held the memory of his. Kisses so sweet. Hands so talented. A body hard and strong. A lover like no other, who could pull a passion from her that she didn't know she possessed, with a shamelessness that scared the crap out of her. She'd been wild last night, fearless in her conviction and wanton in her desire for him.

Her fingers settled on the gold necklace around her neck. She lifted the crystal and turned it slowly. Colors shifted inside, sometimes clear, sometimes cloudy. Her heart beat in turn.

Was this how her mother felt when her father would steal and she knew about it? When he'd lie to her to cover up his compulsion? When he told her he loved her, and meant it?

Clear and cloudy.

She swore she'd never live like that again. Looking the other way while her heart broke bit by bit. Living a life between love and hurt. Knowing she could never save him from himself.

The crystal caught the light, and a rainbow of color flashed brilliantly for a fraction of a second and then was gone. How could something be so beautiful yet so elusive at the same time? Keeping you enthralled waiting for those magic, breathtaking moments of color?

Jillian pressed the crystal to her lips. *I will always remember you.*

Simon shifted, and she felt his morning erection pressed against her lower back. A moan escaped her lips as she reacted to his warm skin and hard body.

She really needed to work on her self-control. But she had a feeling that it was a lost cause with Simon. Every time he touched her, every time he looked at her, was like the first time.

Panic built in her throat. What if she wasn't strong enough to walk away? Would she be caught in the same net as her mother? Would she be doomed to the same fate? Held in place as she waited for those moments of color? Twisting between clear and cloudy?

No. She was stronger than her mother. Love was a dangerous thing. It caused people to make terrible mistakes, and she'd spent her life avoiding that trap. Playing it safe, like with Lance. He'd been perfect because she never really loved him.

But with Simon . . . She was in trouble.

Carefully, Jillian eased away from him. He groaned a little and then settled on his belly. She looked back at him as she stood up. A shadow of a beard hugged his face, his hair was tousled, and he looked completely relaxed sprawled naked across the bed.

Don't do it, she told herself. *Don't make that mistake. He's not the right man for you.*

She grabbed her bag on the way to the bathroom.

Simon opened one eye as the bathroom door closed. He could just imagine what was going through Jillian's mind right about now. Probably a shitload of regret.

He rolled over onto his back and let out a long, slow sigh of contentment. Damn, what a night of mind-blowing sex could do for a man. Although a *morning* of mind-blowing sex would have been nice, too, especially since chances were very good that Jillian had already made up her mind that last night was one big mistake. As true as that may be, he planned on making that mistake as many times as possible.

The minute she turned on the shower, he reached for his cell phone. Simon sat on the edge of the bed and rubbed the back of his neck while the number rang.

It took Paulie only two rings to answer. "It's about time you called. It's already nine a.m."

Simon raised an eyebrow. "How many cups of coffee have you had this morning?"

"Five, not that it matters. I'd still be pissy. Is Jillian okay?"

More than okay, Simon thought. "She's fine. Did you make any progress on that last call to Jackson's phone?"

"All I can tell you is that the call was made from inside Mexico."

"That really narrows it down, Paulie. Thanks."

"Hey, I'm working on it. Mexico isn't exactly the easiest place to track phone activity in. Besides, I want to make damn sure to cover up my trail. Don't want to run into the local authorities."

"No, you don't," Simon agreed ruefully. "But if you could even get it down to a state, that would help."

Paulie huffed. "Shit, I'll do better than that. I've almost cracked the call number. If the call came from a landline, I can give the exact location. If it came from a cell phone, that's gonna take some more time."

Time. It was the one thing Celina didn't have on her side.

"I did have something interesting happen yesterday after you left," Paulie said. "I went into town for a cable and a woman tried to pick me up. Wanted me to take her back to *my place*."

"Let me guess," Simon told him. "Long legs, thick black hair, enough perfume to create her own smog, and built for speed."

"How'd you know?"

"That would be Alexis," Simon told him. "Did you tell her anything?"

"Do I look like an idiot? Women like that wouldn't pick up a geek like me unless I owned the world's largest software company."

Alexis would do just about anything for the right money, even spying. "Maybe she wants you for your computer skills."

"Please, no hard-drive jokes. I've heard them all."

"No, but if she's feeding someone info, I'd sure like to know who. It might not be a bad idea to accommodate her."

Paulie said, "Are you telling me you want me to take one for the team with a drop-dead gorgeous woman? Jeez, I like working for you a whole lot more than Raven. I usually just get shot at with her."

"Well, I wouldn't rule that out with Alexis, either. Just keep her away from the house."

The shower was turned off, and Simon eyed the door. "Anything new on Lance?"

"Nothing. He's been keeping a real low profile."

"What about current site excavations?"

Paulie said, "Unless they have a website or a report posted somewhere, I wouldn't be able to find them. Aren't you going to see Lance today, anyway?"

Simon stood up and walked over to his bag. "Looking forward to it."

Paulie hesitated. "Yeah, I'll bet. Don't hurt him, okay?"

Simon grinned. "Now, why would I do that? What, with him being the guy who was stupid enough to break Jillian's heart and all."

"Now, see, that's exactly why I'm a little bit concerned. We don't need to be causing any trouble in Mexico. Low profile, remember? Think invisible."

Simon glanced out the doors to the balcony. "You have my word as a gentleman."

"Jesus, we're all doomed," Paulie said.

"Call me if you find out anything else."

"Right. Bye."

Simon hung up and tossed the cell phone into his bag.

He could be invisible. Better yet, he could make Lance invisible. It would almost be the highlight of his day.

The bathroom door opened, and Jillian came out, fully dressed in a floral green tank top, beige shorts, and walking sandals. All buttoned up tight.

She stopped when she saw him standing there naked, and her expression turned cool. Her eyes said it all— *mistake*. The disappointment and anger that rose in his mind took him by surprise. He stepped up and slid his hand through her hair. She gasped when he pulled her to him and kissed her hard.

Her hands went to his chest defensively, driving his resolve up a notch. She'd made love to him all night, whether she approved of it now or not. She wasn't fooling him.

Then he felt her lips relax, followed by her hands on his chest. She kissed him back, and the tension in his mind eased, replaced by the heat she possessed.

He broke off the kiss and pressed his forehead against hers. "You can pretend it didn't happen, babe. But that's not going to change a thing. You want this as much as I do."

She closed her eyes as if in pain, and his chest tightened. *Let it go, Simon.* They'd have a few days together, some meaningless sex, and then they'd go back to their separate worlds.

He stepped back, grabbed his bag, and went into the bathroom before he could see her eyes.

Jillian walked out the door of the hotel first. If she could drop off the face of the planet right this minute, she would. It was bad enough to admit to herself that last night shouldn't have happened, but to have Simon call her on it was even worse. He could have just played along and pretended that it never happened and everything would have been fine, but noooo.

She carried her bag to the Jeep parked on the street. Truth be told, it wasn't his fault. She'd lost control and jumped him. What else did she expect him to do? Really, she needed to get a grip on her raging hormones. Every time she got close to him, she lost her mind.

It's just for a few days, she kept telling herself. A few more days of Simon's hands on her body, Simon's mouth on her lips, Simon's...

She had to slow down, because her body was having a moment.

That's when she noticed that someone was sitting in the backseat of the Jeep. She froze on the sidewalk and then turned around, only to run into Simon behind her.

"What?" he asked with a frown.

"Somebody's in the Jeep," she whispered.

His gaze cut to the vehicle, and his expression hardened. He handed her his bag. "Take this and stay here unless you hear shots, and then find cover."

She took the bag automatically as he shoved it into her hands. "You might need help."

He gave her a sharp look. "You can play heroine some other time." Then he headed for the Jeep.

"Fine," she muttered to herself. "But I'm not helpless. Someday you might want my help. *Right.*"

She saw him scan the empty street and then reach into his shirt for his gun as he approached the Jeep slowly. A strange mix of fear and relief swept over her. At least he was armed. Maybe he wouldn't get hurt. Or he could shoot someone, which would be bad, but not *as* bad. She shook her head at the crazy way she was thinking. What had her world come to?

Simon opened the back door and looked inside for a few moments. Jillian held her breath. Then he leaned in farther. Was he talking to the person? Maybe it was just a homeless person looking for a place to crash for the night. Simple, easy, and no one gets killed.

Simon stood and looked at her for a second before waving her forward. Now, *that* was strange. She walked toward him as he checked the street with a frown. Something was very wrong.

When she got close, she noticed a Mexican man sitting in the middle of the seat, his head resting on the back, and he appeared to be sound asleep. However, he looked vaguely familiar.

Simon closed the door abruptly and took the bags from her. "Get in and act normal."

She blinked as Simon tossed the bags in the back and closed the hatch. "Why? Who is he? Why is he in our Jeep? And why aren't you telling him to leave?"

Simon walked around the other side. "Just get in, Jillian."

Her stomach twisted. "Simon—"

But he climbed into the driver's seat and slammed his door, leaving her gaping. *What was going on here?*

She huffed and got into the passenger side.

"What's wrong?" she hissed.

Simon pulled the Jeep out onto the street and glanced in his rearview mirror. "You're not going to like this."

An uneasy feeling prickled across her skin. Then she turned and glanced at the person in the back. It was the same man Simon had run into last night. He wasn't moving. Bruises covered his neck, and it looked crooked, kind of like, like ...

"He's dead," Simon told her.

"Oh, my God." She spun around in her seat and stared straight ahead, hoping she'd either heard Simon wrong or there really wasn't a dead guy in the backseat. She checked the mirror. There really was a dead guy in the back. "Oh, my God."

She grabbed the armrest for support as her head swam. "Why is he here?"

Simon drove calmly through Catemaco like there wasn't a dead guy in the Jeep with them. "My guess would be that someone broke his neck and put him there."

Broken neck. Sure. Happened all the time. She closed her eyes. "Is it my imagination, or is that the same man from last night?"

"Yes. And before you ask, no, I didn't kill him."

She opened her eyes and stared at Simon. "Then who *did?* And who put him in *our* Jeep? After you beat him up last night? Who would know that?"

"Someone who was following us, watching us," Simon replied. "We're dumping the Jeep as soon as possible."

She blinked in disbelief. "You're worried about the Jeep? What about the dead guy *in the Jeep?*"

Simon's lips thinned. "We need to dump him, too."

The hysteria building in her mind hit a whole new high. "What?"

He cast her a determined look. "We have to dump his body."

He couldn't have just said that. He couldn't be serious.

"Simon, we have to go to the police. A man has been murdered."

"We are *not* going to the police."

"Yes, we are," she insisted. "It's the right thing to do."

Simon rounded on her in anger. "What do you think the police are going to say, Jillian? 'Thanks for the body—you can go now'?"

She actually hadn't thought that far ahead. She was still stuck on dead guy. "You can't just dispose of a human being on the side of a road. That's...barbaric."

"So is being framed for his murder," Simon pointed out.

Jillian inhaled sharply as it dawned on her that he was right. They'd been set up. Why? Who would set them up? Who knew they were here?

He turned his concentration back to the road. "We don't have a choice, Jillian. If we call in the police, we'll be the prime suspects."

She closed her eyes. Hell. "Fine. But I'm not watching."

CHAPTER
17

After Simon searched the body and shoved it into a muddy ditch, he drove back to Catemaco and left the Jeep on a side street. Then they carried their gear to the nearest rental place and picked up a different Jeep.

Every step of the way, Simon checked over his shoulder. If someone was following, they were damn good. And that was the part that worried him.

Not only that, Jillian was pale and silent beneath her straw hat. *Accomplice to murder* was probably running through her mind. *Wanted for murder* was running through his. She'd been right. Someone had seen him last night. Followed them. Killed a man and stuffed him in their Jeep. It wasn't easy to break a man's neck. They were dealing with someone very, very good. The only name that came to mind was Kesel.

What Simon didn't get was why Kesel hadn't also called the police in. That would have sealed the murder frame and their fate. So why just put the body in the Jeep? Was it a warning? For what? To get the archives, or to not get the archives? Would have been nice if he'd left a note.

Simon parked the new rental a block away from the café where they were supposed to meet Lance.

"Are you okay?" he asked Jillian as they walked side by side through the city center.

"Fine. Dandy. Great. Why wouldn't I be?"

"Just checking," he said. "Excited to see Lance again?"

She slanted him a stern look. "I'm doing this for you, not me."

Simon tried to contain his grin. She was doing this for *him*. On the downside, Lance hadn't just tossed a dead body in a ditch, either.

They entered a treelined park filled with clowns carrying balloons, families enjoying the day, and street bands playing from every corner. A massive water fountain occupied the center, to the delight of the children dancing in the shallow basin. The café was situated on the edge of the park.

Simon picked Lance out immediately. Wearing expensive sunglasses, an L.L.Bean golf shirt, and starched pants, he sat alone at a table facing the park, sipping a margarita. He smiled when he saw Jillian approach and stood up to greet her.

Jesus, he looked like he'd just stepped out of *GQ*. His jaw was perfectly square, his hair cut just right, his teeth straight and white.

Simon hated him instantly.

He hung back when Lance pulled his sunglasses off and hugged her. Jillian stiffened and broke it off before Lance could give her a kiss, and Simon felt a perverse smugness. They exchanged a few pleasantries before Jillian introduced him. "And this is Simon."

To his growing satisfaction, Lance looked positively confused as he shook Simon's hand. The handshake was smooth and light. Not the kind of hands that dug in the dirt for artifacts. Also not the kind of hands that could snap a man's neck.

"Nice to meet you. Are you a friend of Jillian's or a tour guide?" Lance asked.

Simon grinned. "Both."

Lance gave an unsure laugh, and they sat down at the table with Jillian between them. A waiter took their order for drinks and food and left.

Simon leaned back and stared Lance down, who appeared somewhat unsettled by it. All the better.

"So, you said you were here on vacation?" Lance asked Jillian. "What have you been doing?"

She blinked a few times. "Mostly sightseeing and shopping."

"And some swimming," Simon added.

Jillian kicked him under the table. "Yes, and swimming."

Lance smiled a little too tightly. "That sounds wonderful. Mexico is a beautiful country."

"It certainly is," Jillian agreed.

The drinks arrived, and Simon noted that Jillian took a big swig of her margarita, gave a little shudder, and asked Lance, "So you came down here to work a dig?"

Lance nodded excitedly. "A Mayan site in the northern region of Oaxaca. Would you like to see it? I'd be happy to drive you back with me. Then perhaps Simon could pick you up tomorrow."

Simon stilled.

Jillian said, "Thank you, but I'm afraid our time here is already booked solid."

Lance kept his smile, never missing a beat. "I see. Well, perhaps I could coax you back to Mexico sometime?"

Over my fucking dead body, Simon thought and took a drink.

"Perhaps," Jillian said and shifted in her seat.

The food arrived, and Simon ate while Jillian and Lance exchanged civilized conversation about Mexican art and artifacts.

He was a little surprised when Jillian finished her margarita and ordered a second. She barely touched her food, though. In fact, she hadn't eaten all day. And she hadn't discussed her little secret with Lance. At this rate, she'd be passed out before she remembered to ask who he'd betrayed her to.

Simon leaned over to her and whispered, "It's getting late."

The look she gave him was sad and raw, catching him off guard. Granted, he wanted to kill Lance for a variety of reasons, but mostly for hurting her.

"Could you give us some privacy?" she asked, her voice fragile but determined.

As much as he really wanted to watch Lance's face to see if he was lying, he couldn't deny her. Not after shaking her up so badly this morning. But there was no way he was going to go far. If he saw so much as a tear, he was going to slug Lance.

"I'll be waiting for you when you're done," he told her.

She nodded and downed a good portion of her second margarita.

Simon said a curt good-bye to Lance and headed back in the general direction of the Jeep. Forty feet away, he stepped into a doorway and watched Lance's face. Jillian had her back to Simon, but her shoulders were tight as she talked.

His cell phone chirped, and Simon reached for it without taking his eyes off them. "What?"

Yancy answered with a gruff, "What? What kind of way is that to answer the phone?"

Simon grinned. "How's it going, old man?"

"Who you calling old? You're coming right up behind me, you old fart. Pretty soon you'll be playing bingo in the basement of the local VFW."

Yancy knew exactly how old Simon was, so why was he talking crazy? Unless... A bad feeling settled in Simon's gut as he played along. "Says you. How's the weather?"

"The nights are getting colder."

Damn, Yancy was in trouble. Simon gripped the phone. He had to know how much. "Are you keeping warm?"

"Oh, you know me. I can handle a little chill."

Which meant that Yancy was safe for the time being. Someone must be watching him, though. "Maybe it's time to think about moving south."

Yancy huffed. "No, thanks. A bit of nasty weather isn't going to push me out. I'll just put on an extra layer of protection."

So he was keeping his guns handy. Good. Simon rubbed his forehead. "Any idea if this is a big storm system or a small one?"

"Small one. Maybe last a day or two. But I've been

watching your weather. Looks like you might be getting the big, bad one. Better think about battening down the hatches."

So if Yancy had the small storm, then it was one of Kesel's minions or someone working for the kidnapper, or someone else that Simon didn't know about yet. Yancy could probably handle that. Unless they decided to use him as a little extra incentive.

The big storm could only imply one thing: Kesel.

"Storm clouds are already moving in," Simon told him. "But I'm staying just ahead of it."

Yancy said, "Let me know how you make out after it passes."

If it passed, and if he was still alive to tell the tale. "I will. You, too."

"Don't worry about me. You just keep the valuables safe and dry."

The valuables. Simon looked across the park, where Jillian was sitting with dickhead Lance. "You have my word on that."

"And just so you know, you can't always trust that old jacket of yours. You never know when it might give out on you at the worst possible time."

Old jacket giving out, old friends betraying him. In other words, trust no one. "I hear you. Call me if you need me."

"Bye."

Yancy disconnected, and Simon closed his eyes for a moment. "Shit."

Kesel walked around the abandoned Jeep. So Bonner hadn't lost his touch, after all. He'd managed to shake Kesel, which didn't happen often.

No sign of the dead Mexican. In fact, the Jeep looked completely clean, probably wiped down. According to his GPS, it had only been sitting here for about thirty minutes. Hardly enough time to find another ride. They were still in the city.

He climbed back into his SUV and dialed his cell. Alexis picked up. "Yes, darling."

He drove toward the main highway outside Catemaco. "What has your surveillance uncovered?"

She made a long humming sound. "Is that any way to begin a conversation with a lady?"

You're no lady was on the tip of his tongue, but he needed Alexis's special skills. "Sorry, sweetheart. I'm in a bit of a hurry."

"You're always too busy for me," she said, and Kesel could tell she was pouting.

"I promise that when this is all over with, I'll stop by for a good, long time," he said, checking the streets as he drove. "Did you make contact with anyone in the house?"

"Of course. I met the boy in town. Paulie is his name. Sweet, a little shy. Tall, thin, and smarter than he looks."

Kesel scouted the highway ramps up ahead. They'd have to pass by here to get out of town, if they hadn't already. Since Mexico was a big place, this might be his best bet to pick them up again. "Did you spend any time with him?"

"I asked to go back to his place, but he mumbled something and left in a big hurry. I don't think he kisses a lot of girls."

"Then get him drunk or drug him. Whatever you have to do, but get inside that house." Kesel pulled the SUV onto an access road just before the highway ramp and turned around to face to the road.

"That takes all the fun out of it," she replied.

He killed the engine. "It's not about the fun. It's about money, remember?"

She let out a long sigh. "I suppose. I'll have something for you tomorrow."

"Good." He hung up. Now all he had to do was wait.

Jillian was feeling pretty good by the time she left Lance and headed across the plaza, and she couldn't even blame it on the three margaritas. A heavy weight had been taken off her shoulders, and she wasn't sure if it was because Lance told her he hadn't shared her secret with anyone, or if it was because she was going back to Simon.

Lance hadn't changed a bit. Not a hair out of place. He talked the same, walked the same, and had the same smooth, practiced ways she'd never really noticed before. He was like plastic in a landfill, never disintegrating. She had thought seeing him again was going to be painful and force old memories to the surface. But when he looked at her, she felt nothing. No searing heat, no breathless expectation, nothing at all.

The park still buzzed with a colorful, carnival-like atmosphere and Latin music. She smiled at the children laughing and running around. The sun filtered through the leaves and warmed her face. She loved Mexico.

"I gotta keep you away from the tequila, babe."

Jillian spun around to find Simon standing behind her, looking good enough to eat. Her body trembled with anticipation, and her heart raced. She felt... alive. It occurred to her that perhaps it was because being with him was the most dangerous thing she'd ever done. She was starting to really like it. That was bad, but in a strangely good way.

So she took the few steps between them, lifted her head, and kissed him, slowly, just to taste him. His scent filled her mind, sweeping her into the whirlwind of passion she'd grown to know and love. He slid his hands around her waist, and she pressed her body against his. Somewhere in the back of her mind, she heard *Don't do this*, but she ignored it. Thank God for margaritas.

He moved his mouth to her ear. "On second thought, I think we should pick up a few bottles for the road."

She laughed, and he leaned back to smile at her. Then he laced his fingers in hers as they walked.

"How did it go with Lance?" he asked once they were in the Jeep.

Jillian leaned back in the seat. "He said he didn't tell anyone. In fact, he'd forgotten all about it."

Simon started the Jeep and pulled out onto the street. "And you believed him?"

She nodded. "Lance wouldn't lie to me."

Simon gave her a quick look. "Did he tell you anything else?"

"He wanted to get back together."

Simon slammed on the brakes, and she was glad she'd remembered her seat belt. He stopped them in the middle of the road. When she looked at him, he did not look at all pleased. In fact, there was something a little scary in his expression.

"What did you say?"

She smiled. "I told him the same thing he'd said to

me when he left. I would just like to be friends. Long-distance friends."

Simon shook his head and stepped on the gas. "What an asshole."

She smiled, feeling all warm inside. In fact, she was feeling a little more than warm. She slid the straps of her tank and bra over her shoulders to cool them. "So where are we going?"

Simon checked the rearview mirror as they merged onto MEX 180 South and then eyed her bare shoulders. "Acayucan. Just north of San Lorenzo. We'll hole up for the night and head out to the site first thing in the morning."

Jillian watched the scenery go by for five minutes. She could just sit here and be a good girl. "Long drive?"

"A couple hours."

Or she could do what she *really* wanted to do. Because being a good girl was no fun. Her life until now was a case in point. She smiled. Screw it. "So, it's a road trip."

Simon eyed her with growing curiosity. "Exactly."

She twisted around in her seat to face him to make sure he couldn't miss it when she pulled her straps low enough to show off considerable cleavage. She could tell he was having a hard time watching both her and the road. "We might have to make a stop along the way. You know, to cool off, stretch. Relax."

"Jesus," he hissed and gripped the wheel as he tried to stare straight ahead. There was a sizable bulge in his pants. "You aren't making this easy, babe."

She leaned close to his ear and whispered, "You want to play a road game?"

His jaw muscles clenched. "I think we already are. It's called torture Simon while he's driving."

Jillian reached over the gearshift and honked the horn. "Your side. You first."

Simon gave her a steaming-hot look and cut off the nearest driver as he pulled the Jeep over at the next exit.

They arrived in Acayucan after 5:00—later than he'd planned, but frankly Simon didn't care. He could have stayed parked on the secluded road in the back with Jillian all day. In fact, naked with Jillian was at the top of his priority list right now, and he was pretty sure it wasn't going to get bumped anytime soon. All he had to do was keep her drunk on tequila so that she wouldn't regret it the next morning.

She slept as he drove through the side streets of the city. If anyone was following them, they were going to have to work at it.

He finally pulled into the parking lot in back of a small hotel and shut off the engine. Jillian didn't wake up. For a while, he just looked at her. Her hair was mussed and sexy. Her lips were full and sexy. Her body was soft and sexy. If she got anywhere near the horn again, he was hers for the taking.

And that was the problem. Because sooner or later, this was going to end. He should know better by now. She might want him in bed, but there was no way she'd be able to live with his past sitting squarely between them.

Her love of history went deeper than her ethics. It was tied in with that second vision, and every day was just another day that solidified the attachment.

When they finally found the treasure and he handed

it over, that would be when she'd hate him. Forever. That would be unforgivable. The sadness that swept over him now was a small taste of what it would feel like.

Sex wasn't love. But maybe sex was all he deserved.

Jillian stirred, her eyes flickering open before settling on him. He committed the slow smile to memory.

"Hey," she said softly.

"Hey."

She sat up and yawned. "Acayucan already?"

"You fell asleep. Must be the heat."

A blush rose on her cheeks. "Must be. I haven't been sleeping much lately."

"You think that'll get any better?" he asked with a grin.

Her blush deepened. "Probably not." Then she gazed at the back of the hotel. "Is this where we're staying?"

He opened the car door and stepped out. "I hope so."

"I'm starved," she said, getting out and stretching her arms over her head, her long body distracting him more than he should let it.

He pulled their bags from the back. "I've got a few snacks in the bag. We'll have to wait until after dark to go out."

She frowned in concern. "You think we're being followed?"

"Possibly." *Definitely.* He closed the hatch. "There's something else you should know."

She sighed. "I hate when you start a sentence like that. It can never end well."

"I talked to Yancy. They're watching him. They know we were there."

Her eyes widened. "Oh, God. Is he okay?"

Simon gave a short laugh. "Don't worry about that old fossil. He may not look like it, but he can take care of himself. The bad news is that I think this is bigger than just the kidnappers and Kesel."

Her expression turned serious. "Kesel is here? Why do you think that?"

"I'm pretty certain that the Mexican worked for the kidnappers and was following us to make sure we were doing our job. Then for some reason, Kesel killed the Mexican. Maybe to get him out of the way. Maybe to push us or scare us."

"He would kill for that?" she said, sounding stunned.

Simon shrugged. "Doesn't take much to get on Kesel's hit list. I just don't know why Kesel would take that kind of risk, or for who. He's just a paid mercenary."

"So he's working for someone who wants the lens," Jillian said.

Simon eyed her. "Someone who will stop at nothing to get it back. Someone who is giving Kesel carte blanche and enough money to take these kinds of risks."

Jillian shook her head. "What kind of world is this?"

My world, Simon thought grimly. The big question was, how much did that "someone" know about the archives? He decided to keep that question to himself. He picked up the gear. "And Alexis hit on Paulie for information."

Jillian blinked at him. "What did he do?" Then she raised her hand. "Wait, don't tell me. I don't think I can handle it on an empty stomach."

"Turned her down."

That drew a hint of a smile. "Alexis must not have been very happy."

Simon started walking to the back entrance of the hotel.

"You don't know Alexis. She doesn't give up that easily. She wants inside Mancuso's house, and she'll find a way. I told Paulie to go for it next time. Find out what she's after, who is paying her. Just don't bring her home."

Jillian ran to catch up with him. "You told him to *what?* Simon, that's using her."

He opened the back door. "She's using *him;* what's the difference?"

Jillian gaped. "You shouldn't be pimping Paulie out for information."

"Trust me, it wasn't a hard sell. You've seen Paulie. You've seen Alexis."

Jillian narrowed her eyes. "It's still not right."

He shrugged. "If it gets us some answers, I don't care. No one gets hurt."

"That's not the point," she said, a coolness returning to her tone.

"The game here is survival, Jillian," Simon told her, the resentment growing in his belly. "You play it, or you die."

She glared at him silently, but he knew exactly what she was thinking—*I hate your world.*

She walked into the hotel without saying it.

CHAPTER
18

Acayucan was not like the other cities Jillian had seen on this insane journey. This was a crossroads of sorts, a merging of highways in the center of the isthmus. But more than that, it was possibly the truest Mexico they'd been to thus far, unspoiled by tourism.

The city itself was lovely, a mix of old colonial buildings and new architecture. The streets glowed under yellow lights, and music echoed between the narrow passages. Bright spotlights showed off the most distinguished places. Tucked in between were small shops that sold tobacco and tequila and curiosities that captivated her as they walked along the sidewalk. But it was the promise of food that drew her to the central market, still busy at 10:00 p.m.

"Looks like we're having Mexican again tonight. What do you feel like eating?" Simon asked her. His fingers were laced in hers, the feeling so comfortable now.

"Anything. Everything." She peeked at the trays of tortillas topped with an array of ingredients, many of which she'd never tried before.

"What's that?" she asked him as she motioned toward a basket full of tightly rolled, browned tortillas.

He leaned close. "Flautas. Filled with chicken or cheese and deep fried."

Her mouth watered. "I want that. With chicken and cheese."

He nodded. "I'll order."

She stopped him. "No, wait. I want to."

The lights illuminated his widening smile. "Are you sure you can handle it? Most folks don't speak English here."

She narrowed her eyes. "That sounds a lot like a challenge."

He shook his head. "Nope. Just hungry. Go for it."

She smiled at the woman behind the counter. Mentally she pulled the words together. "*Dos flautas, por favor. Quisiera hacer un polka con su quesero.*"

The woman's eyes widened, and then her face broke into a huge smile. "*Si. Veintidós pesos.*"

While Jillian got money from her bag, the woman fixed two plates quickly and handed them to her. She turned triumphantly to find Simon grinning at her.

She raised her chin as she handed him her hard-won prize of flautas, black beans, and rice. "Dinner."

He took the plate with a funny look on his face. "I'll never doubt you again. How long was that Spanish class?"

"It was only a six-week class, but I did very well. I think that woman was surprised when I ordered."

He laughed. "Actually, I think she was more surprised that you asked her for a polka with her cheese maker."

Jillian stopped just before taking a bite, her eyes growing wide. "I did? Are you serious? Why didn't you say something?"

"I didn't want to ruin your big moment."

She started laughing, mostly at herself and for the poor woman, who had been so gracious. "Okay, fine. My Spanish needs some work."

Simon chuckled along with her, and then his smile faded into a direct flame that curled her toes. *Don't do that to me,* she thought. *None of this is real. I can't let it be.*

They walked through the market after they finished their flautas. In the darkness, she enjoyed the atmosphere and the action, but Simon was focused, watching. When he looked at her he smiled, but she could see the strain in his face. How did he live like this? How did he function when he had to look over his shoulder all the time? This was his world. His choice. Maybe that's why he was trying to get out. Maybe he wanted to change, to leave this madness behind.

She was lost in thought when Simon grabbed her by the arm and whispered, "Act natural. Turn around slowly and start walking back to the hotel."

Her heart raced as she tried to control her growing panic. She kept her cool, though, and turned. Out of the corner of her eye, she spotted a Mexican police officer coming up behind them.

Oh, damn.

Simon stepped up beside her and took her hand. He guided her through the market, cutting between the lanes to shorten the distance. All the while, Jillian was praying.

She didn't know what else to do. Whatever could scare a man like Simon was enough to scare the crap out of her.

They made it to an alley, where Simon pulled her to the side and stopped to peer around the corner. His body was completely still in concentration. Her heart was beating painfully in her chest, and she was sure she was going to hyperventilate before he spoke.

After what seemed like an eternity, he whispered, "We're clear. I think that's enough sightseeing for tonight."

"Fine with me. In fact, I think you've pretty much cured me of sightseeing for the rest of my adult life," she muttered and followed him down the alley.

Simon cast her a quick glance, catching the fear in her eyes. Was she afraid of the police, or him? He couldn't blame her either way. Running from cops was a knee-jerk reaction for him and just the opposite for her. She probably thought he was just being paranoid, but he had good reason.

They exited the end of the alley onto a wide street that led back to their hotel, and he slowed to a more leisurely pace, the past stalking him.

Jillian kept looking at him, wary and wondering what was wrong. She wouldn't ask. Probably too afraid she might not like the answer. Or maybe she thought it was her fault. Damn. He couldn't do that to her.

He cleared his throat. "You want to know why I hate Mexico?"

She nodded. "Yes."

God, he hated saying it, reliving it. But for Jillian, he would. Because he didn't want her to obsess that any of this was her doing, and she would.

"When I was eighteen, I came to Mexico as part of a church group. We were supposed to help the needy build new homes, schools, clinics." He smirked as he stared straight ahead and remembered the day he arrived. "Fresh out of high school. I was going to change the world. Except I didn't know how big or how screwed up the world was."

He glanced at her. She was listening to every word, blue eyes so wide and beautiful under the streetlights. Was that why he was telling her this? He didn't know. Didn't care. She needed to hear it.

"There was one village," he continued. "Dirt-poor. And I mean, dirt-poor. I'd never seen anything like it. These people didn't have a pot to piss in. Whatever we did never seemed to be enough. Then one day, a crew of archaeologists set up camp on the outskirts of town and started digging up a grave.

"You should have seen the stuff they pulled out of that hole. Gold, textiles, statues, pots. Armed guards watched the site day and night. They were there for six months. Stripped the site bare and hauled all that treasure away. Left nothing behind but a big hole.

"The townspeople went through it afterward to see if there was anything left, but there was nothing. No one in town got a penny. I learned the entire contents went to a museum in the States."

Jillian whispered, "I'm sorry. That wasn't right."

He nodded. "I know. I was so mad, I decided to do something about it. So I started asking around if there were more graves like that one. Turned out there were quite a few.

"I started looting them with some locals from another

town. We'd go in at night, clean out anything that looked valuable, and sell it for peanuts to a guy in Oaxaca. Every penny I made went back into the village."

He looked at her and waited for condemnation. There wasn't any. She just walked next to him, watching him like she wasn't breathing.

"And then one night, a couple years later, someone decided they didn't like me anymore and set me up. The police were waiting at my next target. No trial, no nothing. Just tossed me in jail with the murderers and rapists. Five months of hell."

He paused as emotion filled his throat. "No one from the village came to get me out. I thought I was going to be there forever. And I would have, if it hadn't been for Mancuso and Yancy. They heard about my skills and bailed me out."

Jillian's voice was hushed. "And then you started working for them?"

He nodded. "Yeah. I figured that was the least I could do after they saved my sorry ass. A few years later, I went out on my own."

It was so quiet, Simon could hear his heart beating in his ears. He couldn't look at her.

Finally, Jillian said, "Thank you."

He felt his throat tighten. Her capacity for compassion and faith was endless. But the longer he kept her here, the sooner that would die. "You're welcome."

They were almost back to the hotel when one of his cell phones rang. He checked his pockets.

"Yours?" Jillian asked.

He looked at the screen of the first one, and his heart sank. "Jackson's."

"Oh, God," she said. Simon ushered her into a nearby doorway and answered.

"Simon?" Celina answered frantically. "Is that you?"

Jillian was watching him intently.

"Yeah, it's me. Are you okay?"

"No," she said with a sob. "He says if you don't have something by Friday, he's going to start hurting me. Cutting me."

He clenched his jaw. "That won't happen, Celina. Put him on."

There was a bunch of clunking before a warbled, disguised voice came over. "I see that got your attention, Bonner."

The kidnappers knew his name now. They must have gotten it out of Celina. "We're moving as fast as we can," he told the bastard. "If I get Celina back with any parts missing, I will track you down and—"

"Save it. We both know I'm in control here. Just trying to give you a little more incentive."

"I have all the incentive I need," Simon replied. "If I don't get Celina—whole—you don't get the treasure. So back off and tell your henchmen to stop following me, unless you want to find them dead like the Mexican."

"What Mexican?"

Simon paused. He didn't know? Then who was the Mexican working for? Christ. This was getting damn messy.

"So how will the exchange work?" Simon asked.

"You find the treasure. You call me at the number I'm going to text to you. I'll be there with Celina in twenty-four hours. You give me the treasure. I give you your ex."

Simon watched Jillian watching him. This was never

going to work. The treasure was in a location. How was he going to give up the location without losing Celina?

"If you break the deal, I destroy the lens," Simon replied.

Jillian's eyes widened.

Sorry, babe. "Now put Celina back on."

The phone rattled again before she came on the line. "Are you close?"

"We're close. It'll be all right."

"Thank you, Simon. I know you don't owe me this—"

"It's okay," he said. "It won't be long."

He hung up.

Celina flipped the cell phone closed and placed it on the table next to the $65 mini voice disguiser they'd just finished using. Such a simple little device. Amazing how powerful it could be.

"You think he bought it?"

She smiled sweetly at Lance, who was sitting across the hotel coffee table from her. "Of course. Simon is a smart man, but his loyalty has always ruled his heart. He'll find the treasure."

"He's making a mighty big sacrifice for you."

He'll make an even bigger one later. Celina reached for the pitcher and poured cold lemon water into Lance's glass. "Don't worry, love. I told you I'd take care of everything. By this time next week, we'll have what we need to buy our freedom. Donovan will be nothing more than the memory of a good deal gone wrong."

"My deal gone wrong," Lance said. "I still don't know what happened. I was so careful, Donovan was careful. How could the FBI have known about that buy? Donovan's five million dollars cash lost, plus all of my artifacts. I was lucky to escape the exchange with my life." He took a big swallow of his water.

She smiled. "Don't worry. We'll fix it. Donovan will get his five million dollars' worth of treasure back soon enough, and we'll keep the rest. Everything will be fine."

He frowned, concern marring his handsome face. "What about the Mexican man Simon was talking about? Who was he?"

She leaned back in her chair, her smile set. *So handsome and yet so weak.* "Probably just some local looking for easy money. Nothing to worry about, I'm sure."

"Maybe. Or maybe he was working for Donovan."

She sipped her drink. *Weak but smart. She just had to keep him in the dark until the end.* "Now, how could that be possible? Donovan is in the States, waiting for his money. He doesn't even know Simon is in the picture."

"You're probably right." Lance gulped down more water. "Do you think Simon killed the Mexican man?"

She pressed the cool glass to her throat. "Only if it was in self-defense." *Another one of his faults.* Simon could never see the merits of getting rid of trouble permanently.

"Then it must have been Kesel. He's getting close. You realize he's going to be a problem."

She swirled her drink. *Smart but weak.* "Kesel is just a man. Flesh and blood like anyone else."

Still, the color drained out of Lance's face. "I mean, he already killed Jackson. In cold blood."

She gave a little shudder for effect. "I know. That was horrible. We never expected anyone to get hurt. It wasn't part of the plan, but we can't predict the future, either."

Lance loosened his collar nervously. "If Kesel sees us first—"

"He won't," she said in a soothing tone. The last thing she needed was for her main man to get cold feet. Not now. "Besides, we have a plan for that, too. We simply tell Kesel that Jackson stole the lens, not us."

Lance nodded. "Right. And what if he doesn't buy it? What if he's not happy with just getting his lens back? He's already killed twice for it."

"Then we might have to resort to a more permanent solution," she said sweetly. "It could be the only way we can be together forever."

He nodded, looking unsure. She needed to solidify his bond to her. So she set down her drink and stood up. His eyes narrowed as he watched her settle on his lap.

"But that's a last resort, and I doubt it will come to that," she said as she pressed her lips to his jawline. "I love you so much. I can't wait until this is all over with and we can be free."

His hands went around her waist. "I love you, too. I'd do anything for you."

She nipped his lips. "And so would I."

CHAPTER
19

Jillian stood at the open window of their hotel room. The moon was nearly full, hanging low in the steamy Mexican night sky. Stars twinkled overhead, oblivious to this little planet and all its troubles. A warm wind soothed her skin and sleep-deprived mind. The city slumbered under a blanket of darkness.

If it wasn't for the blue light on the horizon, it would be a perfect night.

You have a gift, Jillie.

Not quite, she thought sadly. In fact, right now she'd give up just about anything to get rid of it. A woman's life was in her hands. Jillian knew exactly how Celina felt. Less than a year ago, Jillian had been kidnapped and terrorized by a man exacting revenge on her father. She couldn't imagine what poor Celina was going through.

Or Simon. He felt the same responsibility she did and more. He was a good man. But no matter how hard he tried to get out of this world, he never would. It would come back to haunt him and anyone he loved. Just like it had with her father, and look at the carnage her father's life had left, even years later.

Jillian felt Simon come up behind her and nuzzle her neck. His arms wrapped around and cradled hers as he rocked her gently. She closed her eyes at the surge of energy that zinged through her body. It passed, followed by an ache that lingered in her bones.

"You gotta sleep, babe. We have a long day tomorrow," he said in her ear.

"Do you see it?"

He looked over her shoulder out the window. "The light? Uh, sure. It's in the east."

She smiled a little. "South."

He turned his head south. "Oh, right. I see it now. Big white light."

"It's blue."

He didn't say anything for a moment. "Just because I can't see it doesn't mean it's not there."

She warmed at his attempt to make her feel better. "It doesn't bother you that a crazy woman is dragging you across Mexico on a wild goose chase for a legend that might not even exist?"

"Naw. Happens all the time."

She laughed.

"When did you first notice it? The vision?" he asked.

She tensed slightly at the question. He'd shared his darkest moments with her tonight. It was only fair that she share hers. "When I was about eight. I was staring at a vase in my house one day, and I saw the shadow of a man put his hands around it and put it into a bag. At first,

I thought I was watching a ghost." She paused. "Then I saw it was my father."

"Shit," Simon said softly.

Jillian continued, "So I asked my mother why my father put the vase in a bag. She told me I had a gift. That I could see things that other people couldn't. But I was never to talk about him like that again. He was a good man."

"I'm sorry."

She felt Simon's embrace tighten around her, felt the warmth and the sincerity there. "It's okay now. He's better. He was a thief for a long time, but he paid for his crimes."

Simon kissed her hair. "So did you."

Yes. And I can't do it again. I'm not that strong.

"Come on," he said and tugged her back to the bed.

"I thought you wanted me to sleep," she said and eyed him.

He sat on the edge of the bed, pulled her against him to kiss her belly. "What kind of guy do you think I am?"

"Horny?" she ventured. "Insatiable? Inexhaustible?"

He grinned up at her. "True, but only with you." Then he pulled her until she fell across the bed on her stomach. Before she could twist around, he straddled her bottom.

"Well, this is a little kinky," she said, breathless from the excitement racing through her body.

Then she felt his hands on her neck, warm and strong. He pressed his fingers to the tight muscles and smoothed out the tension.

"Relax," he whispered.

She sighed and sank into the bedding while his fingers

worked their magic. "You really aren't afraid that I'm crazy? A freak? What if I suddenly snap and kill you in your sleep?"

"That would definitely solve all my problems," he said and pressed a nerve that sent a shock wave down her spine. His thumb slid along the muscle, and she felt herself relax despite the conflicting sensations.

She gave in to the rhythm and strength of his caress, lulling her toward sleep. Her eyes closed, and the last of the tension eased out of her body.

Simon heard her breathing even out and felt the fight go out of her. He continued to stroke her satiny skin, feeling the heat through his fingers. Perfect skin. Perfect hair. Perfect clothes. Perfect everything.

And now he understood why. If he thought he was a freak, he'd probably try to be perfect, too. Or maybe not. He never cared what anyone thought of him. But Jillian did. She'd grown up knowing that her father was a thief. No wonder she walked the straight and narrow.

And now he'd brought her to the dark side with all the thieves and killers.

Good going, Simon.

Donovan was sipping his morning coffee on the balcony when his cell phone rang. He checked the number and frowned. This could be trouble.

"Donovan here," he answered, bracing for the worst.

"Raul is dead," Walsh said.

Donovan swore softly. "How bad is it?"

"A farmer found him and called the local police. We were able to intercept and clean it up. He didn't have any identification on him, so that helped. We should be okay."

"Should be? I'm not sticking my neck out for 'should be,' Walsh. Is it cleaned up or not?"

"It's as clean as it's going to get."

Which meant it wasn't.

"Did Bonner kill him?"

"They had a run-in, but Bonner let him go."

So someone else killed him. Another raider? Was the word on the street already? Another player he hadn't foreseen. How many were there? "Is the job in jeopardy?"

"I don't think so. I can't believe that anyone would be able to put you and Raul together."

That much was true. They were worlds apart.

"Is the couple in danger?"

"That I don't know."

Donovan tapped his fingers on the fine-bone-china cup. All the years of waiting. All the years of hoping were now at stake. "Can we protect them until they locate the archives?"

Walsh exhaled loudly. "Possibly, but we're trying to stay low so they don't detect us. I'm walking as fine a line as I can right now. Any closer, it could blow up in our faces."

A seagull drifted across the blue sky. Donovan had waited a long time for this, longer than he could remember. There wouldn't be many more opportunities, and none like this one. He thought about his wife waiting for him in the States and all the sacrifices she'd made for his obsession. He wanted to end it now, to go out in a blaze of glory and to quiet the passion in his soul once and for all. This treasure was like no other. It would be enough.

"I've worked too hard for that to happen," Donovan said. "Keep your distance. If Bonner is half as good as I've heard, they'll be fine."

"I hope you're right," Walsh said.

Simon woke up to sunshine and an empty bed. The shower was running, and he could hear Jillian singing. He listened to her soft, lilting voice. He could get used to this. Sleeping with Jillian, touching her, listening to her, arguing with her. Living with her.

He closed his eyes. *Don't go there, Simon. You are not the right man for her.* He knew in his heart of hearts that was true. Every time she looked at him, she saw trouble. He couldn't even deny it. There were a shitload of skeletons in his closet. He couldn't ask her to live in there with him.

He rolled over onto his back and checked the clock.

6:00 a.m. Time to move out. He got up, retrieved his phone from his bag, and yawned as Paulie's number dialed.

"Hey," he answered. "Is Jillian okay?"

Simon glared at the phone. "What about me?"

"You can take care of yourself."

"Trust me, so can Jillian. She has more skills than she lets on. Did you know she can handle a weapon?"

Paulie gave a laugh. "Seriously? Good for her. I wouldn't doubt that Raven taught her."

Simon shook his head. Someday he was going to have to meet Raven.

"How's it going with Alexis?" he asked Paulie.

"We have a date tonight," he said. "She's very excited."

Simon grinned. "I'll bet. Just a friendly warning. She could ruin you for life."

"Shit, sounds good to me. But just in case, I'm gonna try to tap into her cell phone and place a GPS on her somewhere."

"Somewhere?"

Paulie laughed. "It's a tough job, but someone has to do it."

"Right," Simon said. "I talked to our kidnapper last night. He's getting antsy."

"Jeez, it's only been a few days. What's he want, miracles?"

A miracle would have been real nice right about then. "Looks like. He text-messaged me a phone number to call when we get close. I want you to track it down."

"Will do. Just send it along. I have some news on the kidnapper's call to Jackson's phone. I managed to trace the number and associated GPS signal. Unfortunately, the phone is registered to a nonexistent company in Mexico City. That's the good news."

"What's the bad news?"

"The call originally came from southern Veracruz. But I'm watching the GPS, and the signal keeps moving."

Simon rubbed his eyes. "Let me guess. They're following us?"

"You got it. Probably homing in on Jackson's cell phone signal."

Which might not be a bad thing, because that would mean Celina was moving with them. Maybe the kidnapper was planning on following this through. A ray of hope emerged.

Simon heard the shower being shut off and lowered his voice. "One more thing. We had a run-in with a dead body."

"'scuse me? I could have sworn you said 'dead body.'"

"I did, and before you ask, no, I didn't kill him. But someone saw me rough him up when I caught him following us. The next morning there was a stiff in the backseat of our Jeep."

"Crap. Jillian must have wigged."

"A little," he admitted, although not as much as he'd expected. He gave Paulie the location where he'd dumped the body. "Someone should have found him by now. I need to know who he was and who he was working for."

"Wow, this just keeps getting better and better. I'm amazed you have any living friends."

Simon told him, "Be careful. Some of them I killed myself."

"I'm shaking," Paulie came back. "I'll keep an ear to the airwaves. Have you found any clues to the archives yet?"

Simon looked over as Jillian came out of the bathroom wearing khaki short shorts, a thin pink tank top, and no bra. Blood made a mad rush from his brain, and he almost forgot what he was going to say. "Jillian saw the priest at Tres Zapotes, so we know the lens works. We just don't know how or why."

Her expression dimmed, and he hated it.

"Or where the treasure is," Paulie noted.

"Right. Today we're going to check out San Lorenzo. If that's a bust, we'll head up to La Venta."

"Sounds like a plan," Paulie said. "Be careful."

"*You* might want to check if your health insurance covers you in Mexico," Simon told him. "Talk to you tomorrow."

He hung up and said, "Morning. Sleep well?"

Jillian walked past him to put her toiletries in her bag. "The most sleep I've had in a week." Then she turned to him. "Thank you."

He arched an eyebrow. "For what? Not jumping you? Granted, it was a huge sacrifice."

A blush bloomed on her face. "For that and for..." She hesitated. "For understanding."

"No problem." He grabbed his bag.

"And, Simon?"

He stopped to look at her.

"I'd like to be present next time you call Paulie." She batted her eyelashes. "For the *entire* conversation."

Simon studied her. "You don't trust me?"

She crossed her arms and lifted an eyebrow. "Do you really want to address that particular issue? Because that could take all day."

He grinned. "True." This was getting fun. "So how do you propose to keep an eye on me when *you're* in the shower?"

A smile spread across her face as she met his gaze and then gave his naked body a long once-over that turned up the heat, not that he needed the added encouragement.

"Live in fear, Simon."

The boat ride down the Chiquito River to Tenochtitlán, the oldest of the Olmec ceremonial sites at San Lorenzo, was hot and sticky and crowded with tourists by the time they boarded at noon. Jillian watched the lowlands coast by and wondered how the Olmecs could have carved a complex of waterways and a city this large by hand and sheer will.

The morning spent at the San Lorenzo museum had been thrilling, with Olmec heads, pieces of stone pipes, and remnants of statues and altars that had survived the bitter siege of the Olmec people in 900 B.C. Even Simon had behaved himself.

Yet her excitement had ebbed when she had failed to see the priest or any of the stonecutters on the grounds. Or anything at all.

She tried to control her growing fear. For the first time, her vision was failing her, and she didn't know why. Maybe she was tired or stressed from the chaotic tilt her life had taken. How rotten would it be to lose her damn vision when she needed it most?

"You're quiet," Simon said as he leaned close to her ear. "Something wrong?"

She should tell him the truth, but she couldn't face his disappointment, either. Besides, they were going to the actual archaeological site, so perhaps that would improve her vision. She smiled over her shoulder, where he was standing behind her holding on to an overhead bar. "Just a little drained from the heat. You?"

He cast a quick glance around at the other passengers. "So far, so good. But if you notice anyone taking a special interest in us, let me know."

She eyed him. "You gonna rough him up?"

His gaze cut to hers. "You want I should call in my friend Rocco, instead?"

She gave a laugh. "That scares me, because I'm pretty sure you're serious."

He grinned and looked out over the flat river basin. "Naw. No friends named Rocco."

That was probably true, Jillian thought. His world of "friends" seemed awfully small.

The boat slowed and docked along the edge of the muddy river. As they walked up the embankment toward the site, her heart sank. The ruins were little more than earthen mounds and grass. Active archaeological excavations were under way in the distance, and a tour guide was leading most of the sightseers toward the more interesting finds.

"Not much left of the Olmecs here," Simon noted astutely. "Where do you want to start?"

"South," she said, although she wasn't quite sure why.

He nodded, and they tracked across the plain to the south. Scraggly trees and scrub soon blocked out the others.

After fighting underbrush for ten minutes, they stepped into a wide, grassy clearing. Jillian pulled the lens from her shorts pocket and scanned the plain. Nothing. She closed her eyes, knowing that Simon was waiting patiently for her verdict.

"We need to keep moving," she told him and took the lead. She didn't know where she was going but didn't worry about getting lost. If they got disoriented, all they had to do was head east and find the river.

After ten more minutes, they entered another clearing with an expansive view of the distant mountains. Jillian said a silent prayer and drew the lens out again. For a few long moments, nothing happened. Then a familiar prickle flowed across her skin. *Yes.*

Everything faded from the edges inward until all she could see was the tiny world captured in the lens. Then that tiny world became everything. The landscape changed as ancient peoples marched by in a long procession. Drumbeats rose in her ears, voices chanting. Elaborate feather headdresses crowned the shaved heads of men, women, and children as they danced in single file. The chant strengthened, and she felt herself swaying to the hypnotic rhythm.

I know this, she thought, anticipating the cadence and phrasing. Drawn deeper into the vortex, she felt at one with the people. Her eyes grew heavy and nearly closed, but then she heard him calling her.

She forced her eyes open. The priest stood before her. He spoke slowly and with great passion.

I don't understand, she tried to tell him after a few moments, but her mouth was heavy and sluggish, and the words wouldn't come.

Please tell me where it is. I need to know, she begged.

He stood and pointed behind him. She lifted the lens to the mountain range and froze. A column of blue light shone brightly from just beyond the ridge.

The light. The archives.

She brought the lens back to him, but he was gone. The world fell away, the ancients blurred, the chant faded, leaving only her name ringing in her ears.

Then everything went black.

CHAPTER
20

Simon couldn't bring her back. He checked his watch. She'd been passed out for five minutes, but it seemed like a lifetime. There was no color in her skin, and her breathing was shallow. Against the green grass, she looked like death.

"Come on, babe," he whispered, his voice raw as he poured water onto his wadded-up shirt and pressed it to her forehead again. She moaned softly. He drizzled more water over her scalp and mentally calculated how long it would take him to run back to the main site to get help. If she didn't come to in the next thirty seconds—

Her eyes fluttered open, and he thanked God. Which was damn big, because he hadn't talked to God in a long time.

Slowly, Jillian's eyes focused on him. Color rose in her cheeks. She licked her dry lips. "Hey."

"Are you hurt anywhere?"

She laughed weakly. "Just my pride."

He helped her to a sitting position and gave her some

water. That's when he realized his hands were shaking. Sweat ran down his face and chest. He was a wreck.

Jillian stared at him. "Are *you* all right?"

"Fine. I just wish this was scotch. What happened?"

Her eyes widened as if she just remembered. She scrambled a little unsteadily to her feet and scanned the vicinity, one hand gripping his arm for support. She pointed a line across the field. "They were here. A ceremonial procession, I think. Then the priest appeared. He showed me—"

Jillian stopped and faced south, standing perfectly still. "What's over those mountains?"

He frowned, not liking the direction. "Southern Oaxaca. Why?"

She turned to look at him, her eyes bright. "That's where it is."

Simon stared at her in disbelief. "How do you know?"

"Because that's where the light is. It wasn't just a glow in the sky. It's a beam, a beacon for the Archives of Man."

He looked from the mountains to La Venta, their next stop in the opposite direction. Mancuso had said to stick to the Olmecs. There were no known Olmec sites in the direction Jillian wanted to go.

"You have to trust me, Simon," she said as if reading his mind. Her gaze held steady and sure.

Time is running out.

"I know I'm right," she added.

Celina's life is on the line. And then it occurred to him that Jillian was aware of all those things, too. They meant as much to her as they did to him. She was willing to step off the path, and she wouldn't do that unless she was absolutely certain.

Trust me, her eyes begged silently. Because she knew how hard this was for him.

He said, "Then we head south."

Simon leaned on the front grille and watched the traffic zip by no more than ten feet from the gas station. A young kid pumped gas into the Jeep under the canopy of corrugated steel. The old filling station was like many in Mexico—built cheaply, deteriorating, and boasting everything from gas to tires to questionable food. A giant mound of used and abused tires edged up to the road. Old dogs lay in the shade. Dust rose with every step. And they were heading south.

He still couldn't believe it. This is what he wanted her to do—tell him where the treasure was. To lead him. So why did his stomach twist every time he thought about it? Maybe it was because he was afraid of what would happen to her next time she used the lens. Because *he* sure wasn't looking forward to it.

The young attendant finished pumping gas, and Simon paid him. The boy eyed the generous tip and disappeared in a flash. Simon got in and parked the Jeep on the side of the building before heading inside to see how Jillian was doing.

He could hear her voice as he quietly pushed the screen door open. Bottles of water sat on the counter between her and a Mexican man in his fifties who was concentrating on every Spanish word she was trying to say.

Simon crossed his arms and leaned against a wooden column to enjoy the show.

"*No petro,*" Jillian said again, using her hands to try to help in the translation. "*Cebu.*"

The man smiled and nodded as Jillian kept asking for an ox before finally noticing Simon. He pointed to the steamed tamales in the case behind the man. His eyes widened in comprehension, and he waved to the case. "*Ah. Cebo. Tengo solamente tamales.*"

Jillian said, "*Si, si. Muy bueno. Cuatro tamales, por favor.*"

While the man bagged the tamales, Simon came up behind her. "How's it going?"

She turned, beaming. "I just ordered dinner. I think my Spanish is improving."

He smiled back. "I guess it is." Then he took the bag from the man and gave him a few extra pesos for his patience and kindness. "*Gracias.*"

Jillian said, "I just need to use the restroom. Be right out."

Simon went to the Jeep and tossed the bag in the backseat. He was about to climb in when he spotted a police car driving by from the north. One of the two officers inside looked at him and said something to the driver, and the car immediately slowed down.

"Shit," Simon said softly. *Not now.*

Jillian stepped outside with an armful of water bottles, and he held his hand up. She stopped in her tracks, her smile fading as she looked around. "What?"

The police car made a U-turn, kicking up dirt, and headed back to the station. Simon half turned and pretended to be rolling down the door window as he put the keys under the mat. "Get back inside, Jillian. Lock yourself in the bathroom and don't come out until everything quiets down. Keys are under the mat. Anything you need is in the Jeep."

"No," she said, shaken but stubbornly standing her ground.

He didn't argue with her. He just shut the door and walked past her to face the cops.

"Trust me," he said as the police car stopped right in front of him.

Jillian stepped back inside the station, frantically trying to figure out what to do next. She peeked out a grimy window and saw two officers get out of their car to talk to Simon.

What if they had discovered the dead Mexican? What if they tied him back to Simon? No way was she going to leave him alone, and no way she going to let them take him away.

Think, Jillian. Think.

She'd seen the Jeep was parked on the side, twenty feet from the door, but it was in sight of the cops. There was one entrance on the side and one in front, which made neither safe to use. What she needed was a back door. She skirted around the racks and aisles. The man behind the counter was reading a newspaper and hadn't seemed to notice the police car yet.

She slipped into the back room, where crates were stacked to the ceiling. The back door creaked a little as she pushed it and stepped into the blinding sunlight. Tires littered the entire rear lot behind the building, piled twenty feet high in places.

She ran to the corner of the building and looked around it. No sign of Simon or the cops, but she wouldn't make it to the Jeep without them seeing her. The Jeep was out, for now.

Male voices rose, and her pulse raced. She had to help him. What would Raven do?

She crinkled her nose. Well, for one, Raven would have weapons. No weapons here. Just water bottles.

She lay her head back against the building. What now?

That's when she spotted an old, rusted-out truck sitting on a worn dirt path that wound around the tire mountains. The truck looked ancient but big and powerful. An idea began to form. It was crazy. It probably wouldn't even work.

The conversation out front grew louder and more heated.

She dropped the water bottles to the ground and ran back inside. She might not be Raven, but she could come close.

Simon was in big trouble, and he knew it. The officers were becoming increasingly agitated at his lack of cooperation. They kept looking at the Jeep and checking his identification. For some reason, they weren't buying the tourist line.

All he wanted to do was get out of this as quickly and quietly as possible. He opened his wallet and made a show of the money he had inside. Neither one of them bit.

Just his luck. Honest cops.

When he heard them say, "Come with us," he knew this would get ugly. Still, chances were good they'd leave the Jeep alone and Jillian could get out safely.

Simon was about to put his life in the hands of fate

when a rumbling sound as loud as a freight train rose from behind the building. The roar grew, accompanied by a chorus of belching and pops that sounded a lot like gunfire.

One of the cops stepped back to investigate. A plume of dust swept around the building from the rear. Dogs whimpered under chairs, and a horrendous, tortured, screaming whine permeated the air.

It grew louder and closer. Then the pile of tires by the side of the road exploded, sending bouncing projectiles in all directions. The road quickly became a deadly obstacle course as cars screeched to stops in both directions. The two cops scrambled for their car, yelling at each other.

Then the Jeep backed up behind him in a cloud of dust with Jillian at the wheel. She reached around and opened the rear door.

"Get in," she yelled.

He threw himself in as the Jeep lurched forward. The door slammed shut, and he lost his balance when they took a hard right.

It wasn't until he got on his knees that he learned why. They were fishtailing on a dirt road behind the building.

"Where are we going?"

Jillian was concentrating fiercely on the rough road, while still managing to hit every pothole. "Trust me."

Like he had a choice. He looked behind him. No cops. Yet. It wouldn't take long. When he turned back around, they hit a low ditch that sent the Jeep airborne. It bounced once on the road pavement and vaulted into the other ditch.

Simon's head smacked the roof, and then he skidded

right as Jillian wrenched the Jeep around and onto the road.

"Take it easy, Jillian."

"If you don't have anything constructive to add, then be quiet," she snapped.

When he finally pulled himself onto the backseat, he checked the carnage in their wake. Through a screen of dust, tires littered the road between them and the flashing lights of the cop car. An old pickup truck was buried in the pile. People were out of their cars and wandering around.

Simon rubbed the lump on his head and climbed between the seats to drop into the passenger side. Jillian's hands were white on the steering wheel. Both of them were breathing hard in the silence.

"Did you get the tamales?" she asked.

He pulled a map from the glove box. "In the back. Think I landed on them, though." He checked the rearview mirror. No red lights. Always a good sign.

"They're probably still fine." She handed him a water bottle. "Thirsty?"

He took a big swallow and handed it back to her. She finished it in one gulp and tossed it over her shoulder carelessly. A few more minutes of silence followed.

"Take a right at the next turnoff, about ten miles away. We need to get off the main road for a while."

She nodded once, eyes glued to the road, fingers glued to the wheel. "Good thinking."

"Wanna fill me in on what just happened?" he asked. "Or save it until we get some tequila?"

"Oh, we're *definitely* picking up some tequila." She regripped the wheel, and the Jeep lurched unevenly along.

He waited.

She blinked a few times and finally said, "I paid the guy behind the counter one hundred dollars for his truck. Drove it out behind the building, put it in drive, set a cement block on top of the accelerator, and jumped out."

He stared at her in wonder. "Brilliant move aiming it for the tires."

"Thank you. It's actually a little frightening how easily it came into my mind. I just wanted to cause a distraction and block the road long enough for us to disappear."

Simon started grinning, then chuckling, which gave way to a full belly laugh. After a few moments, Jillian smiled.

"One hundred dollars," he said, still amazed. "Never underestimate."

"What?" she asked, taking her eyes off the road for the first time. The Jeep swerved onto the shoulder and nearly flipped before Jillian pulled the wheel around. "Sorry."

Then he remembered something that made him more nervous than he'd been all day. *She couldn't drive.* Anything she'd learned was from watching him. His gut instinct told him to tell her to pull over and let him take the wheel.

He glanced at her white knuckles and at the absolute concentration and determination on her face. She'd gotten him this far, and he wasn't about to burst her bubble after she'd saved his ass. He took a deep breath and crossed his arms to relax in the seat. "No problem. But you might want to take your foot off the brake while you're driving. Kills the gas mileage. Got a ways to go before we stop tonight."

She nodded and eased her foot off the brake.

Simon pulled out his cell phone and dialed Paulie's number. He answered on the first ring.

"What's wrong? Is Jillian okay?"

Simon turned to look out the back window. "Why do you always assume something is wrong?"

"Because you already called me today, which means something went wrong."

"Jillian's fine. We just had a bit of trouble," Simon told him. "The flashing-red-lights kind."

Paulie sighed. "What do you need?"

"Information, for now," he said. "We're heading south toward Matias Romero, Oaxaca. I need to know if the authorities put an APB out on us. Can you do that?"

"Sure can. Wait. South? Why are you heading south? I thought the plan was to follow the Olmec trail?"

Simon glanced at Jillian. "South is where the archives are."

Paulie said, "Okay. Anything else?"

"No. Just call if you hear anything."

Simon hung up the phone and slipped it into his pocket.

"So what's the itinerary?" she asked.

Damn good question. He checked the map. "We'll stop for the night and ditch the Jeep as soon as possible. They took down the license plate number."

Jillian said, "No problem. I ripped the plates off the old truck. They're in the back."

Simon turned slowly and stared at her in utter astonishment.

She raised an eyebrow. "Hey, I paid a hundred bucks for them."

CHAPTER
21

Some local cops spotted Simon Bonner at a filling station north of Matias Romero," Walsh said. "They stopped to make sure and got a little overzealous. Tried to bring him in, but both he and the woman escaped."

Donovan paced the balcony, the glorious sunset wasted on him. At least she was still alive. Without her, they would never find the archives. Never. They'd been hidden for thousands of years. There was a reason why.

"Do we have anyone on them now?" he asked.

"Based on where they were heading and the time they left, they're probably near La Ventosa by now. I'm trying to clean it up from here, but they caused one hell of a commotion at the filling station. I have my hands full calming the authorities."

Donovan puffed on his cigar. "Pay them off."

"I will, but there comes a point where it just gets too big and too loud. Let's hope Bonner knows to keep a low profile from here on in."

And finds the archives soon, Donovan thought. He wasn't the only one getting restless.

Walsh said, "There's something else you should know. We picked up a man following them. It took some legwork, but we learned his name is Kurt Kesel, a gun for hire. He's been implicated in a slew of assassinations and nasty jobs. Spent some time in prison. I don't know why he's after them, but at this point, he's not interfering with their progress."

Donovan rubbed his temple. Was he working for another collector? "Can we take him out?"

"Quietly? Probably not. Plus he's already disappeared off our radar. This guy is a pro."

The cigar glowed as he drew on it. "Then we'll deal with him when we have to."

Jillian weaved the Jeep between potholes large enough to swallow them whole. A tiny rural farm town made up of wooden and weathered structures leaned into the rutted dirt road.

Simon pointed to one place where several townfolk were gathered on the porch, eyeing them with keen interest. "Pull over there."

She parked the Jeep and turned off the ignition.

"I'm going to see if we can get a place to stay for the night," Simon told her.

She nodded, distracted by her surroundings.

"Are you okay?" he asked.

She turned to him and smiled. "This kicking-ass thing takes a lot out of a girl."

He watched her intently. "Gotta get used to it."

Right. She peeled her cramped fingers off the steering wheel. Never happen.

Simon opened the door and stepped out. "I'll be right back." Then he leaned in. "By the way. You kick ass pretty damn well for a civilian."

Jillian smiled as he shut the door. The events of the day swept through her bones. Her brain was going a mile a minute. She was dusty and hungry and so wired she couldn't stand it.

The crazy plan had worked far better than she'd imagined. She still couldn't believe she'd actually pulled it off. No wonder Raven loved this. No wonder she was addicted to it. It was scary and terrifying and fun as hell.

Jillian sighed and exited the Jeep to stretch her tight muscles. The smell of manure mixed with the humid, sultry air. The sun was hanging low over the mountains, waning to a warm red glow.

She spotted a little girl watching her from a doorway of one of the shacks. Big brown eyes studied her quietly. Her hair was long and uneven. Her fingers were dirty, and Jillian almost gasped when she put them in her mouth to suck on.

She appeared to be about three years old, but her eyes were ancient, seeing far more than she should ever have to. There was no smile for Jillian. No reaction. Nothing.

Jillian swallowed the emotion in her throat as she surveyed the town with brutal honesty. The stores and buildings were little more than rough-cut boards slapped together to form walls. Rusted tin roofs dipped in the waning daylight. Sheets covered the broken windows and doorways.

Two rows of shacks on either side of the road made up

the town center. Three men, dirty and ill clothed, stood barefoot and watched her from the front porch of one.

She'd never seen such poverty. Manhattan had its poor, but nothing like this. *Dirt poor,* Simon had told her, and he was right. She probably had more money in her pocket than anyone in this town made in a whole year.

This was their everyday situation. Did the children go to school? Did they laugh? Did they realize there was more to this world than what they could see?

At that moment, she wanted to give them everything she owned, do something to make this better. Like Simon had. Who could see this and not want to do anything in their power to make it right? He was a good man. He had tried to make it better.

Somewhere in the back of her mind, a whisper said, *You're falling for him.*

Slowly, the rest of reality overcame her, snuffing out the last of her excitement. How many laws had she broken today during their grand escape? That was not the real Jillian, and she had to remember that. She'd give anything to help these people, but she wouldn't break the law to do it. She couldn't live like that.

Simon walked out of the shack with keys in one hand and a small bottle of tequila in the other.

"We have a place to stay for the night," he said and handed her the tequila.

She opened it and took a swig that made her shudder. Then another. Simon watched her curiously. "The accommodations are not going to be stellar."

She nodded, never taking her eyes off the depressing scenery. "That's fine."

"Getting to know the town?" Simon asked as he took a drink from the bottle she offered him.

"Not much to see," she admitted, and then she looked at him. "How do you fix this?"

He put the cap on the bottle. "You don't. Let's go."

Reluctantly, she abandoned the discussion and climbed into the passenger side of the Jeep. Simon drove them to the edge of the town and parked behind a shack on a low hill surrounded by a cornfield.

While Simon switched the plates, Jillian went inside to survey the night's accommodations. A single overhead bulb shed a meager light that didn't quite reach the corners.

It was a two-room shed with a battered metal roof, bare boards for walls, and screens in the two windows. New blue curtains fluttered in the breeze, looking out of place.

Wide wood planks covered a floor that had been neatly swept. A clean blanket was thrown over the bed in one corner. One handmade table and two mismatched chairs took up the other side. A narrow door led to the tiny bathroom, which consisted of a stained toilet and a sink. One towel hung on a nail.

As humble as it was, she couldn't help but think she had the best room in town tonight.

She made a meal of cold, squashed tamales, a bag of chips, and tequila in two glasses she found in a box on the floor. Simon entered and gave the place a cursory glance before pulling up a chair. He tossed a pile of folded maps on the table between them. "Time to regroup."

"Give me a minute." She tossed the tequila down and felt it burn her throat. Then she shook off the shudder.

Simon grinned at her, and she warmed. And not from the tequila. Then his smile faded, and he reached for his glass. "There are a few things you should know."

She groaned. "You have got to come up with a better opening line."

He drank two shots of tequila in a row, and she knew it was going to be bad.

Finally he said, "The kidnappers are following us. Using Jackson's phone as a tracker."

She refilled both their glasses. "Okay."

He eyed her. "Okay? That's it?"

Jillian clinked her glass against his. "All relative now. What else?"

Simon watched her down the tequila in one shot. As soon as she stopped drinking, she was going to hit the wall. Between blowing up the garage and passing out at San Lorenzo, she'd had a long day.

"Kesel is probably following us, as well."

She gave a little shake and poured more tequila. "Yup. Dead guy."

"Uh-huh. And now the cops."

Jillian shot the entire glass and grinned at him. "So basically you're trying to tell me that everyone is following us. Half of them are waiting until we find the archives to jump on us. The other half of them could jump us at any time."

He could tell by the plastered smile on her face that he needed to talk quickly. "Exactly. We need a plan."

"Okeydokey," she said, picking at a tamale as he spread out the map.

He circled Mancuso's town with a pen. "This is where

we started, where you first saw the light. Can you remember where you saw it?"

She raised an eyebrow. "I was a little wasted on tequila at the time."

He grinned. "One of my fondest memories." He handed her the pen. "Draw a line in the general direction of the light."

She drew a short line pointing south. Then he circled Tres Zapotes, where she'd had the first sighting of the priest, and she drew her line in the direction he had pointed. They went through the other sightings—Catemaco, Acayucan, and today at San Lorenzo.

A pattern began to form, converging on a single location. She was right. And it was triangulating to just southeast of this spot.

"We're close," she observed.

They *were* close. This was really going to happen. And all the worries he'd had about how they were going to pull it off and get out alive were now coming to the forefront.

"Maybe that's why you seem to be getting more involved with every sighting," he noted.

She yawned. "Maybe."

She was fading fast. He marked a route on the map, trying to stay clear of the main roads, which was going to be tricky in this part of the country.

"I think our best course of action is to keep heading south until we are parallel with the light you're seeing. Then head east. We'll follow the beam until we run out of road. From there, it'll be on foot to the archives."

She stared at the map for moment. "And then what? We leave breadcrumbs for everyone following us? We wave a white flag?"

From the look on her face, she understood what they were up against. They were on their own. They couldn't trust anyone, including the police. "I could call in Paulie—" he began.

"No," she said, tracing the route with her fingers. "It won't do any good."

Simon watched her faith die in front of him. "We don't have to do this. We can leave now. Create new identities, go to a place where no one will find us. Start over."

Her gaze rose slowly to meet his. "And let Celina die."

"She might anyway," Simon told her truthfully.

Jillian smiled weakly. "And she might not."

A touch of relief replaced the horrible feeling in his gut. "We'll think of something."

She nodded wearily and laid her head down on her forearms. "Sure."

Crash city. He refolded the map. "Bedtime, babe."

She was already asleep.

Simon woke up to an empty room and sat up with a start. Moonlight shed a ghostly glow over everything. The wind had died down, turning it hot and sticky in the shack. The bathroom door was open and dark.

"Jillian?"

No answer. He tamped down the flash of panic. She was fine. Probably just looking at that damn light again. Simon threw off the sheet, pulled on a pair of shorts, and jammed his feet into shoes before stepping outside.

The full moon illuminated the cornfield and sparse collection of trees. A dog barked in the distance, but Simon couldn't see much over the cornstalks that crowded the shack. He checked the Jeep first. She wasn't in or around it.

"Jillian?" he yelled louder.

For a heart-pounding moment, all he heard were insects in the darkness. He turned south and slashed through the cornfield, calling her name. A thousand scenarios dominated his thoughts. What if she was lost in the field? What if she wandered away in her sleep? What if she changed her mind and decided she couldn't handle this anymore?

In a grassy clearing at the edge of the field, he found her, wrapped up in a white sheet, staring up at the mountains. Moonlight grazed her delicate features, and blond hair floated over her shoulders in the breeze. She didn't seem to notice when he approached—a bad sign—and he braced himself for the worst.

"I'm okay," she said suddenly.

"You could have answered me," he said, his voice rough.

Dragged from a past only she could see, Jillian turned to his worried face and saw the residual concern in his eyes. That was her fault. She'd scared him. "I'm sorry. I wasn't sure if your voice was real."

He swore softly and looked away, his face lost in darkness. "You see it?"

Jillian gazed at the narrow blue beam reaching into the heavens. It was perfect now. Crisp, clear, with ribbons of clouds that danced along its length. She held her hand up, silhouetted against the blue.

"It's so beautiful. I could stand here all night."

Her voice didn't sound like her own. She felt a strange yearning flow over her and sighed at the way it called to her soul. She was drawn into its simple splendor, a gift from the past. How long had it been here with no one to appreciate it?

"Will you be able to let it go?"

No, she felt herself say, mesmerized and lost. It was so close. *Never. This belongs to me.*

"Jillian, come back."

She heard his voice, and part of her splintered. *Simon.*

His name rolled through her mind, cleaving her from the light—bit by bit. She felt pressure in her chest like she was being torn in two. Despair filled her mind.

You can't have both.

I want both, she replied desperately.

You have to choose.

I can't. I don't even know who I am anymore, she thought.

You have to find out.

And then she was free, released from the grip of turmoil and delivered whole. Strong hands held her arms. Soft lips pressed against hers. She moaned and leaned into the safety of Simon's embrace.

She kissed him with complete and careless freedom. For now—for this brief moment in time—she chose him. Relief flowed across her mind. For tonight, she was free from the decision. Betrayal could wait until tomorrow.

She shrugged off the sheet and let it drift to the grass at her feet. Simon inhaled deeply as she pressed her bare body to his. The breeze brushed her skin like a lover's first touch. She felt alive, naked and vulnerable in the unknown wilderness. The air was cleaner, the night sounds soothing, and the grass soft and welcoming beneath her feet.

She pulled Simon to the ground with her. He followed silently, knowing what she needed more than she did. He'd always known, from the very first time he touched her.

Why did it have to be you? The one man who could tempt me from the past? The one man I could give it all up for?

Simon buried his fingers in her hair, holding her while he kissed her face over and over, each kiss full of compassion. As he braced himself on his elbows, his knees nudged her legs wider, and she obliged. He growled softly and trailed kisses down her throat, between her breasts. Warm palms cupped her, fingers rolled her nipples gently. She arched her back for more and opened her eyes to the stars. The universe gazed down on her—immense yet strangely intimate.

Sensations overwhelmed her as Simon rediscovered every curve and tender valley. He rubbed his cheek against her belly, his shadow of a beard igniting the fire that had been smoldering. She moaned when he dipped lower, easing to her core. His strong hands wrapped around the inside of her thighs.

She pulled in a deep breath when he touched her with his tongue, exhaled when he closed his lips around her, and cried out when he sucked.

She gripped his hair with her fingers as pressure built with every flick and nibble and drag of his tongue. The intensity became unbearable, and she tried to move away. Simon would have none of it, his grip tight and sure. With one last choked cry, she succumbed to the raging climax. It ripped her apart, scattering her starry world before slowly, magically, coming together in mindless peace.

In her private ecstasy, she felt Simon lie down beside her. Felt him gather all her shattered pieces into his arms and stroke her hair. She felt everything—the heat of his skin, the grass cool beneath her skin. The fabric of his shorts and the hard ridge between them. She inhaled his warm, sexy scent. Listened to his every breath.

Will you be able to let it go?

Jillian frowned and shook the intrusion from her mind even as her heart twisted.

"Babe?" Simon whispered roughly.

She pressed her fingers to his mouth. *Don't. Don't say anything. Don't say you like me or care about me or, God help you, love me. Because this isn't real. It's too beautiful. It can't possibly last.*

She replaced her fingers with her lips, silencing anything that might become reality.

Jillian pressed her hand to his chest and pushed him to his back, her lips never leaving his as she straddled his hips. She closed her eyes and let her senses absorb him.

Slowly, methodically, she kissed his face and throat. He tasted salty and warm on her lips. His hands rubbed her arms and back as she worked her way down his chest and belly.

By the time she reached his straining shorts, every muscle in his body was taut and burning. She slipped her fingers under the waistband and slid his shorts down.

A low, feral growl vibrated deep in his chest as she dragged her tongue along his length. With every tender caress, Simon shuddered. A wave of satisfaction flowed over her. She did this to him, made him feel that wonderful. She could give as good as he did.

In a flash, she could tell he was on the edge, and she

stopped. He let out a tortured groan as she settled on top of him and took him into her—inch by amazing inch.

She eased all the way down and moaned at the perfect fit. His teeth bared, and his fingers gripped her thighs tight. For a moment, neither of them moved.

Need and hunger mixed in his eyes. She leaned forward and kissed him gently. He watched her with tormented intensity as she sat back up.

Then she lifted her hips and slid back down over him.

He let out a fierce growl and pushed her off him and back down again as he arched into her. She followed his frantic rhythm, the power building in her core with every lunge.

The world spun out of control, leaving only Simon and their desperate need. Release poured through her, stars crowding her mind. Simon's final thrust matched his loud shout.

She collapsed on top of him, spent. For a long time, she lay there in her perfect world. No worries. No pain. No fear. No decisions. Just Simon.

I love you, she said, in the deepest, most sacred part of her heart. It didn't matter anymore. Because whatever choice she made, she was going to lose.

CHAPTER
22

Kesel sat on the outskirts of the town with no name and watched the shack in the distance, silhouetted by the night sky.

It had been an eventful afternoon. He had not thought the woman capable of pulling off the stunt at the garage. There was more to her than he anticipated.

And more to this situation than he expected. Why were the cops on their tail? He couldn't imagine that Bonner was stupid enough to leave a trail from the Mexican to himself. No, there was something else at play here. Something had changed. Was it the timing? Was it the body? Or was someone else involved?

Whatever the reason, he needed another man and a new vehicle pronto. He opened his cell phone and dialed Carlos.

"Where are you?" Kesel asked him before he even had time to say hello.

"At home in bed. Where else would I be at this hour?"

"What did you learn about Raul?"

Carlos swore. "You woke me up for that? You can't wait until morning?"

"No. What do you have?"

There was a lot of noise on the other end before Carlos came back. Paper was shuffled in the background. "Raul Vega. No family. No job. No address. No nothing."

Kesel stilled. "Fake license?"

"Looks like."

The only reason a man would need a fake license was if he didn't want anyone to know who he was or who he was working for. Warning bells were ringing in Kesel's head.

"Get on the road, Carlos. It's time."

Carlos groaned. "I have relatives coming tomorrow. My wife will kill me if I leave now."

"I don't care," he told him. "Be in La Ventosa by tomorrow morning."

"La Ventosa? Do you have any idea how long that's going to take me? I'll be driving all night."

"Are you in or not?"

Carlos sighed. "I'm in. I'll call you when I get there."

Kesel knew that greed would motivate him. Greed will make a man forget about his family. Greed will make a man forget his honor.

Kesel said, "Come alone, Carlos."

Carlos balked. "What? *Now* you don't trust me?"

"I just don't feel like getting rid of another body."

Simon grappled for the ringing cell phone by the bedside. He flipped it open without looking at the caller. "Paulie, I'm going to kill you if this is before six a.m."

"Nice way to answer the phone," he replied. "Is Jillian okay?"

She made a little sound and snuggled closer to Simon. He forgot about his too-early wake-up call. "Fine. How'd it go last night? I see you survived Alexis. I'm impressed."

"For your information, we didn't do anything."

"Now I'm *really* impressed. How'd you manage that? Drug her?"

There was a short pause. "You really worry me sometimes. No, we just talked all night."

Simon yawned. "I didn't know Alexis was capable of that. What did you talk about?"

"Everything. Anything. She's a nice lady. She hates this business. Says it's killing her. She wants to get away and start over new somewhere."

"Uh-huh. And who's going to finance that? Because Alexis likes her high life."

Paulie said, "We didn't get that far. Right now, she's doing odd jobs."

"No shit," Simon told him. "For whoever pays the most."

"Like your friend Kesel," Paulie added.

That got Simon's attention. He sat up on the edge of the bed. "She told you that? What'd you give her to cough that up?"

"Nothing. Well, I kind of told her about the lens."

"Jesus," Simon muttered. "Paulie, you can't trust her. You'll get us all killed."

"I don't think so. From what I hear, you don't want to cross Kesel, and she's doing just that. She told me that the word on the street is that he's after our lens because someone stole it from him."

Jillian stirred behind Simon, and he lowered his voice. "He was the one who found the lens?"

"Yup. And it seems Kesel has serious betrayal issues. He wants whoever screwed him."

Simon rubbed his eyes. "That explains why he hasn't moved on us. He's waiting until we hook up with the kidnappers. They must be the ones who took the lens."

"That's my thinking, too. You realize this is all going to hell the minute you turn over that treasure to the kidnappers. I don't think Kesel is too particular about who he kills."

Simon stood up and looked out the window. "Don't worry. I'll shake him long before that."

"Glad to hear it. And now for the good news."

Simon muttered, "About time."

Paulie continued, "There's no APB on you or Jillian."

Now that didn't make sense. "Those cops recognized me. I'm sure of it."

"If they did, it wasn't from this train wreck. Weren't you in trouble here before?"

"A long time ago." Too long. This was different.

Paulie said, "I can't help you there. And your dead body hasn't surfaced, either. I've checked every wire I got. Nothing."

That was impossible. The body had to have been discovered by now. It was right by the road. Even a big animal couldn't have dragged it out of that ditch. It hadn't rained recently—

"You don't sound happy," Paulie said, breaking the silence. "This was the good news, remember?"

"Something's not right," Simon murmured, half to himself.

"Sorry, bud, that's the best I got. How's it going on your end? Any new disasters to report in the past twelve hours?"

Simon glanced at Jillian, who was sleeping like an angel. *Nothing I can tell you about, Paulie.* "We're closing in on the site. Probably be within walking distance today."

"Walking? Through the jungle?"

"Ancient civilizations don't usually provide a paved road up to the door of their hidden treasures," he said.

"Crap. Now I gotta worry about venomous snakes," Paulie said.

Simon shook his head. "It's not those kinds of snakes you should be worrying about."

Paulie added, "By the way, tell Jillian that Raven called. I stalled for her, but Raven's not particularly patient. Jillian needs to call her sister immediately."

"I'll let her know. And, Paulie, call tomorrow. *Later* than six a.m."

"Wimp," Paulie said and hung up.

Simon tossed the phone into his bag. The sun was rising through the window, casting a golden glow over Jillian's face. He wished he could lie on a beach somewhere with her or take her out to dinner and watch her laugh. He wished he could treat her right instead of . . . this.

As he stood there, he realized that he couldn't live with himself if anything happened to her. He'd dealt with a lot of death in his life and somehow survived. But losing her . . . he wouldn't survive that.

Jillian was glad that Simon chose to do the driving, because the back roads were barely passable. She would have gotten them stuck a hundred times by now. As it was, she had developed a hell of headache from all the bouncing around.

She ducked instinctively as yet another low-lying branch smacked the windshield. The Jeep rocked from side to side as they crawled along two worn tire tracks in a dense forest. The mountain terrain was slow going, and it was already noon.

Simon asked, "Can you tell how much longer we have to suffer this damn road?"

She checked the map. "About two kilometers. Maybe we'll be there by tonight."

That got a little smile out of him. "I'll just be happy to get off this road without wrecking the Jeep."

Oh, God. She hadn't even thought about that.

"On the upside, not many people will be able to follow us through this," he added.

She *had* thought about that one. "Do you think Celina is with the kidnappers who are following us?"

"I sure hope so."

Jillian nodded. So did she. "How long were you married?"

He gave her a quick glance before concentrating on the pothole landmines. "Almost two years."

Jillian smoothed out her shorts. "How did you meet?"

"She was a raider. We became partners. Worked on a bunch of finds. Made some good money. And then things went bad."

"What happened?"

He seemed to brace himself as he answered. "She got bit by the bug."

Jillian blinked at him. "What kind of bug?"

"Greed. Obsession. It changed her, just like it changes everyone. Whatever we found was never enough. She always wanted more. Started taking risks. Almost got me killed a couple times. Finally, I said no to her. I figured she'd see reason and stop."

"But she didn't," Jillian noted with complete understanding. She knew all about greed. About not being able to stop the madness. The bug had bitten her father, too.

Simon shook his head. "She just went out and found someone who was willing to take those risks."

Now it made sense. "Jackson."

"Jackson," Simon concurred.

"So, you're finding the woman who left you for another man, *for* the other man?"

Simon wrenched the wheel to the right to avoid a huge rut in the road. "That's right. There are very few people in this world who matter to me, and I've lost a lot of them already. I don't want to lose any more."

He seemed to mean every word. Didn't he realize that they probably weren't going to get out of this alive, anyway? Why did he keep going? Faith? Maybe. She'd like to think so. There wasn't much else to hold on to right now.

She looked down and noticed a paper covered in glyphs, in with all the maps. "What are these?"

Simon glanced over. "Mancuso's notes on the lens glyphs. He gave them to me before we left."

She studied each of the five drawings across the top of the paper, and then the words assigned to them. *Moon. Shut eye. Simple circle. Hand. New sun.*

She grabbed the dashboard as the Jeep bounced over a big bump. "Did he say how they relate to each other?"

"No."

She studied the long sets of lines he'd traced below each of the five glyphs. Those must be the intricate writing she'd seen between the glyphs. "Did he get a translation on the writing?"

"No. He said he'd never seen it before."

"That's too bad," she said. "If I had something more to work with—"

"You'll do fine," Simon cut in.

She gave him an uncertain look, and he grinned back. He had far more faith in her than she did.

The road suddenly smoothed out, and the jungle opened up to a grassy plain. Simon blew out a breath. "About time."

Jillian took the lens out of her pocket and swept the sky to the east. The blue beam was there, beckoning over a low mountaintop. "I think we need to hang a right."

Simon replied, "Will do. Stop looking through that."

She blinked and turned to him. "What?"

His expression was grim. "Every time you spend too long with that thing, it takes control of you."

So much for faith. "You don't think I'm strong enough."

"That's not the point."

"That's exactly the point," she countered. "You asked me last night if I'd be able to let it go."

He gave her a strange look. "No, I didn't."

A chill ran up her spine. If it wasn't his voice asking the question, then *whose voice was it?* She swallowed and tucked the lens in her shirt. "Never mind."

They drove in silence for some time before Simon spoke. "How close are we?"

"Close. I can't give you an exact ETA but...It's just a gut feeling."

He nodded. "We have time, then."

She eyed him. "Time for what?"

"To find the location and then go back to a safe place where we can call the kidnappers. We give them the location and the lens in exchange for Celina."

"You mean not find the treasure?" she asked, thrown by the curveball. "Just leave everything and walk away?"

He turned to her. "That's what I mean."

She shook her head. "But they can't get to the treasure without me."

He shrugged. "We tell them they can. Write up some fabricated instructions. Just to give us enough time to save Celina and get away."

Her heart sank, and she tried to control the waver of her voice. "I suppose we could try."

Simon ran his hands over the wheel. "So you're good with that plan?"

She stared at the glyphs in her lap. In a way, it would be a blessing. She wouldn't have to choose. She wouldn't have to decide man's fate. She wouldn't find out why she had this gift. She wouldn't find peace.

"Sure."

CHAPTER
23

Home sweet home." Simon dropped their bags in a nondescript hotel room. He was so sick of hotel rooms. The small mountain town of Pluma Hidalgo, perched on the Sierra Madre del Sur mountains, was a hell of a lot farther south than he'd expected to end up. Never in a million years would he have guessed the archives would be here.

"For tonight," Jillian added. "I need a shower."

Those were the first words she'd uttered in the past eight hours aside from an occasional "yes" or "no." Her disappointment was palpable. She wanted to find that treasure.

Not for Celina.

For mankind and for herself.

Although, if it was really for mankind, she would have argued with him a little. Which meant it was for herself. Not for the wealth or for the thrill of the find. But for answers, knowledge, reverence, to be "the one." Take your pick. The bug came in all forms.

He had hoped if he took her out of the equation, she wouldn't blame herself for whatever happened in the end. She could hate *him* instead. And as much as that hurt, at least she wouldn't live in guilt. She could be free. More importantly, she'd live through it.

Apparently, she didn't see it that way.

She flicked on the light in the bathroom, and he asked, "Need any help in there?"

"I think I need to take this one alone. I'm pretty disgusting."

There was a sadness in her eyes that betrayed her smile. The bug. He hated it.

He hitched his head toward the door. "I'm going to rustle up some supplies and dinner."

Jillian nodded. "Okay."

Fight it, he wanted to tell her. *Don't let it win.* But she just shut the door and left him alone with his thoughts. He had taken it all away from her. Everything she'd ever dreamed of or about. The archaeological discovery of all time. He'd pitted her compassion against her passion, knowing full well which one she'd sacrifice.

She would never be able to forgive him for that. He didn't expect her to.

Jillian stepped out of the bathroom to a quiet hotel room and sat on the bed facing the wall mirror. She looked different. Eyes world-weary and wary. Like Simon's.

This world had done terrible things to him. It'd stolen his heart and his soul and his faith. Now she understood exactly how he felt.

All along she'd thought she would find the treasure

and perhaps answers to the questions that haunted her. *Why me? Why the sight? Why now?*

But a life was at stake, and somewhere along the line, she'd forgotten about that. How could she compare a few selfish moments to a human being? She couldn't.

As for humanity—she couldn't control that, either. This wasn't her doing or her undoing. Besides, Simon was right. One discovery was not going to stop all the wars or the famine or suddenly give every person on this planet a new lease on life. Nothing could do that.

Besides, there was no guarantee the kidnappers would go for the plan, anyway. In which case, she'd get her chance, find her answers, and die.

Wow. Some choice. Maybe she should be glad Simon came up with a plan, after all.

Jillian reached into her bag and removed her cell phone. She pressed the second speed dial after her father's. The phone rang twice before Raven came on the line.

"Where have you been, Jill?"

Jillian lay back on the bed, more exhausted than she could ever remember. Maybe it was the altitude. "Oh, you know. Just busy with the museum." *Liar.* "How was the diving?"

"A bust. Can't get rich off all of them."

Jillian laughed a little. "You don't do it for the money, honey."

Raven laughed with her. "This is true. Plus Dax got some great photos, and no one was eaten by sharks. It's all good."

A great sadness settled over her. "Speaking of feeding the sharks, how's the bonding with Dad going?"

Raven gave a sigh. "Let me tell you, bonding is a hell

of a lot more stressful than stealing. Give me an impossible heist over this any day."

Jillian said, "He loves you, and he's trying *very* hard to make up for everything."

"I know. In fact, he's trying too hard and driving me a little crazy. So how about you come out here to save me from bonding hell?"

Jillian closed her eyes. "I'll have to see when I can get away. Summer's our busiest time…" Her lies trailed off as the burning in her eyes grew.

There was a long pause. "Jill, is something wrong?"

She opened her eyes and noticed a water stain on the ceiling. "I just wanted to tell you that I love you."

Raven's tone turned serious in a flash. "What happened? Are you okay?"

"Please tell Dad and Dax that I love them, too. Promise me you'll take care of each other."

"Jillian, *tell me* what is going on. Where are you? Don't go anywhere. Don't do anything. I can be there in twenty-four hours."

Tears streamed down her face and into her wet hair. "Sorry, sweetie. We can't do it your way this time."

She heard Raven screaming her name as she disconnected.

Donovan was in bed when the phone rang. He fumbled for the phone and checked the incoming number before sitting straight up in bed. "Hello?"

"Pluma Hidalgo," Celina said.

"You're certain?"

"We just got the call. They are heading into the mountains. We need to move fast. When can you be here?"

He mentally calculated the distance and the time it would take to get there. "Six hours."

"Good. Call me for more details when you get close. I won't answer, but I'll contact you as soon as I'm alone."

Donovan stood up and cradled the phone under his chin as he turned on the light and began packing. "You sound stressed, Celina. Having second thoughts?"

She gave a laugh. "Never. This is nothing I can't handle."

He tossed clothes into a suitcase. Everything would go. He wasn't coming back here again. "You think you can handle Kurt Kesel, too?"

As he expected, that question gave her pause. "You are a man of many surprises," she finally said.

You have no idea, lady. "Is he one of the messes I'll need to clean up?"

"Among others. In fact, *everyone else* except you and me."

He checked his gun. "You just make sure you keep an eye on the sparrow, Celina. Because if I don't get that treasure, I'm not cleaning anything up except the trail that leads back to me."

He left out "which means you," knowing he didn't have to say it.

"I've got everything and everyone under control. You just stick to the agreement."

Donovan put the gun on top of the clothes. "You, too." He hung up and dialed Walsh, who answered immediately.

"We're moving in. Our targets are at Pluma Hidalgo. You need to be in position in the next two hours. Can you do it?"

Walsh paused for a few moments, and Donovan heard keys clicking in the background. "Not a problem."

"Stealth is crucial," Donovan added. "I just want all parties on the radar. No one gets near them. Whatever that takes."

"Also not a problem. I'll split my men up to cover everyone."

Donovan closed his suitcase. "Once you get into position, I'll meet up with you."

Simon eased the bathroom door open. It was still dark and quiet, just as it had been when he'd gotten back an hour ago. Jillian had been sound asleep, and he was careful not to make any noise. Then he'd stayed in the shower until he ran out of hot water. He'd shaved and picked up. Hell, he'd even hung up the towels.

Now he stood in the darkness waiting for his eyes to adjust so he wouldn't thump around the room like an idiot. If he did, she'd wake up and he'd have to tell her that the kidnappers hadn't gone for it. In fact, they'd been pissed as hell and given him a drop-dead date—literally. Two days. That was it. That's all they had before Celina started going to pieces.

"Simon? Is that you?"

Damn. "It's me. Didn't mean to wake you."

He felt around in the dark for the bed, found it, and slid in next to her. Jillian turned to face him and pressed her long body against his, making him whole. She was warm and nude, and any thoughts of sleep vanished.

She slid her leg up his thigh and her hands across his chest. How was he going to tell her? How could he explain that their chances of walking away from this were just about nil? The kidnappers couldn't be trusted.

He kissed her, trying to push the miserable phone conversation out of his mind. She felt relaxed and safe in his arms. He'd tell her tomorrow. Tonight, he'd make love to her with every ounce of passion and strength he possessed. Because there might not be many more tomorrows. He had tonight, and that had to be enough.

Jillian wrapped her arms around his neck and made the little moaning sound that he yearned for more than air.

There and then, he decided that he couldn't do it. He couldn't allow his world, his problem, to kill her. And he wouldn't. It wasn't her fault that he had no one he could trust to help them. If he did, they might actually have a chance. But he didn't, which left him with only one choice.

They'd go find the location and the treasure. Jillian would get to see it, maybe find some peace along the way. After that, they'd come back here, and he'd take the lens from her and finish the deal himself. As far as she'd know, the original plan to swap the location for Celina would seem to have worked. At least until he was gone, and by that time, it'd be too late for her to stop him.

Then she'd hate him.

First thing tomorrow, he'd call Paulie and tell him to come and get her.

She kissed his face gently, putting all the amazing compassion she possessed into it. He felt her soul and her essence in each kiss. He inhaled her warmth, caressed her supple skin, reveled in the small sounds he drew from her.

He'd give anything to spend every day for the rest of

his life with her. Anything. His heart, his soul, his life. The truth was, even if he survived this, she'd never forgive him for lying to her. For shutting her out. And if he told her his plan, she'd never let him go through with it alone.

I'm sorry, he thought, and then he made love to her.

CHAPTER
24

Morning broke hot and humid in Cielo Pasado, a small village just east of Pluma Hidalgo. Jillian leaned out the window of the Jeep for a better look. It had been a short but terrifying drive along treacherous mountain roads. Roads barely wide enough for one car, let alone the trucks whose drivers seemed oblivious to the physical limits of sheer rock faces on one side and sheer drops on the other.

Simon had been very careful this morning to make sure they weren't being followed. He'd told her it would be difficult to track the cell phone signal in the mountains, but in all honesty, she still felt like a sitting duck.

Cielo Pasado hugged the lower half of the jungle mountainside with fierce determination and grace, not unlike the people who lived here. The main road ran between two tightly packed rows of wooden buildings and shanties before snaking its way into the distance. Side roads were squeezed into the hillside, where they disappeared in the dense forest. Women in brightly colored dresses walked down the road with children running behind them. Men stood on porches and smoked cigarettes.

A nearby sawmill filled the air with a nonstop buzzing. Roosters and other livestock carried on in between the lulls. The air was thick with the smell of drying coffee beans and moist vegetation.

But it was the view that stole the show. Morning fog had finally relented, leaving behind an impossibly blue sky and scattered clouds that looked down over the jagged peaks. The mountains were steep, deeply creviced, and covered with green trees. They stretched north, blue and hazy to the horizon.

The mountain in front of her was the one. Finally, after traveling across most of Mexico, she'd found it. She could feel its ancient pull from here, but she held on to the present. This was no time to lose focus. She wouldn't think about tomorrow. Just today. Just get through today.

On a narrow dirt path on the outskirts of town, Jillian fashioned her hair into one long braid while Simon checked the burro and supplies. She popped the straw hat on her head. It was already hot in her tank top, light camp shirt, zip-off pants, and hiking shoes. She realized that she looked like a real-life tomb raider. For some reason, that didn't bother her as much as it should.

Simon led the mule toward her. "It's all uphill from here."

"I noticed. You sure know how to show a girl a good time, Bonner."

He focused on her with unnerving, sensual singularity, and she felt the heat rise in her face. Would that *ever* go away? She hoped not.

"I aim to please, ma'am," he said low and tipped his felt Indiana Jones fedora.

"And you do," she said, surprised by her own nerve.

Simon laughed. "Always nice to get a good performance review. We have enough supplies for a few days."

He handed her the reins to the burro, and she scratched the animal's head. "What if it takes longer than that?"

"It won't," Simon replied, sounding supremely confident as he set his GPS.

"So...ever been this way before?" she asked, gazing into the deep forest.

"Nope," he said.

"No guide?"

"I'm a tomb raider, babe. That would be embarrassing."

"Ah. As opposed to getting lost in the mountains forever."

He grinned.

She took a deep breath. "Adventure time, then?"

"Yup."

"Good thing you're good," she said.

His lifted his gaze to hers. "So are you. Better than you think."

The unexpected compliment warmed her, which was pretty impressive considering how hot she felt inside and out.

He shoved the GPS in his pocket and eased a long machete from a hip holster as he scanned the vicinity. She eyed the gleaming edge with dread.

"For the undergrowth?" she hedged.

He turned grim. "And anything else that gets in our way."

As he led them into the jungle, she towed the burro behind him. Within minutes, all sounds from the town faded away and they were engulfed in a green world. Birds chirped and flew overhead. Sunlight speckled the forest floor as she walked single file behind Simon.

Jillian noted that some of the forest on either side had been clear-cut. Stumps littered the landscape, ugly and stark.

People have to eat, she thought to herself. Especially these people.

"I talked to the kidnappers last night."

Jillian turned her attention to Simon up ahead. "You *did?* What did they say?"

He slashed at some vines. "It's a go. We trade the location for Celina. The only caveat is that we have to tell them how to get inside."

Relief poured through her. "Thank God. You could have told me this sooner, Simon. It would have made me a very happy woman."

"There's bad news, too."

The moment of relief passed. "Of course there is."

Simon continued, "If we screw them, they'll be back for us. But if it all goes well, we're free and clear."

Except for the part where she was an accomplice to giving man's salvation to a bunch of thugs. Jillian sighed. *Give it up. Nothing you can do to change it. Just be grateful you might live through this.*

"And you believe them?" she asked.

"I have to."

Jillian gave silent thanks and ventured, "So we're going in?"

"I think it's the best way to ensure our continued survival."

She couldn't help but smile. *Inside.* It was almost more than she had hoped. "Glad I brought my camera."

"Right," he said. But he didn't sound right. His mind was elsewhere. Maybe on tomorrow. Maybe on next week. Maybe far away from her. The realization brought a new fear.

"So," she said, gathering her nerve. "After this you head home to New York?"

Simon shot her a curious glance over his shoulder, then shrugged. "Probably. I'm retiring. What about you? Back to the museum?"

What about her? She hadn't dared entertain any thoughts of the future. The museum was still there. Her work. Her life. But somehow, it all seemed rather...boring. Painfully boring, in fact. Except that Simon would be there, too. Which led to a whole other emotional time bomb that she wasn't willing to think about just yet.

"I don't know," she replied honestly.

"Thought you loved your work."

"I do." And she did. But now she wasn't so sure that's what she wanted to do forever. "I just need a vacation, I think."

He turned and grinned. "This isn't a vacation?"

She smiled. "Not quite. I want a vacation where I don't have to worry about any dead bodies showing up in my car."

Simon sliced a low branch. "Doesn't everyone."

That was it. No "Hey, how about we get together after this?" No "I'd like to see you again after I don't need you to find treasure for me anymore."

Jillian concentrated on her footing. It was a lot less depressing than her future.

*   *   *

"God, I hate the fucking jungle," Carlos said and slapped at his neck.

Kesel was tempted to kill him right then and there, sitting in the forest. But he needed another man on his side. At least until he didn't need him anymore.

From his vantage point above the town, Kesel could see the road and the side road where Bonner and Jillian had disappeared into the jungle. He lowered the binoculars. Celina should have no trouble tracking them.

"So now what?" Carlos asked.

"We wait."

Carlos swatted a bug off his arm. "Until when?"

Kesel turned his binoculars to the dirt road that wound through the jungle. "Until Celina shows up."

"You really think she'll show?"

Kesel smiled for the first time today. "I'm positive."

"They're all on the move now," a man said over the two-way radio in Walsh's Land Rover. "You want us to follow each group as they go in?"

Donovan shook his head and told Walsh, "Tell him no. Just follow the last group. They'll all end up in the same place."

Walsh nodded and relayed the message to his men before signing off. He started the Land Rover and pulled it out onto the dirt road for the short drive to the insertion point. "All set. We can go in now."

Six feet, solid in his camouflage outfit, and sporting a short crew cut, Walsh looked like a dangerous man to be up against. And he was. Donovan was glad he sat on his side of the game.

Even with the A/C cranked, Donovan wiped the sweat from his brow. He should be wearing shorts in this heat, but the jungle could be a nasty place. Pants were hotter, but safer.

Walsh stared at Donovan, his blue eyes missing nothing. "Are you sure you're up to this?"

"Are you calling me old?" Donovan asked him, only half-serious.

Walsh grinned, which turned his normally stoic expression boyish for a split second. "No, sir."

"Nice to know the training is still there," Donovan said with a huff.

"Yes, sir."

Donovan laughed. "Now you're just sucking up."

"Wouldn't think of it, sir."

Donovan tried to turn up the A/C. "I don't have to tell you what an important and expensive mission this is. We'll only get one chance. If we blow it, there will be a lot of unhappy people asking why."

Walsh didn't even look at him. "Don't worry. I have no intention of anything going wrong. Out here in the jungle, we rule."

Lance stumbled over a root for the fifth time in the last twenty minutes, and Celina gritted her teeth. Ignoring him, she concentrated instead on her prey's trail. She had had decent footprints in the dirt for the first part of the trek but had to be more diligent in the undergrowth. Luckily, Simon had done a good job with the machete. Fresh gashes made for easy tracking.

She moved silently through the dense forest. Lance made enough noise to wake the dead.

"Yuck," Lance said from behind her. "That mule of theirs is a crap machine."

Celina glanced back and smiled. "It certainly appears that way. We need to move a little faster, honey."

"Yeah, well, this backpack weighs a ton." Lance stopped, looking winded and downright laughable in his jungle gear. With the ivory safari hat and matching shirt and shorts, he'd be perfect in a made-for-TV movie. Unfortunately, he also stood out in the surrounding greenery like a big, stupid bull's-eye. Although, she didn't care as long as someone shot him instead of her.

She adjusted her shoulder harness and gun. "Sorry, but I need to be able to move in order to track them."

He didn't look convinced and slapped a mosquito. "How much longer?"

She looked at the tracks. "I can't tell for certain. We're about thirty minutes to an hour behind them, though. They will stop for the night. We'll be able to catch up then."

Lance squinted at her. "What about us? Don't we sleep?"

"We'll be fine, I promise. This is my specialty, remember?"

He gave her a strange look. "Yeah, I know. Shouldn't we have a donkey like they do, instead of one backpack?"

She turned back to the trail. "Once we catch up with them, we'll be able to use their supplies."

Lance tromped behind her. "But they only have enough for two people."

Exactly, she thought.

"Here!" Jillian yelled suddenly.

Twenty feet ahead of her, Simon stopped and turned.

She was stock-still in the shadow of a steep knoll, holding the lens up toward the summit. Despite a full day of hard hiking, she beamed with excitement.

He stepped back to where she stood and gazed at the hill. It was a good forty feet high, with a flat top, and was as wide as far as he could see. The sides were heavily encased in moss, giant leaves, and vines.

"Stay here," he said and hiked to the right to scout it out. All the way, the hill maintained the same slope, the same structure everywhere, seeming very possibly man-made.

Pay dirt.

This was usually the time when adrenaline hit him, but all he felt right now was relief.

By the time he got back, Jillian had tied the mule to a nearby tree and given it some water. She met him as he approached, her eyes bright. "This is it. I know it is."

He started pulling the gear off the mule. "I believe you're right."

"So what are you doing?" she asked while he started sorting the camp equipment. He could hear the enthusiasm in her voice. She wanted to run up that hill, race inside, find the treasure. *Rookies.* Dead stuff didn't go anywhere.

"This is a good place to spend the night. Give me half an hour, then we'll head up. It's only five p.m., but the sun will go down fast in the mountains. I want camp ready when we get back."

Jillian bit her lip as she looked up at the hill, but she didn't argue with him. They set up camp quickly. Jillian was practically fidgety as he went through what they'd carry in their small packs—headlamps, water, the lens for her, gun for him—just your average hiking gear. He helped her with her pack and then sprayed more mosquito repellent on her as she danced from foot to foot.

"Are we ready yet?" she asked impatiently. Her hat was on, her body tense, eyes bright.

He grinned. "I can see we're going to have control issues here."

"Oh, you have no idea."

He spun around to the familiar voice.

On the edge of camp, Celina stood pointing a gun at them, and Lance was behind her. It was all so wrong; Simon thought he was imagining it.

Celina smiled, pleased. "Hello, Simon. Long time no see."

She looked perfectly fine. No bruises, no sign of abuse, no signs of struggle. No sign of having been kidnapped.

His disbelief was replaced by a betrayal that hit him square in the gut. Reality settled over him, and fury rose in its wake—powerful, lethal, and full of pain.

No. Not with so much at stake here. She wouldn't do this to him. She couldn't be that crazy. She couldn't use them like this—Jillian and everyone else drawn into this mess. People *he'd* drawn into this mess. Because he'd trusted Celina. He'd believed her. He'd believed. How could he have been so stupid?

"Fuck," he hissed.

CHAPTER
25

For a moment, Jillian's mind shut down. This wasn't right. Celina wasn't supposed to be here. She was kidnapped, hurt and helpless. But she was holding them at gunpoint. And Lance was here—

Then it all came crashing down in a sickening, gutwrenching wave that threatened to bring Jillian to her knees. Lance had lied to her. Celina had lied to Simon. It was all a lie, all of it. There was no kidnapping, no death threats, no one in danger. She and Simon had gone through all this—the fear and torment and trouble—for nothing.

For worse than nothing.

For betrayal.

"How could you do this?" she said, stuttering the words from sheer emotional overload.

Lance stepped forward, looking ludicrous and completely out of place in his color-coordinated jungle wear. "Jillian, I'm sorry—"

"Shut up, Lance," she snapped. Then she faced Celina and the gun. "How could you do this to Simon?"

The woman had the nerve to grin. "Money."

"I don't mean that," Jillian said, trying to maintain her self-control through the rage. "Do you have any idea what he has done for you? Gone through for you?"

"Found me the archives?"

"He cared about you," Jillian said tightly.

Celina laughed lightly, her voice ringing across the woods. "That's sweet. But, of course, I would expect no less after all Lance has told me. He said you were the most trusting soul he'd ever met. Always finding the good in everyone."

"Well, I guess you proved me wrong. There is no good in either of you," Jillian replied as she cut Lance a sharp glare. He shoved his hands in his pockets and stared at the ground. What had she been thinking? How could she ever have dreamed he was the right man for her?

"Lance, darling, check Simon for weapons," Celina said.

Lance's head snapped up. "What?"

Celina gave him a placating smile like a patient mother. She was using him, just like she'd used everyone else. Jillian seethed. *Lance, you idiot.*

As Lance followed the order, Jillian's eyes met Simon's. Judging from his absolute stillness and silence, he was furious but under control while Lance patted him down.

She didn't need her psychic skills to know what Simon was thinking—all this was his fault. He never should have trusted Celina. He should have walked away and let humanity screw themselves.

She wanted to tell him she understood, that it wasn't his fault. Being human and caring were not wrong. The problem was the people who didn't think that way.

"No weapons on him," Lance announced.

Celina narrowed her eyes. "Check his pack."

Jillian gave a sigh. Sure enough, Lance found the gun in the pack. This was bad.

"Now her," Celina said.

Lance stepped up to Jillian. She looked him dead in the eye. "If you touch me, I'll kill you."

He froze.

"Just take the pack and give it to me," Celina snapped, losing patience fast.

Jillian slipped the pack off and handed it to Lance. He hesitated before turning back to Celina. "I really am sorry."

"You're a dead man, and you don't even know it," she whispered.

Lance blinked furiously. Then he handed the pack to Celina.

She passed Lance a gun. "Cover them."

Then she riffled through the pack until she found the pouch. The lens slipped out into her hand and caught daylight with a vengeance. Jillian's gut twisted at the way Celina's eyes lit up. The bug.

Celina slipped the pouch into her pants pocket and tossed the pack back to Jillian. "You carry this."

Celina pulled out a second gun and checked it. Jillian shrugged the pack onto her back. "I can't find the treasure without the lens."

"You'll get it when you need it." Celina turned to

Lance. "You stay here with Simon. If he moves, shoot him."

Lance looked from Celina to Simon, a frown darkening his face. "Where are you going?"

"I'm taking Jillian to find the treasure for us."

"But I thought we were doing this together."

"This is my specialty, remember?" she said with a demure smile. "Unless you want to shoot Simon now?"

Lance blanched. "Well, no..."

"Then it's settled."

Say something, Lance, Jillian thought. *She's lying to you. Call her on it.* But he didn't. He wasn't strong enough to fight Celina.

Jillian's attention turned to Celina, who walked over to Simon and said, "I didn't expect you to be such an easy target. You're getting soft in your old age, darling."

Simon didn't bite. For a moment, Jillian worried that he might do something stupid like try to tackle Celina with a gun in her hand.

Celina put her hand to her chest. "Although I was very touched when you tried to save me with that crazy plan to give us just the location."

Jillian said, "You were crazy enough to take it."

Celina eyed her, and then Simon. He didn't move a muscle. Her smile grew. "Oh, you didn't tell her, Simon? Why am I not surprised?"

Simon watched as Celina came face-to-face with Jillian. "We turned down the offer. In fact, we cut the deadline in half knowing that you two were trying to weasel out. Wouldn't want you changing your mind at the last minute."

Jillian stared at Celina, unwilling to face Simon. Was

she telling the truth? Why would he lie to her? Why would he tell her they needed to find the way inside—

The answer came quickly and with a sting that radiated through her being. Because he was going to come back alone. Without her.

She looked at him then, and the raw emotion in his face confirmed her fears.

I trusted you with everything I had, she said silently. *My heart, my body, my soul. And even that wasn't enough to save you.*

"Well," Celina said happily into the silence. "Let's go find us a treasure."

Donovan trudged behind Walsh, who wasn't even sweating, despite carrying a fully loaded pack.

Maybe he *was* too old for this, but he'd be damned if he'd allow his sixty-four-year-old body to let him down now. He was so close he could taste it.

Walsh's radio beeped softly, and he stopped to answer it. He was listening and nodding silently when Donovan finally caught up.

"Just hold your positions," Walsh said and signed off. He checked his GPS while he filled Donovan in. "Jillian and Simon pitched camp about three miles ahead beside a large knoll. Celina and Lance just showed up, and now Celina and Jillian are climbing the hill. We have a report that Kesel and an unidentified man are about a mile behind. Two miles ahead of our location."

Donovan's heart was racing, and not just from the unaccustomed exercise. "They found the archives. It must be buried in the hill."

Walsh eyed him with the calmness of a man who

hadn't spent his life waiting for this moment. "Don't give yourself a heart attack. We have a long way to go."

Donovan waved his hand. "Not on your life. Lead the way, boy."

Anger radiated across his body as Simon stood his ground and stared Lance down from ten feet away. In the five minutes since Celina and Jillian had left, he hadn't even dared to speak. That's how close he was to losing it. Not that there was much else to lose at this point. But if this was going to be his last stand, he wasn't leaving anything on the table. If it killed him, he was going to find Jillian and get her out of this alive—even if she never wanted to see him again. Even if she walked away from this freak show of a life he'd built for himself. He couldn't blame her there, but one way or another, he would get his chance to apologize to her.

Lance was going down first.

"You really think Celina is coming back for you?" Simon asked.

Lance looked nervous behind the gun. "She'll be back."

Simon nodded slowly. "Let me guess. She offered you half? She told you that if you went along with her plan, she'd take care of everything? She handled all the dirty work, made all the connections?"

Lance frowned deeply. "This is her area of expertise. I'm just an art dealer."

"So why are you here?" Simon asked with cool deliberation. "Aside from spilling Jillian's little secret, I can't for the life of me figure out why Celina's keeping you around."

The gun wobbled in his hand. "She loves me."

Oh, this was going to be a piece of cake. "Celina is incapable of love. You should have figured that out by now."

Lance pursed his lips. "She does love me. She's doing all this to get me out of a huge debt."

"From the goodness of her heart? Not possible."

"So that we could start a new life together," Lance said, his voice rising with each justification.

He needed to keep Lance talking, second-guessing himself and Celina, until he realized just how deep he was in this and how disposable he was in this entire scenario. "Uh-huh. So why didn't the two of you go get Jillian? Why send Jackson?"

Lance pulled off his hat and wiped his forehead with his sleeve. "Because I can't go back to the U.S. until I pay off the debt. Plus Kesel got wind that Celina took his lens."

Celina stole the lens from Kesel. It figured. That explained why Kesel hadn't moved on Simon all this time. He was waiting for Celina to show up. Kesel was working for himself. This was personal. And Lance was in one whoop-ass pile of trouble. "So Celina set up the kidnapping to force her husband to go get the treasure for you?"

"Jackson wasn't supposed to die," Lance said with a look of dismay. "I didn't realize how badly Kesel wanted his lens back."

"Now you know," Simon told him. Good ol' Lance was sweating like a pig. Time to turn up the heat. "Kesel will kill you both when he finds you. And he *will* find you."

Lance's face flushed in the heat. "Celina said he wouldn't be a problem. She'd take care of him."

"She didn't." He paused to let that sink in, then gave Lance a cursory look. "Or maybe she has. Ever hear of the sacrificial lamb?"

"What do you mean?"

Simon smiled wide. "I just figured out why you're still here."

Lance blinked about a hundred times before taking a step back. "No. She wouldn't do that to me. She loves me."

Simon took two steps forward. "You think? She sacrificed her own husband for this. She nearly got me killed when *we* were married. You aren't detecting a pattern here?"

He raised the gun. "Shut up, Bonner. Just shut up. And don't move or—"

"Or what? You'll kill me? I think that's probably in Celina's plans, anyway—" Then Simon stopped talking, timing his ruse carefully. He looked into the forest behind Lance and listened.

Lance's eyes darted around. "What?"

"Keep your voice down. I heard something," he whispered.

Lance was getting more nervous by the second. "Like what?"

Simon held a hand up to silence him. He had to play this just right. "Quiet."

Lance twisted his body while he kept the gun on Simon. "I don't hear anything."

Simon stared at one spot in the forest behind him. "If it's Kesel, you probably won't. He's only half human."

"Celina said he was just a man."

"Haven't you learned, Lance? Celina lies. I'd watch my back if I were you, because she's not going to."

Lance turned his head to look at the forest, and Simon leapt forward, grabbed Lance's arm, and shoved the gun up. Lance yelped in pain as Simon twisted his wrist and punched him square in the face.

He went down like a rock. Simon took the gun from Lance's limp hand. Then he snagged his backpack and slung it over his shoulder as he raced for the hill.

Lance was on his own—the sacrificial lamb. He deserved no less for what he'd done to Jillian. Although in truth, Lance would be no more than a speed bump for Kesel.

Jillian stopped in the tangled vines that covered the plateau of the monument. And it *was* a man-made monument. On the way up, she'd discovered stepped stones that reached the top level. Not that Mother Nature hadn't done her damnedest to cover the entire structure with trees and roots. They were making progress at a snail's pace.

"Keep moving," Celina said for the hundredth time. Jillian was getting pretty sick of being poked in the back with a gun. They had to be getting close. The plateau could be only so big. It was time to play her one and only card.

"I can't," Jillian said as she stopped and turned to look at her. "I'm lost. I need the lens."

Celina glared and handed her the pouch. "Don't try anything. Or I'll call Lance and tell him to kill Simon."

Bitch. Jillian took the bag. "You never loved him, did you?"

"Love is overrated. A waste of energy and time with no return on investment. Gold is forever," she said without even batting an eye.

As Jillian slipped the lens into her hand, she recalled her conversation with Charlie back at the museum. *Vases last forever. You can't mend a broken heart. That makes hearts more valuable.*

Looked like Charlie was right. Hearts *were* more valuable. Breakable, but also more courageous. Risking all for love.

Halfway up the climb, Jillian had realized that Simon had lied to her to save her. Because he loved her. He never got past that point. Probably didn't think about how it would hurt her if she found out. It was pure love—right or wrong, fair or not. Now Jillian understood why her mother had loved her father despite everything he'd done to her. Why she'd believed he'd come back.

She'd had faith in love.

And so did Jillian. Right or wrong, fair or not. Clear or cloudy.

"Love is forever," she said to Celina and stared at the lens. "But you'll never know."

Then she turned her back to Celina to scan the sky. The blue beam was dead ahead and very close.

"Go."

Jillian pushed ahead between the trees and undergrowth, ducking branches and wrestling with vines. Just when she was about to give up, the forest relented and she stepped out into a small circular clearing crisscrossed with roots. Waning sunlight glowed over a paved courtyard.

The jungle hadn't encroached here, as if showing reverence to the low stone doorway seasoned with fifteen thousand years of nature and weather. Above, around, and behind it, the forest protected its ancient secret.

With dread, Jillian lifted the lens to the doorway. *Please don't be the place,* she pleaded silently. *Please don't be here.*

The priest, smiling at her, didn't listen. Her heart sank. He was bathed in blue light, magnificent, and so pleased to see her. He thought she was the one to save mankind.

"I'm sorry," Jillian whispered.

A gun poked her in the back, and she winced.

"What is it? What do you see?" Celina demanded to know.

Jillian closed her eyes and opened them. The priest was gone. Only the blue light remained.

Then she realized that she hadn't felt its pull. In fact, she didn't feel anything at all. For the first time in days, her mind was crystal clear. "Nothing. It's a doorway."

"No shit. Give me the lens."

Jillian hesitated, eyeing the stone pavers. All she'd have to do was drop the crystal lens and it would be over. Celina would shoot her and then kill Simon.

She squeezed the lens in her fist. No. She had to believe that Simon would come back to her. Have faith in love.

Jillian relinquished the lens and walked toward the doorway. She could make out parts of glyphs hidden under the vegetation. They looked just like the ones on the lens, and her mood dimmed even more. With any luck, the way would be blocked.

A heap of soil and ground cover forced them to duck to look inside. Behind the heavy swags of vines and leaves, the entrance opened to a tunnel that led into complete darkness.

Celina shone a flashlight down the length, illuminating cobwebs. There was no way to tell how long the passage ran or to where. She shoved Jillian's shoulder. "You first."

Jillian pulled off her straw hat and shoved it into her pack. Then she climbed forward, swatting webs and hanging moss out of the way. As they moved deeper, centuries of built-up roots and vegetation decreased, and they were able to stand. Still, Jillian's boots sank into two inches of slippery mud as the tunnel began sloping downward, and she had to work to keep her balance. Moisture settled over them like a cloud. The outdoor light faded quickly, plunging them into a strangely alien world lit only by Celina's flashlight.

Jillian moved ahead slowly as time ticked by. How long had they been in here? Ten, twenty minutes? All the while, she wished for a pile of stones or a wall to block their path, but so far, the way was clear. Luck wasn't with her today.

She took a step forward. Suddenly, the floor gave way, and the ground fell out from under her. Her back slammed onto slick stone, and she screamed as she slid into a dark abyss. Her shoulder smashed into a solid wall, which also gave way, sending her hurtling blind to unknown depths. She clawed at the stone beneath and around her, trying to stop her descent.

Then the floor was gone, and she fell into total blackness.

CHAPTER
26

Kesel hauled Lance up by his collar until they were nose to nose. "Where are they?"

Lance wasn't looking too good. Sweat pooled around his neck and in big rings under his arms. One of his eyes was swelling shut.

"Who are you?" Lance stuttered.

"Kesel," he said softly. Lance's good eye widened in recognition. "If you can't tell me where they went, you're no use to me."

"They went up the hill," Lance sputtered, and he flailed as he tried to point behind him. "That hill right there."

Kesel noted a fresh trail on the steep slope.

Lance babbled on. "Celina was the one who took your lens, not me. She used me, too, you know? She's lied to me from the beginning. I didn't want to get involved in any of this. It was all her idea."

Kesel returned his attention to Lance wriggling in his grip. "Think he's telling us the truth, partner?"

Carlos came up behind him, smoking a cigarette.

Lance's expression changed to horror when he saw Carlos. Kesel could feel him shaking.

"Hey, Lance. Haven't seen you since—" Carlos paused for a moment. "Since you showed so much interest in buying Kesel's lens. Next thing I know, Celina steals it from me and you don't come around no more. I can't tell you how heartbroken that made me."

Lance turned white as a ghost.

Carlos dropped his cigarette on the ground, stomped on it, and gave Lance a solid slap on his cheek. "Let's go see what your girlfriend is up to."

Simon heard a woman's scream, but he couldn't tell if it was Jillian's or Celina's. Either way, it gave him a direction, and he crashed through the vegetation until he came to the stone entrance. He swept the clearing with his gun, but nothing moved. Nothing made a sound.

There were two sets of damp footprints leading to the doorway. Donning his headlamp, Simon climbed through the opening and scanned the long, straight corridor.

Stepping carefully, he moved into the narrow tunnel. The footprints had disappeared in the thick layer of gelatinous mud, but there was nowhere else to turn, so he moved forward. Simon shone his light from left to right, top to bottom, watching for traps and trouble. Because *this* was just too easy. There should be signs of animals foraging or living here. This was a perfect hideout for some very large, very dangerous wild creature—

He froze as he noted fresh scrapes in the moss on the walls just ahead. Behind him, there were no marks, and up ahead the tunnel continued undisturbed and unspoiled except for the new spray of mud that was dripping everywhere. Something had happened to them right here. The hairs on the back of his neck rose.

Trap.

Simon pushed on the surrounding walls and ceiling. Nothing. He kneeled and pressed through the muck against the floor. Nothing.

Short of their having been transported via alien technology, he had no idea where they'd disappeared to or how. Or if Jillian survived the trap.

He clenched his teeth against the onslaught of helplessness. He had to believe that she was okay. She was smart, resourceful, and stubborn as hell when she wanted to be. She'd find a way to save herself, no thanks to him.

Male voices rose behind him. Shadows covered the pinpoint of light at the opening, and he heard Lance whining. Looked like Kesel finally caught up with him, because there was no way Lance would come up here of his own accord. Time was up.

Simon cinched his pack tighter, braced himself, and took a step forward. The floor swallowed him whole.

Jillian sat on the cold floor and rubbed the side of her head, where a lump was forming from the hard landing. Her mind felt fuzzy, and she wanted to throw up.

That was one hell of an entrance. Apparently, the Seer got no preferential treatment from the ancients.

Jillian fumbled through her pack and pulled out the headlamp that Simon had put there. To her relief, it was still intact and working.

After gingerly fitting it to her head, she scanned the darkness to see what kind of new mess she'd fallen into. The air was still, dry, and cool. Nothing stirred the fine layer of dust that blanketed the floor. It appeared to be another tunnel made entirely of stone, only shorter, with a turn at each end. She hoped one of them would actually lead somewhere instead of just dropping into oblivion.

Of course, a whole new danger could be lurking around every corner. On the upside, there was no sign of crazy Celina or her gun. Either she hadn't fallen into the trap, or they'd separated on the way down, which meant she could still be here somewhere.

"Good," Jillian muttered to herself. "She wanted in, she's in."

Jillian was feeling pretty good about that, until she remembered that she was "in," too.

She rested against the wall and forced her scrambled brain to think. She'd fallen through the floor, which meant she was inside the monument. How far down she'd tumbled she couldn't tell. The fall had been too rapid and disorienting.

But for the moment, she was free of Celina, and she planned to keep it that way. She wasn't going to help Celina find the archives. Even though the nutcase had the lens, she didn't know how to use it.

Which meant there was hope that the archives were safe. All Jillian had to do was find a way out. A nice doorway with a big exit sign that led to the jungle would be perfect.

Right. She scanned the monotony of gray stone. The ancients didn't seem to be into clear signage.

On the other hand, perhaps they'd left something behind for *her.* She concentrated on the length of tunnel, calling upon her vision to show her the way. But despite her best efforts, it refused to obey, leaving her dizzy from the attempt. She rubbed her aching eyes.

Then a woman's angry tirade broke the silence, bouncing off the stone.

Celina was alive, and she sounded pissed. What were the chances that she'd dropped her gun on the way down? Probably not good, and certainly not worth the gamble.

Running seemed like a very good option. Jillian lurched to her feet, holding the walls for support as her head rebelled at the sudden movement. There were only two directions to go, and she chose the one opposite from Celina's voice.

Jillian got to the corner and turned it carefully. It opened to another corridor, and she moved forward, through a longer straightaway that split off in two identical-looking directions.

Jillian stopped at the split and held her swimming head. What kind of place was this? It was like a damn maze.

She glanced behind her and realized that it *was* a maze. Dread replaced the headache with sickening speed. The walls seemed to close in around her.

Why? Why would they do this to her? What was the point?

Jillian heard Celina yell her name, closer now. She stumbled toward one of the paths, panic driving her forward. She turned a corner and came up against a dead end.

No. She spun around and scrambled frantically back to the junction to take the other path. One junction led to another, rooms opened to four choices, and dead ends abounded. Before long, every turn looked the same, and she found herself hyperventilating. Her head throbbed. She had to stop to catch her breath.

What was she doing? This was insanity.

As she forced herself to calm down, Simon's words came to her: *You're better than you think.*

Just the thought of him was enough to ease the fire in her skull and slow her breathing. He had faith in her skills. She inhaled and exhaled slowly, concentrating on the control it gave her. He needed her to be strong. He had enough to worry about keeping himself alive.

Celina's ranting reverberated through the maze. Jillian turned her head slowly and glared in the general direction.

If Celina wanted the archives, she could spend eternity down here finding them. She deserved to die alone with her beloved treasure. That woman had used and sacrificed every man she touched under the guise of love.

But Celina would not ruin Simon.

And at that moment, her priority suddenly became very simple—*save Simon.*

He believed in her, he trusted her, and Jillian was not going to be the woman to break him. She felt resolve gather in her belly and solidify into a single, cohesive, powerful force. She was going to finish this. Not Celina's way. Not Raven's way.

Her way.

Jillian turned right and walked with purpose, mentally charting her last few turns. There didn't seem to be a pattern to the—

She froze at the end of the passage, where her headlamp caught a break in the stone—a hand glyph had been carved delicately into the wall. She moved closer, and with her fingers, she traced the carving to make sure it was real.

The hand symbol that Mancuso had depicted. This meant something. If only she had the lens...

A flash of memory from this morning hit her. She reached into her backpack and withdrew the folded wad of Mancuso's notes.

"Jillian!" Celina screamed from somewhere behind her, louder now.

Stay calm, Jillian willed herself as she opened the paper. Under each glyph Mancuso had drawn the lines— a short series of connected right angles—some vertical, some horizontal. The hand was the fourth glyph across the top.

"Okay. So what does it *mean?*" she whispered.

The ancient walls weren't talking.

Think, Jillian. Precise interconnected lines, going in different directions and of varied lengths. No pattern. Not an alphabet. Not writing. They just flowed down the page like a...like a map.

Jillian looked up at the long tunnel she was in. If the wall the hand was carved on was the first long line and it angled right...

She followed the corridor exactly as shown on the paper directly under the hand. The next passage was long but had a left branch in the middle. Jillian checked the next turn on the paper. A short left.

It matched.

The next question would be: where did it lead? She had a good idea it was the archives, but the ancients wouldn't have put their greatest treasure here without also providing a way to get them out. There had to be an exit to the outside somewhere.

And that's the thought she clung to as she followed the lines on the map.

Donovan and Walsh arrived at twilight to find an empty camp, one indifferent burro, and no sign of anyone. Donovan rested his weary bones on a rock while Walsh disappeared into the shadows to connect with his men.

Donovan wiped the sweat off his face with a handkerchief. He *was* too old for this. His days of adventure were over long ago. But there was no choice—he had to finish what he'd started.

Walsh didn't understand. It was just another mission to him. He hadn't grown up here and seen the worst that Mexico had to offer. The suffering, the strife, the hopelessness—so cruel and relentless that by the time Donovan was sixteen, he'd lost all faith in Mexico and left his country. His home.

He took a deep breath. Now he was back, a wealthy man by anyone's standards. This time, he was going to stay until the job was done.

Walsh materialized over his shoulder and knelt next to Donovan to whisper his report.

"My men are in position as instructed. All our parties went inside via an entrance up top. Celina and Jillian first. Followed by Simon, and then Lance, Kesel, and the unidentified man. No one has come out. You want to move in?"

"A doorway?" he asked.

Walsh nodded. "Made of stone."

His excitement began to grow. There had to be a structure underneath. "Tell me about the hill."

"One of my guys did a rough recon. Looks to be a square formation with equal sides. Each side measuring approximately one hundred feet. The top level is flat."

Man-made. Donovan couldn't believe it. They'd found the archives. The sheer adrenaline rush overrode his exhaustion. He stood up, energized. "Tell your men to hold their positions."

"You don't want to follow them in?" Walsh asked.

He had the archives within reach. After all these years, his debt to his homeland was nearly paid. He could be at peace. "That won't be necessary."

Donovan took a cigar out of his pocket and slipped off the wrapper. He inhaled the cigar's sweet bouquet, and then carefully clipped the end. He could see Walsh's disapproval as he flipped open his lighter and lit the cigar over the flame.

"We came all this way. Why wouldn't we continue?" Walsh said.

Donovan puffed and enjoyed the pleasant taste and smooth finish. "Because sooner or later, they have to come out with the archives."

There was a potent pause. "And you don't care who wins in there?"

Donovan watched the cigar's glow. "Frankly, I don't."

CHAPTER
27

I hate mazes," Simon muttered.

What was it with ancient civilizations and mazes? Was it like some kind of torture device? He shone his headlamp at two passages in front of him—door number one or door number two.

He was about to choose door number one when he heard Celina yell Jillian's name. It bounced off the walls in every direction, making it damn difficult to figure out where it originated.

But it meant that Celina was alive—and she didn't have Jillian.

He let out a breath he didn't realize he'd been holding. Hopefully, Jillian had survived the hellish tumble down here. She didn't answer, but then again, she would know better than to answer Celina.

If he got his hands on Celina, he might just have to kill her this time. She'd totally lost it. She'd been crazy before. Now she was dangerous, completely consumed by the bug. Nothing and no one was going to stand between her and the archives.

Which meant he had to find Jillian before Celina did.

He chose a direction, hoping it led to Jillian. Minutes passed as he traversed the maze, backing out of dead ends and feeling like he was going around in circles.

Celina was not helping. Her shouts just bounced around, adding chaos to an already confusing situation.

When he noticed big footprints in the dust, he realized he'd already been this way. Worse than that, the prints gave his trail away to anyone looking for them.

Damn. He retraced his steps quickly and followed the path not taken. Another set of prints showed up, smaller. A woman's. They didn't stop or backtrack or even appear to change pace. Could be Celina. She'd dealt with mazes before.

Something on the floor caught his eye, and he bent down to pick it up. It was a piece of straw hat.

Simon grinned. "That's my girl."

Kesel limped through the maze on the badly twisted ankle he'd gotten as a result of trying to land on his feet. He had a compact flashlight in one hand and his gun in the other as he swept each corridor. No sign of Lance or Carlos, but they were here somewhere. He'd seen them disappear and had tried to avoid the floor trap, but it had just been too steep and slippery.

The apparatus had separated him from Lance and Carlos as each descending layer spun and twisted. He'd been in enough of these to know it was part of the design. The creators wanted to make sure whoever came down here wouldn't find his way out unless he had the lens and knew how to use it.

He didn't have the lens, but he sure as hell wasn't going to die here. Fuck everyone else.

He heard moaning and rounded a corner to find Lance and Carlos in a heap. Lance was sprawled on top of Carlos, who was pushed against the wall, his neck twisted at an unnatural angle.

Kesel reached him and felt his throat for a pulse. Nothing.

Looked like the treasure was all his now. Not a bad deal. Unfortunately, he'd also lost his second gun, and he didn't relish the thought of navigating this labyrinth alone on a bum ankle.

Lance leaned against the opposite wall holding his shoulder with a vacant look on his face. Blood trickled down the side of his head, and his one eye was now a full-blown shiner.

"What happened? Where are we?" He sounded half-drunk.

Kesel balanced on his good leg and considered his options. Lance was no threat. Shooting him would make a lot of noise and give away his position. Better to just leave him. He was too weak and too stupid to get himself out of this.

A woman's voice resonated from somewhere up ahead. Kesel concentrated on the scattered echo. He couldn't make out the words, but the direction was certain.

He stepped over Lance.

"You're in hell," Kesel told him. "Put in a good word for me."

Jillian stood just inside a massive colonnade with Mancuso's paper clutched in her hand, awestruck to her soul.

Rows of white pillars were spread before her, each one at least twenty feet high and four feet in diameter. Every column was covered in intricate etchings and magnificent glyphs that stretched from the smooth floor to the gleaming ceiling.

The chamber was massive, seeming to go on forever. A blue glow emanated from the center. She wandered toward it, adrift in the ancient architecture.

She stopped at the first pillar and traced the past with her fingertips. A light glowed from within the stone, revealing a transparent relief. Three-dimensional drawings emerged in stunning detail.

Jillian realized that she was looking at a drawing of a human liver, cut away to show the layers. Next to it was a visual procedure showing a piece of the liver growing. Lists and paragraphs surrounded the pictures. A large amount of text was shown beside a medical procedure of the fully grown liver being put into a patient.

The ancients had successfully grown and transplanted human organs. She shook her head in disbelief and scanned up the column covered with other medical discoveries—text, tables, instruments, and illustrations.

Jillian moved to the next column and pressed her hand to it. This one portrayed the planets with shocking accuracy, impossible landscapes of the Moon, telescopes, pictures of sunspots, and the Milky Way. Rows upon rows of what looked like calculations worked as dividers. Rockets, spacecraft, and other floating machines were explained.

"Unbelievable," she whispered as the magnitude of the find dawned on her. This would change the world.

She moved from pillar to pillar, finding plans for

engines that appeared to operate on plain air, floating bridges that spanned seas, entire pre-planned cities, plant farms growing on the oceans.

Writings, brilliant landscapes, maps, drawings, charts, sequences of lines and dots filled miles of space. Never in all her years of working with art had she seen anything like this. A lifetime of discovery awaited.

She spun around, taking in the enormity of the archives. Rows of columns radiated in every direction, each revealing something new and fascinating. The salvation of humanity; this was what they meant. A knowledge far superior to our own.

One particular column caught her attention. It was covered with drawings only halfway up, and then tiny faces—thousands upon thousands of them—dotted the rest of the way. She moved closer to study it.

A row of images started at the bottom and spiraled around the column. It occurred to her that it depicted a continuous story. She circled the column, following the evolution from the phases of ancient man to a full-blown, flourishing, highly organized global society.

How had they known this? she wondered as she followed the story. Society had thrived, but eventually, abundance changed to greed and indulgence. She watched technology turn to weapons. Peace to war. Images showed how it spread across the planet in horrifying realism until the world was engulfed in fire and ash covered the skies.

The last diagram showed a desolate, scarred world—and ancient man struggling to survive once again.

Jillian realized that this was the story of man. The Archives of Man were not just one civilization. This was the culmination of all ancient civilizations, all their experiences and failures.

Tears clouded her vision as she surveyed the faces of those who had died long ago. She pressed her hands to the warm stone, connecting with a culture that hadn't been touched in thousands of years, yet was trying desperately to keep this story from happening again.

"I understand." This was why she was chosen. Mankind had been this way before. She was here to stop the cycle. "I know what you want me to do."

Then reality dimmed her excitement, and she looked back to the way she'd come. She wasn't alone in here. Sooner or later, Celina or someone equally bad would stumble onto this place.

Jillian had to protect it from anyone who might exploit it. She'd rather die than allow the archives to be chopped up and sold to the highest bidder. If this meant she died protecting it, so be it.

And Simon would be broken.

You can't have both.

I want both, she thought.

You have to choose.

Sadness washed over her, because there was really no choice. How could she put her love before the fate of an entire world?

The blue light beckoned between the columns. *Her* blue light. She walked between the columns to where the room opened up to an antechamber fifty feet square. In the center, a round pool of azure liquid shimmered with a light of its own. And floating on top was a model island city with complexes of buildings, plazas, and pyramids, hills, rivers and valleys, ports, roads, and waterways etched in white stone.

This had been their world.

"These people didn't fool around, did they?"

Jillian turned to find Simon's grinning face behind her. Relief overwhelmed her as she flung her arms around his neck. He was safe. He was here. She didn't have to choose.

He held her tight and kissed her hair.

"I thought I'd never see you again," she said, clinging to his heat.

"I *am* a tomb raider."

She laughed and pulled away to look at him. "How could I forget?"

He turned serious. "I'm sorry for not telling you about the deal—"

"I know why you did it," she said. "Kiss me, Simon."

He did, soothing the fear in her heart and making her whole once again. Everything would be all right. Together they would be fine. Together they could save the world.

He broke off the kiss and looked around. "We don't have a lot of time. Did you find an exit?"

She blinked. Exit? No. "What are you talking about? Did you *see* this? Look at the columns. The writings. There's an entire library of knowledge here. Knowledge that can cure diseases and help mankind."

He eyed her. "I saw it. It's nice. I figure we're below ground level, so there must be a ramp out of this room big enough to drag the archives out—"

She swept her arms wide. "*These* are the archives. You can't drag these out. This is what we've been looking for."

Simon glanced around and frowned. "And we don't need it anymore. Celina and Kesel are right behind us."

She took a step back, shielding the model with her body. "*No.* They can't have this."

Simon's expression hardened in the blue light as he approached her. "Jillian, we need to leave now."

He didn't understand, and he never would because he wanted to keep her safe.

You can't have both.

It wasn't fair. It wasn't right. She shouldn't have to make this choice. She felt her heart clench from the treachery of the inevitable.

"I can't," she whispered. *I know who I am.*

Simon stared at her for a long time. "And I can't leave without you." He reached for her.

A gunshot zinged through the air, separating them. Simon spun behind one column, and Jillian ducked behind another.

Celina's yell filled the subsequent silence. "No one's leaving until I get my *fucking* treasure."

Donovan had just about finished his cigar when he heard a lot of chatter on Walsh's radio. In the light of a single lantern, Walsh frowned as he spoke to his men. "Bring them here."

Walsh looked at Donovan. "We have company."

He stood up, a little stiff from the makeshift chair. "How many?"

Walsh took out his gun and checked it. "Three men. Probably looters on the prowl. I can handle them."

Donovan sighed. He really didn't want this to get any

bigger than it already was. "I wouldn't mind hearing what they have to say."

Walsh turned his head toward the sounds of approaching people. "Don't count on them talking."

Moments later, one of the three barged into the circle of light looking none too happy. He was a thin young man, about twenty-five years old with a shaved head and wearing a Bad Company T-shirt with the sleeves cut off over blue jeans.

The other two brought up the rear, but Donovan couldn't get a good look at them in the darkness.

"State your business," Walsh said.

"Hey, it's a free forest," the young man said. "And I'm pretty sure that abducting tourists at gunpoint is illegal. You gotta badge in that monkey suit of yours? 'Cause I haven't seen a single badge yet, and I'm not telling you anything until you produce one."

Then the young man crossed his arms and glared at Walsh.

Unruffled, Walsh replied, "*Abduction* is a strong word. We're simply making sure you don't injure yourselves. This is dangerous territory."

The young man huffed. "That's a big pile of crap if I ever heard one."

Donovan smiled despite himself and stepped forward. "What my associate is trying to say is that we have this territory staked out for an archaeological dig. The guards are here to protect it from looters."

A voice came from the back. "Now, now. Do we look like looters, Donovan?"

From the shadows, a tall elderly man emerged. It took

a moment for Donovan to recognize him. "Elwood Yancy. I thought you'd be dead by now."

Yancy stepped up and shook Donovan's hand. Forty years melted away, just like that. "I thought you'd given up trying to save the world."

Donovan shook his head. "Not the world. Just Mexico."

The young man looked from Yancy to Donovan. "Are you kidding me? You *know* this guy?"

Yancy hitched his head toward him. "Meet Paulie. A good kid, if a wee bit impatient. And I believe you know Mancuso."

Donovan laughed out loud when Mancuso approached, wearing his trademark white suit and hat. Nothing had changed. The dealer still looked as dapper as ever. They shook hands, and Donovan turned to Walsh. "Tell your men everything is fine. They can go back to their posts."

There was a whisper of movement before the forest closed in again. Only Walsh stayed, ever alert.

Paulie raised his hands. "What's going on? Who are you, and why are you here?"

Donovan exchanged glances with Yancy and Mancuso and then shook his head ever so slightly.

Yancy slapped the kid on the back. "Better you don't know. Just be glad it's him and not someone else."

"Fine," Paulie said with a huff. "Have your little secrets. All I want to know is, where are Jillian and Simon?"

Donovan pointed to the hill. "In there. Along with a few others. A man named Kesel and an unidentified man. Lance Fairfax and Celina Jackson."

Paulie gawked. "What? Celina? That's impossible. She was kidnapped."

Donovan shook his head. "It was a ruse. She used it to force Simon to finish the task her husband, Jackson, was supposed to do—get Jillian and find the archives."

"Unbelievable," Paulie said, glaring at him. "You knew all this and you just let them drive all over Mexico so you could get your treasure."

"Better me than the looters," Donovan said.

"Nice," Paulie said. He picked up his backpack from the ground. "I'm going in after them."

"Won't do you or them any good," Donovan said. "Only Jillian will be able to find the way out."

Mancuso put his hand on Paulie's shoulder. "He's right. The structure was designed for the Seer."

"I've got eyes too," Paulie said, pulling his pack on.

"And I got a gun," Walsh responded. "Boss says stay put. You stay put."

Paulie glared at him. "And who the hell are you?"

"Better you don't know that, either," Donovan said.

"There's nothing else we can do?" Yancy asked. "They're friends."

Donovan understood what that meant. "I'm sorry, but our best hope is to wait."

CHAPTER
28

Simon peered around the column. Celina could be any-where. Kesel could be anywhere. But it was Jillian who really worried him. His worst fears had come true—she didn't want to give this up.

Her back pressed to a stone column, she crouched across from him, staring at the city model—lost in the past. How was he going to compete with that?

"Stay here," he whispered.

Jillian turned to him and blinked.

What do you belong to? he wanted to ask. *The past or the present?*

Then she nodded. He could only hope she meant it. He slipped from pillar to pillar, into and out of the shad-ows. Blue light cast an eerie glow over the floor, and he watched for movement.

Minutes passed and no sign of Celina, but the hairs on his neck were standing straight up. Had he missed her? He turned back toward Jillian's location when he heard something that chilled him to the bone.

"Come on out, Simon. I got your girl."

He swore and slipped behind a column where he had a clear view of the center room. Celina was using Jillian like a shield, holding a gun to her head.

"Don't be a hero, Simon."

Celina was already crazy enough to kill Jillian. Wait 'til she found out there was no gold or treasure here. She'd totally flip. Still, he couldn't risk Jillian's life.

Simon stepped out from behind his cover and walked toward them. Celina pulled Jillian closer when she saw him. "Drop the gun."

He slowed and tossed his gun on the floor. The clatter echoed through the forest of columns.

Simon caught Jillian when Celina shoved her at him.

Blue eyes looked up at him, and she whispered, "You never mentioned that your ex-wife is *crazy*."

"Yeah. Sorry about that," he answered.

"Now. Let's find that treasure," Celina said.

He met Jillian's gaze. They had a slight problem.

Jillian turned to Celina and held out her hand. "I need the lens."

What was she doing? She just got done telling him that *this* was the archives. Did she know something he didn't, or was she just stalling for time? Waiting for him to come up with some brilliant plan to save them both? 'Cause that last part was going to be a little tough.

Celina tossed her the pouch. "If you try to escape, I'll shoot him."

Jillian gave him a quick glance, then took out the lens. She walked away slowly, scanning the chamber. Simon watched her concentrate, his apprehension growing. What if she didn't come back from the past? Would she rather die than give the archives to Celina?

He checked the room for something, anything he could use to his advantage. There was only ancient script that people were willing to kill for.

Suddenly Jillian stopped and focused the lens on the city. She frowned as she watched the blue liquid for a long time, walking all around the perimeter of the island. She passed the lens out over the liquid, and blue spots reflected and dotted the columns.

Out of the corner of his eye, Simon saw movement behind him. Kesel? Shit. Just what he needed. Kesel behind him, Jillian riveted to her lens, and Celina torn between the two of them.

When Simon heard the telltale click, he dove for cover and yelled, "Jillian, get down!" He saw her drop to the floor and crawl into the shadows.

The shot went off, and Celina screamed and spun, her gun falling to the stone floor. She grabbed her wrist, crying out in agony.

Kesel hobbled into view, his gun on Celina and his mind on revenge. "Who did you think you were fucking with? Some lowlife digger?"

Simon knew Kesel wouldn't let any of them out of here alive. He wasn't crazy. He couldn't be fooled or bought. He was a killer. As soon as he'd dealt with Celina, he'd come after them.

Simon searched the area for Jillian, but he couldn't see her. He had to figure out a way to get around the pool to her without Kesel seeing him.

Meanwhile, Kesel said, "I want my lens, you bitch. Where is it?"

This just kept getting better and better. Then he heard Jillian say, "This lens?"

What the hell?

He shifted to the other side of the stone column and peered around the curve just in time to see her walk toward Kesel. Her expression was cool and serious as she swung the felt bag from side to side like bait.

Simon growled. Once he saved her ass, he was going to have a little talk with her about the dangers of walking *into* the line of fire.

To her own amazement, Jillian wasn't even shaking when she said, "Do you want your treasure?"

Kesel watched her with dark eyes—soulless and without emotion. Even battered and wounded, he was a dangerous man. Maybe more so. Injured animals were fearless and unpredictable.

She spoke firmly. "I give you the lens, Celina, and the treasure. And you let me walk out of here."

Kesel's eyes narrowed. He wasn't buying it. Then Jillian held the bag by her fingertips over the floor. "Or I could just *drop it*."

Kesel went very still. That got his attention.

Celina said, "She's bluffing. She'd die before she destroyed that lens." Then she leaned toward Kesel. "Besides, she's not the only one in this room. Simon's unarmed, and I believe you have a score to settle with him."

Jillian inhaled. *No.*

"Is that right?" Kesel said, looking interested.

Celina smiled. "Make me a partner and I'll tell you where."

"Don't bother," Simon said from behind Jillian.

Kesel immediately turned his gun on Simon.

Through gritted teeth, Jillian said, "I was *trying* to save you."

His gaze cut to her. "Doing a damn fine job, too, babe. But this is between me and Kesel." Then his eyes shifted to the main entrance. He had a plan to escape. Well, so had she, right up until he decided to play hero.

"I've been waiting for this moment for a long time, Bonner," Kesel said.

Simon stepped forward. "Go for it, asshole."

Her breath caught. He was going to sacrifice himself so she could make a break for it. After she'd chosen the archives over him. She gave a last look at the civilization she was about to abandon.

Make your choice.

And she did.

"Kill him and you'll never see the treasure. Ever," Jillian said, holding the bag to drop. "I'm the only one who can get it, and this is your only chance, Kesel. The treasure in exchange for me and Simon. Last offer. If you don't accept it, you get no toys to take home."

"Don't bother negotiating," Simon told her. "He won't let us out alive."

Celina said, "Take it. Take the treasure. We can always track *them* down later."

"Shut up, Celina," Kesel said. He glared at her. "I didn't give a damn about it before. But stealing it from you? That's worth a few minutes of my time." He looked at Jillian. "Deal. Now find it."

He was lying, of course, but so was she.

Jillian slipped the crystal out of the bag and swung it out over the blue liquid. "It's under the model. The whole thing will rise up when the crystal reaches the bottom of the pool."

Simon was watching her, his eyes wary. *Trust me,* she thought. *Believe in me.*

She let it drop. The crystal plunked into the thick liquid and disappeared instantly. Nothing happened.

"She lied," Celina said. "I told you she'd never—"

The floor started to vibrate, and the model began to shudder and rise. The liquid in the pool rippled and sloshed over the sides. Stone ground against stone. Dust floated down from the ceiling overhead.

"Yes!" Celina shouted, her eyes wild.

Jillian looked at Simon and cut her eyes to the main entrance. He blinked confirmation.

They both took a step back from the pool as the floor trembled. A piece of the ceiling broke off and crashed to the city model, showering them with thick liquid.

"No!" Celina screamed in horror at the pool. "You're destroying it!"

Just as Kesel raised his gun toward them, Simon kicked it out of his hand and threw himself at Kesel. With a hard thud, they landed on the floor next to the pool, trading bone-crunching punches.

Celina just stood and screamed at the pool as the island rocked and split into pieces.

Simon yelled, "Jillian, go!"

She eyed the ceiling as it made its slow descent, pushing the columns and all their knowledge down into the ground. Burying history yet again. A few of the columns twisted under the pressure and buckled with a spray of stones. The place was coming down, but she didn't care. She wasn't leaving without Simon.

Jillian picked up a nearby chunk of stone and ran toward the two men. She threw it at Kesel's head. It hit and bounced off with no apparent effect. Neither man could get a good footing in the slippery blue liquid on the floor, and she had to step back to avoid getting knocked over.

All she could hear were meaty blows and pained grunts. They rolled over, and she caught a glimpse of Simon's bloodied face. Kesel outweighed him by at least fifty pounds and was using all that extra leverage to crush Simon's neck.

She was about to throw herself on Kesel's back when Celina grabbed her neck from behind. "You ruined everything!"

Jillian reacted without thinking, reaching behind her to scratch Celina's face. The grip around her neck eased up and Jillian twisted, using Celina's raging momentum against her to throw her aside. Celina came around swinging, catching Jillian in the head hard enough to make her see stars. Then, Celina kicked her in the gut.

Jillian stumbled backward, sucking air. She braced herself against a column. The ceiling was noticeably lower now—ten feet away and still dropping—although Celina didn't seem to notice as she smiled and stalked her.

Jillian heard Simon give a feral growl and turned to see him use his legs to push Kesel off him. Kesel made a grab for Simon, missed, and disappeared over the edge of the pool with a splash.

Then she had other things to worry about as she dodged Celina's next blow and ducked under her arm. Celina's fist connected with the column, and she howled. While Celina gripped her hand, Jillian picked up a nearby stone and whacked her in the back of the head with a sickening thud. Celina dropped.

Screw self-defense class. Nothing beat a good, heavy rock.

Jillian swayed on her feet and turned to see Simon on his side, grabbing his throat as he spit up blood. She dodged debris on her way to him and helped him to his feet. Cuts and blood covered his face and arms.

Simon glanced at Celina and rasped, "You okay?"

Jillian managed a smile. "Never better. You?"

Simon looked over at Kesel, who was sliding under, his eyes wide. He grappled for the edges, but the liquid sucked him down. He didn't ask for help. He just stared at them with those soulless eyes and slipped under. Jillian almost felt bad for him, but she had bigger problems.

The ceiling was low enough to touch now, and whole sections were crashing around them. There was a great wail as the main entrance they planned to use disappeared under a pile of rubble.

They covered their heads as stones filled the air like shrapnel, and dust rolled toward them in a cloud.

Simon waved at the air and yelled, "That's bad."

She nodded. "I know another way. Help me move Celina."

They grabbed Celina by the arms and half dragged, half carried her to where Jillian would find the exit. To where the priest had shown her before he'd forgiven her for the choice she'd made.

Just as they ducked into an alcove in the wall, the ceiling dropped to under five feet, their tiny bit of space becoming the only refuge. Jillian pounded against the back wall, but it didn't budge and there was nowhere else to go.

"It's here. I know it is," she said to Simon.

"I believe you," he replied, and settled Celina against one wall. The ceiling disintegrated beside them, filling the alcove with dust and debris.

Simon pulled Jillian against him, covering her body with his. Exhausted and drained of any hope, she held on to him with all her might, feeling his heart beating against hers and his warmth when he kissed her.

"I love you," she said.

His response was lost in the final destruction.

CHAPTER
29

As dawn approached, Donovan watched the site implode. They had vacated the area when the ground started shaking last evening. Now he stood nearby as entire sections continued to collapse. Yancy and Mancuso stood next to him in silence. Sitting on a rock with his head in his hands, even Paulie was quiet.

Walsh came up beside Donovan and asked in a hushed voice, "Any orders?"

He pressed his lips together. "We wait until the site settles. Then we'll launch a rescue operation."

Walsh stared at the ruins. "You think that's a worthwhile mission?"

"I do," he said.

Walsh nodded and vanished from his side.

The jungle had come alive with the promise of morning. The mountain range in the distance was etched with gold. How many ancients had stood in this spot as they toiled to build the archives? To save their culture from extinction and to make the next world better?

He'd tried to do that, and he'd failed. He was going to have to accept that. His final gift to Mexico would never be. He couldn't save even this much.

And the lives. He swallowed the lump in his throat. This wasn't supposed to happen. They weren't supposed to die. He hadn't cared in the beginning, but their struggle to do the right thing, their sacrifice... He cared now.

"I knew it!" Paulie suddenly yelled behind him. "I knew you'd make it!"

Donovan spun around to see Celina emerge from the forest with Simon and Jillian behind her—all of them covered from head to toe in grime and dirt and blood.

Paulie jumped up and ran past Celina, who broke free and headed directly toward the group. She frantically scanned everyone assembled, no doubt looking for a partner in crime.

Sure enough, her eyes narrowed when she saw him. "Donovan?"

He grinned. "Hello, Celina."

She raced to him and grabbed him by the arms. "Thank God you're here. You wouldn't believe what I've been through. Those two tried to kill me. Kesel and Lance tried to kill me. But I can still get you the archives. We found a tunnel out. The deal can still be on. There's enough in there—"

He cut her off. "Celina, the Ministry of Culture would like to have a few words with you about your smuggling activities."

Her mouth dropped open. "What?"

"As well as your involvement in the death of your husband, and anything else I can think of to charge you with."

Her eyes widened. "You're a *cop?*"

He smiled, feeling better by the minute. "For the people of Mexico, I am."

"You lied to me," she said as Walsh's men took her into custody. "You son of a bitch. You lied to me!"

Celina screamed all the way through the forest. Donovan pulled a cigar from his pocket. It wasn't going to be such a bad day after all.

After big hugs from Paulie and Elwood, a marriage proposal from Mancuso, and some cleanup, Jillian felt a lot better. At least until she surveyed the full extent of the damage. The site was pocked and battered. The structure had been reduced to a pile of rubble, and under it all was a forgotten world.

Jillian closed her eyes at the sting. She'd tried her best. In her heart, she knew there was nothing more she could have done. Sadness filled her, but also a strange sense of freedom.

She couldn't do it all. Just as that civilization had passed into oblivion, so would others. Perhaps the fate of man was to reinvent himself over and over until he got it right. Would the archives have made a difference? Would anyone listen?

There were no answers here.

Jillian gave a sigh and wandered over to meet Donovan. He was an older man with gray-shot hair and hazel eyes. His brown skin and broad face belied a distant Mayan ancestry. His hunched shoulders betrayed his failure.

He looked up at her somewhat sheepishly when she shook his hand and said, "Thank you."

He grimaced. "Don't thank me for using you for my own selfish dream."

She smiled. "Yancy told me who you are. I understand why you did it."

"Doesn't make it right," he said with a sadness that tugged at her heart.

"You've made a dent in a major smuggling ring. I think it was worth it for that alone."

He gave a little grunt. "Perhaps. Unfortunately, it got a bit out of control, and there were too many casualties."

Jillian nodded silently. Jackson, the man they found in the Jeep, Kesel, and probably Lance. Or maybe he escaped.

As if reading her mind, Donovan asked, "Is anyone else coming out of there alive?"

"I don't think so."

He stared over the ruins for a long time before speaking. "You know I left Mexico long ago. Left it open for anyone to walk in and out with our culture. All of this is my fault. I should have been working with the authorities a long time ago to prevent it. Making a difference."

"You can't do it all, Donovan. Sometimes you have to live in the present."

"Perhaps." He turned and smiled at her. "Did you see it?"

She understood what he was asking her. He was the right man to tell. He was the right man to take it from here. "The Archives of Man is a library, a culture's collective knowledge. No gold. No artifacts. Just irreplaceable knowledge. I'll try to write down what I can remember."

His tired eyes met hers. "Is there nothing left?"

She hesitated and then said, "The archives are still there."

Donovan stared at her. "What?"

"It wasn't destroyed, at least not all of it. The knowledge was recorded on the library's supporting columns. They just sank into the ground." She nodded toward the site. "All you have to do is move a few thousand tons of stone."

His eyes lit up. "You haven't told anyone else?"

She shook her head. "And I won't if you don't want me to."

"I don't want you to."

Jillian grinned. He understood. Donovan would do the right thing.

She noticed Simon waiting for her on the edge of camp. He'd trusted her with the most important thing he could—his life, and she'd been right. When the last of the chamber collapsed, the pressure blew out the hidden entrance, giving them an exit.

Her heart filled her chest when he smiled, looking more beautiful than any relic. More amazing than a room full of history. More promising than any legend. It was time to write her own history.

"Good luck," she told Donovan and walked away.

Mancuso's beach looked quiet at 1:00 a.m., but Simon knew she was out here. A big moon dominated the Mexican sky, illuminating the strip of sand. Dark waves stretched lazily to the shore.

As he made his way to the beach, he realized what a welcome change this was from the jungle just two days before. He'd finally caught up on his sleep. His wounds were healing nicely, thanks to Jillian's TLC. Mancuso's house had filled up with Yancy, Paulie, and Jillian's sister, father, and brother-in-law. As soon as Jillian had called them, they'd swarmed in like... family.

Family. He'd have to get used to that. Maybe. Maybe not.

Jillian hadn't said she loved him again. She'd taken care of him, made love to him, treated him the same as before. But the words weren't there. Had she only said it before because she thought they were going to die? He didn't know, but he was going to find out tonight. He couldn't wait any longer.

He found her, naked except for the sarong tied around her hips as she stood silhouetted against the moon's reflection across the water. The breeze swirled her hair behind her. She turned and smiled a smile that was meant only for him. Flawless skin and ivory breasts gleamed in moonlight.

His pulse quickened as he came up beside her. "See anything?"

"Just the moon," she said. "You?"

The woman I love. "The moon's okay, but I like the view from here."

She laughed when he pulled her close and kissed her, breathed her into his soul. Her skin, her lips, the way she moved, talked, walked; he'd never get tired of any of it.

"I have a confession to make." She leaned back and peered at him with her clear blue eyes. "I've been meaning to show you something."

He stilled as she opened her hand between them. The crystal lens glowed in the moonlight. He shook his head in disbelief. "How?"

"You owe me a new necklace," she said with a sly grin.

He realized he hadn't seen her wearing the crystal necklace since they got back. "That's the crystal you dropped into the pool?"

She nodded. "When I was standing next to the pool, the priest appeared and showed me that the model was sacred, never to be touched. Disturbing it in any way would seal the chamber. I took a chance the crystal would be enough."

"A fail-safe," Simon noted.

She nodded. "Yes. The ancients didn't want the archives falling into the wrong hands, and they managed that risk by leaving it up to the Seer to decide. For me to decide."

He wrapped her up in his arms. "I'm sorry, babe. I'm sorry you had to make that decision."

She leaned into him. "I had no choice. They would have killed us both and desecrated the archives."

It still hurt her, and he knew it would for a long time. "You can't let anyone know you have the lens, Jillian. It's not safe."

"I know. I brought it out here to throw in the ocean," she admitted and relaxed in his arms. "But then I thought, 'What if there are more archives?' Maybe we'd get another shot at it."

The "we" part gave him hope. "Sounds like an adventure to me."

"Me, too."

She kissed his shoulder, and he forgot about the lens as her heat seeped into him, warming his heart.

"Is there anything you want to tell *me?*" she asked softly.

"Just one thing."

He felt her body tense as he lifted her palms to kiss each of them in turn. "The most important thing."

She arched an eyebrow. "Really? Sounds serious."

He kissed her wrists and heard her inhale. "Better than anything you'd find in a museum."

"Better than that?" she whispered.

"Much." He took her face in his hands and pressed his lips to hers. "*Te amo.* Do you know what that means?"

"No," she said, her voice hushed. He saw her eyes rim with tears and held on to his resolve.

"It means I love you, Jillian Talbot. How'd you like to make an honest man out of me?"

She burst into laughter as a tear ran down her cheek. "It's about time, Bonner. I thought I was going to have to tie you up and torture you until you figured it out."

"Hell, if I'd known that, I would have waited."

She put her arms around him. "Oh, no, you don't. Can't take it back now."

He wouldn't dream of it.

She pressed her body against his, her eyes hooded. "By the way, I knew what *te amo* meant. I just wanted to hear you say it." Then a slow, sexy smile crossed her face. "In fact, I've been working quite a bit on my Spanish." She leaned forward and whispered in his ear, "*Quite mis ropas.*"

Simon grinned and reached for the sarong. "I *love* Mexico."

SIGHT UNSEEN
SAMANTHA GRAVES

•

CLUES ONLY THIS PSYCHIC CAN SEE

Can an art thief earn an honest living? Raven Callahan does, with the help of a rare psychic power that lets her read the emotions locked inside ancient objects. But when her partner is kidnapped and Raven is forced to steal a priceless masterpiece to save him, ESP takes a backseat to quick wits, steely nerves, and the lethal skills she needs to survive.

A KILLER ONLY THIS COP CAN CATCH

Ex-cop Dax Maddox made just one mistake on the job, but it took a young rookie's life and cost Dax his ability to see color. Now stalking a killer brings Raven into his life—and floods his gray world with vivid and conflicting emotions: anger and lust, suspicion and awe. Are the criminals they seek one and the same? If so, Dax and Raven's growing need for each other could inspire a madman's terrifying scheme for the ultimate revenge . . .

AVAILABLE FROM GRAND CENTRAL PUBLISHING

(0-446-61838-1)   ($6.99 US / $9.99 CAN)

Discussion Questions

1. Simon Bonner wants to retire from the backstabbing tomb-raiding world so he can live a normal life like everyone else. Do you think that retiring will solve all his issues?

2. Jillian grew up in a family of thieves. Because of this, she has always walked the straight and narrow, following the rules, following the law. In doing so, what has she sacrificed?

3. When they arrive in Mexico, Simon sees only badness and ugliness around him. Jillian sees the same things he does—the same people, places, and events—but she notices only the goodness and the beauty in them. As the story progresses, though, they each begin to see both the positive and negative sides of things. How does this change them?

4. Jillian and Simon argue about looters and looting. She says he's destroyed history so he can sell his ill-gotten gains to the highest bidder. He says it's better to have the artifacts found and points out that some of his best customers were museums. Who is right? Is it better to have artifacts dug up so they can be appreciated, regardless of how they came to light? Or is it better to never discover a precious piece of a culture long gone if it is done only for commercial gain?

5. Jillian is very different from her sister, who is a capable thief. Raven is physically and mentally strong and has an impressive skill set. How does Jillian compare herself to Raven at the beginning of the book versus the end of the book?

6. Although Paulie is Raven's loyal assistant, what makes him such a good sidekick for Jillian?

7. Simon makes an executive decision to try to cut Jillian out of the final swap with the kidnappers, even though he knows she may never forgive him for it. He does it because he loves her, but is there really another reason?

8. Jillian chooses to bury the archives rather than risk having them fall into the wrong hands. Given the same situation, what would you have done?

9. Do you think Jillian and Simon will live happily ever after? What do you think makes a great romance?

THE DISH

Where authors give you the inside scoop!

From the desk of Carolyn Jewel

Dear Reader,

What was that line Shakespeare stuck in one of his plays? Oh, yeah. *Hamlet*, act 1, scene 2. "There are more things in heaven and earth, Horatio, than are dreamt of in your philosophy." Even if you're not Horatio, and chances are you're not, that's a true statement. When things go bump in the night, maybe it's not the cat knocking stuff over.

Maybe there really is a monster drooling under your bed.

Right. There are things out there maybe you don't know about. Say, for example, the mages in MY WICKED ENEMY (on sale now). A mage is a person who can do magic. Real magic. The kind that can get you killed. Or save your life. Depends on your point of view, I guess. Then there are demons and, more specifically, fiends. They're not people, but they can do magic, too. My advice is watch out for both. Here's the thing you need to know about fiends, though: most of the time they look like normal people. You could walk down the street and never realize that wicked-hot cutie sitting by the coffee shop window isn't human and that if he wanted to, he could destroy your life. Could be your boss isn't human (I've had one or two bosses I'm convinced didn't have a check mark in the human category). For a fiend, learning how to pass for normal is a survival skill. Didn't used to be that way, but it is now. That's just a heads-up for you. Here's another one: they're good at it because they have to be. They end up enslaved to some effing mage if they're not careful. And sometimes even if they are.

With the magekind, it's hard to tell where you stand, mostly because they started out human. They don't have as much trouble pretending to assimilate. Human but not very, if you see what I'm getting at. It's enough to make you wonder, isn't it? I mean, do you even know who you are? Really and truly? Be honest. Maybe you just wake up one day and realize your entire life has been a lie. The man who raised you is a mage who crossed over to evil centuries ago, and now everybody and their brother wants you dead.

Maybe you get headaches. Bad ones. You know, a flash of pain from the supraorbital process down to your maxilla. Hurts like heck. And they're getting worse. And worse. Then you see stuff that turns your stomach. So you run.

Right into the monster's arms.

It could happen. It happened to Carson Philips in MY WICKED ENEMY.

Watch yourself out there. That's all I'm saying.

carolyn jewel

www.carolynjewel.com

♥

From the desk of Samantha Graves

Dear Reader,

When I wrote my first romantic suspense, SIGHT UNSEEN, I discovered that I loved exotic locales. The research was intense, but that only made these amazing places more amazing.

In my latest book, OUT OF TIME (on sale now), I got to visit Mexico with all of you. I have never been there, but someday I'd love to see it for myself. In lieu of that day, I did the best I could with guidebooks, videos, travelogues, maps, photos, and even an online Speed Spanish class. What did we do before the Internet?

My fascination for Mexico turned into Jillian's passion, as well. She embraced this culture and its people with an open heart. Her wide-eyed appreciation became a symbol for how she viewed life and people—seeing the beauty in everything.

Simon's dislike for Mexico has nothing to do with the country itself, but with the betrayal he experienced there—a betrayal that marred him with a cynicism that shaped the rest of his life.

During the story, both characters must face the truth as Jillian begins to see the ugliness and Simon begins to see the beauty. It could have been Mexico or Guatemala or Santa Barbara—all places contain both ugliness and beauty. What you choose as truth is up to you. What you do with that truth defines you.

In the end, Jillian didn't let the ugliness change the fact that there is beauty, and Simon didn't let the beauty change the fact that there is ugliness. They simply found their common ground, accepting both as part of life and choosing to see the truth in their love for each other.

I hope you enjoyed both.

All the best,

Samantha Graves

www.samanthagraves.com

P.S. In case you were wondering, *"Quite mis ropas"* means "Take my clothes off." Happy reading!

From the desk of Paula Quinn

Dear Reader,

Few authors get to see their characters come to life before their eyes, but I did. You met Graham Grant, the hero in A HIGHLANDER NEVER SURRENDERS (on sale now), in my previous release, LAIRD OF THE MIST. I met him in Grand Central Terminal. The Scottish Village there hosts a fashion show that was about to begin. I like kilts. I'll watch.

Donning a kilt of black leather and matching jacket that he held closed at his chest, model and former rugby star Chris Capaldi stepped onto the stage like he owned it. His tousled mop of deep amber hair eclipsed killer green eyes that sparkled with confidence and a hint of wickedness. All he did was smile and a horde of women behind me started whooping and cheering in a dozen different languages. Oh, yeah, he knew the ladies were digging him, and he fed the frenzy by sliding the jacket off his bare bronze shoulders and curling his sulky mouth into a grin so salacious I swear every woman in attendance sighed at the same time. Grand Central was never so hot.

There was my Graham Grant. Six feet three inches of pure rogue.

Chris has graciously agreed to star in my next Grand Central Publishing release about a notorious rogue and a beautiful rebel he can never have. From the moment Graham meets the bold and passionate Claire Stuart, he wants to take her, claim her. But Claire has far more dangerous undertakings ahead than surrendering to a wickedly alluring Highlander. Amid betrayal, honor, duty, and ultimately love, she must put this vision in his place in order to save her sister's life, and her own. Pick up a copy of A HIGHLANDER NEVER SURRENDERS and journey with Graham to a place that has remained untouched until now—his heart.

Enjoy!

All the best,

Paula Quinn

www.paulaquinn.com

LOOK FOR

THE NEXT NOVEL OF

ROMANTIC SUSPENSE

FROM

SAMANTHA GRAVES!

Want to know more about romances at Grand Central Publishing and Forever? Get the scoop online!

GRAND CENTRAL PUBLISHING'S ROMANCE HOMEPAGE

Visit us at www.hachettebookgroupusa.com/romance for all the latest news, reviews, and chapter excerpts!

NEW AND UPCOMING TITLES

Each month we feature our new titles and reader favorites.

CONTESTS AND GIVEAWAYS

We give away galleys, autographed copies, and all kinds of fun stuff.

AUTHOR INFO

You'll find bios, articles, and links to personal websites for all your favorite authors—and so much more!

THE BUZZ

Sign up for our monthly romance newsletter, and be the first to read all about it!